The New Kids

As Katie, Molly, Eric, and Greg rounded the corner, identical frowns crossed each of their faces. Some girls, none of whom Katie recognized, and a few boys in Stevenson jackets had taken over their space in the quad.

"Hey, that's our cherry tree!" Katie exclaimed, tossing her red ponytail indignantly.

"And those are our benches!" Eric growled.

Just then the warning bell rang. Katie knew she should go back to her own homeroom, but instead she lingered at the edge of the quad. One of the Stevenson girls was still sitting on what until this morning had been the gang's bench, and Katie stared at her. She couldn't help wondering if the school merger between Kennedy and Stevenson would really be so easy after all.

COUPLES

COUPLES

SEALED WITH A KISS!

M.E. Cooper

SCHOLASTIC INC.
New York Toronto London Auckland Sydney

No part of this publication may be reproduced in whole or in part, or stored in a retrieval system, or transmitted in any form or by any means, electronic, mechanical, photocopying, recording, or otherwise, without written permission of the publisher. For information regarding permission, write to Scholastic Inc., 730 Broadway, New York, NY 10003.

ISBN 0-590-41263-9

12 11 10 9 8 7 6 5 4 3 2 1   8 9/8 0 1 2 3/9

Printed in the U.S.A.   01

First Scholastic printing, January 1988

SEALED WITH A KISS!

Chapter
1

Katie Crawford slipped on a pair of dangling silver and turquoise earrings, then shook out her long red hair. She leaned toward her reflection in the mirror and wrinkled her nose. Too much mascara? Not enough? With a shrug, she hurried back over to her bed to grab her bookbag. She couldn't stand still long enough to fuss with her makeup this morning. It was still January, but the sun shining in her bedroom window was brighter than it had been in weeks and today was the start of a new semester. It was spring term at last!

Someone was honking a car horn in the driveway as she trotted down the stairs, the heels of her new brown boots clattering noisily on the polished wood. Mrs. Crawford poked her head out of the kitchen as her daughter reached for

1

the hall closet door. "No time for bacon and eggs, honey?" she asked, putting a hand up to the scarf that held back her thick red hair.

"No, thanks, Mom." Katie pulled her jacket on and wrapped a jade-green muffler around her neck. "That's Greg outside. He's picking me up early — he promised me something special for breakfast."

Mrs. Crawford laughed. "More special than bacon and eggs?" she asked teasingly.

Katie grinned and blew her mother a good-bye kiss. "Have a great day!"

"You, too! See you this afternoon."

The bright sunshine was deceptive; when Katie stepped outside, she was hit by a gust of cold winter wind. She was also just about knocked out of her boots by another bossy blast from the horn of Greg's Mercedes — or rather, his mother's Mercedes. Katie waved a hand as she approached the car, which was parked at the bottom of the Crawfords' driveway. "Trying to wake up the whole neighborhood, Montgomery?" she called cheerfully.

Greg poked his sandy brown head out of the open window on the driver's side and grinned. "I wouldn't have to honk if you weren't so slow, K.C.," he countered. He looked pointedly at his watch. "Besides, they've probably been up for hours by now!"

Katie reached the car. "Come on, I'm not *that* late!" she protested, leaning her elbows on the door to rub noses with Greg. Only then did she realize her boyfriend wasn't alone. Grinning at Katie from the backseat were Eric Shriver and her best friend, Molly Ramirez. Her usual seat in the front was occupied by an enormous Brewer's Bakery bag overflowing with freshly made doughnuts.

"All aboard for Kennedy High!" Eric announced, stretching his arm over into the front seat to grab the bag of doughnuts. "You showed up in the nick of time, Katie. I've been dying to dig into these!"

Katie got in and pulled the car door shut, then looked back at Eric with one eyebrow raised as Greg pulled out onto Magnolia Street. "Looks like you didn't wait," she observed, pointing at the powdered sugar that decorated Eric's chin and the tip of his nose.

Eric widened his eyes innocently. "Who, me?"

"He only had two," Molly told Katie, reaching into the bag herself and pulling out a plump jelly doughnut. "And if I know Eric's appetite, that was just a warm-up."

Katie turned back to Greg. He was whistling, his blue-green eyes narrowed against the bright morning sun. She held back a giggle as she popped open the glove compartment to look for Greg's Vuarnet sunglasses. He reminded her of those corny Old Spice commercials, she thought. Or was it Irish Spring? Resting one arm on the back of his seat, she leaned toward him to slip the sunglasses over his ears. It was a good excuse to get closer and sneak another kiss even though

3

Greg pretended she'd almost made him drive off the road.

Snuggling under his right arm, Katie poked Greg in the chest with her index finger. "There are a few crumbs on your crewneck, too, Monty," she teased. "How many doughnuts did *you* manage to put away in the five minutes it took to drive from Brewer's to my house?"

"None!" he declared as Eric shouted, "Three!" and Molly said, "Seven!"

Katie laughed and nuzzled Greg's neck. He squeezed her shoulder. "Well, I guess that's okay," she conceded to the others. "After all, he's a growing boy."

"If he grows any more he'll pop through the car roof!" exclaimed Molly. At five feet exactly, she was more than a foot shorter than Greg.

"Too true," agreed Katie, who had to look a long way up at him herself. She glanced back at Molly and Eric as she bit into a cinnamon twist. "What are you guys doing here, anyway?" she asked through a mouthful. "I mean, besides eating my doughnuts?"

"This is a happy-first-day-of-spring-semester car pool!" Eric's carefree expression then gave way to a sober one. "Do you realize, Katie, that this is not only the start of a new semester, but it's also the start of our last semester at Kennedy?"

Katie's dark brown eyes widened. "I keep forgetting that!" she exclaimed, turning to face forward again. "I mean, time is going by so fast. It doesn't seem possible!" She studied Greg's sharp,

4

handsome profile as Eric and Molly began chattering in the backseat about their new classes — how glad they were to be through with Ms. Fairclough's trig course, but would precalculus with the infamous Mr. Hansen really be any improvement? Greg didn't turn toward Katie, but she could tell by the smile touching the corner of his mouth that he knew she was looking at him. He reached up and brushed his hand against her cheek. Katie's body tingled warmly. Greg's touch was relaxing and exciting all at once. As she half-closed her eyes, her thoughts ran over the events of the past few days. She and Greg had spent almost every waking minute of their short winter break together. Ice-skating at the old Capitol Ice Skating Rink in Rose Hill with Molly and Eric and the rest of the gang; waiting impatiently for the mailman, since colleges and universities with rolling admissions were already sending out acceptances; staying out late every night and working out together in her basement during the day; taking long, lazy drives through the frosty countryside . . . more wonderful memories to add to my collection, Katie thought with a contented sigh. She and Greg had only been dating since October, but sometimes it seemed like a lot longer. They were so close. Katie was happier heading into the end of her senior year than she'd ever imagined she could be, and it was mostly because of Greg. She knew she'd made the same kind of difference in his life, too.

Greg seemed to read her mind. They were

stopped at a red light and he bent over to plant a kiss on top of her head. "Feeling good?" he whispered against her hair.

"Yeah," Katie answered softly. She tipped her face up to his and their lips met in a sweet, brief kiss. "I feel fantastic."

"Me, too," Greg said. He glanced casually over his shoulder before he drove through the now-green light. Katie was pretty sure she could read *his* mind this time. To an outsider they might have seemed like a funny foursome. Katie had gone out with Eric before she started dating Greg. Breaking up with him had been very painful, and for a while things had been more than a little awkward between them. *And* between Eric and Greg. But there were no hard feelings now, and the fact that Molly and Eric were good friends had helped keep them all together.

Molly's enthusiastic voice broke into Katie's daydreams. "Katie, I talked to Ted last night and he said I could expect to hear from James Madison any day now. He said he heard at the end of January last year!" Molly's boyfriend, Ted Mason, was a freshman at James Madison University in Virginia. It was one of Molly's top choices, although she was also applying to schools in her home state of California.

Katie tried to wriggle out from under Greg's arm, but he wouldn't let her. She turned her head as best she could, meeting Molly's eyes. "I know you'll get in," she said with conviction. "There's no doubt in my mind."

6

"Doesn't Ted have any pull there?" joked Eric, pushing up the cuffs of his new fleece-lined denim jacket. "Couldn't he threaten to quit the football team unless they accept you?"

Molly waved a doughnut at him. "I think I might have a chance to get in without Ted's help, thank you very much!" she protested.

Eric grinned. "You're right, you do," he said. "After all, if I were interviewing a black belt, *I'd* take her. I'd be afraid of the consequences if I didn't."

"Oh, you!" Molly waved the doughnut again, and this time Eric grabbed it from her and took a huge bite. "You should be afraid of the consequences right now, you rat! Just because you got into Williams early decision and are set for life doesn't give you the right to make the rest of us panic even more than we are already!"

Eric wiped the doughnut crumbs from his mouth with the back of his hand before putting a muscular arm around Molly and pulling her close. "Aw, you aren't panicking, are you?" he said, mussing up her hair. "You know you'll get in everywhere you applied and so will Katie. Now, that loser Montgomery, he's another story. He's lucky he's still a junior and has a whole year to get his act together!"

Katie giggled and Greg snorted. "Thanks for nothing, Shriver!" he said.

"How's Ted doing, anyhow?" Katie asked Molly.

Molly's blue eyes glowed the way they usually

did when she talked about Ted. "Oh, he's doing really well," she said brightly, running a hand through her dark, tangled curls. "This term is starting out better than his first one. He's even psyched to try out for the baseball team, which is something, considering what a tough time he had when he played for the Rose Hills Ramblers. Well, he said he really feels like he's a part of things now. He's adjusted, you know?"

"That's great." Katie nodded thoughtfully. She squinted, trying to picture herself strolling confidently around the snowbound Dartmouth campus, or feeling at home in the warm California atmosphere at Berkeley. She sighed. "Isn't it crazy to think that next year it'll be us? A year from now we'll be halfway through *our* freshman year, wherever we are!"

"Whoa!" Greg shook his head as he turned onto Main Street about a mile from the high school. "Let's take this one day at a time. You guys still have a whole semester at Kennedy to get through!"

"You know, I'm really going to miss the place," Eric observed, his voice serious.

Molly hunched down in her seat, pushing her knees up against the back of the seat in front of her. "That's why we have to make our last semester the best one ever," she pointed out.

"It will be my best, I know it," Katie said fervently. "I'm really going to be ready for the gymnastic finals this spring! Since Sara Weiss isn't at Potomac High anymore — she moved out of state — the competition's going to be weak. We *have* to win the title again." Her eyes sparkled. "I want it so badly."

"I hope the swim team has a good season, too," Eric contributed. He was captain again this year. "But if I know us, we'll probably finish around fourth or so in the league." He shrugged. "I guess I won't mind. I keep having to remind myself that winning's not the only thing that matters."

"Well, it matters to me," Katie said firmly. She and Eric had never really seen eye to eye on the matter of competition. "I feel like we have so much at stake this year because we're the defending state champions. We just have to win."

Greg glanced at Katie, his eyes mischievous. "You really want to be number one again, huh?" he teased. "No matter what it takes?"

"Don't tell me you don't want the same thing for yourself and the crew team," she retaliated. "You talk all the time about how this spring you're going to be the undefeated, undisputed crew kings of the county!"

"Actually, there isn't much chance of that happening." Greg made a sad face. "Without you as coxswain we just won't have that winning edge." He flashed her a meaningful smile and she laughed. Last fall she'd joined the crew team to be a cox for Greg's boat. With Katie on board, the team had swept by four other teams to win the Kennedy High Invitational Regatta — and she and Greg had fallen in love. "Besides," Greg argued, "I row just for the fun of it."

9

Katie shook her head and sighed in exasperation. "Your problem," she explained, winking at Eric and Molly, "is that you've always had everything — boats, cars, everything. You don't know what it's like to want something as much as I want to win the all-around individual medal. I'm too old for the Olympic trials, so this is as far as I'll go. It's my last chance!"

Greg grinned good-naturedly. "You're right, tiger!" He gave her knee an affectionate squeeze. "There isn't anybody who can beat you this year. You'll definitely be number one. Although," he concluded gallantly, "you're already number one in my heart."

"Oh, gee," Katie said with a giggle. Molly groaned and Eric threw half a doughnut at Greg, but hit the rearview mirror instead.

"Hey," Eric interjected, changing the subject. "I just remembered something. What do you think the new kids from Stevenson are going to be like?"

Like in Rose Hill, the teenage population of nearby Carrolton, Maryland, had been declining in recent years, only at a much faster rate. The school board had recently announced its decision to close down Stevenson High School and divide the student body among three other schools. As a result, Kennedy High was getting almost a hundred transfer students starting this semester. This fact hadn't really hit Eric, Katie, Greg, Molly, and the rest of their crowd at Kennedy yet — they'd all been too busy with holiday fun and then finals to wonder how the closing of Stevenson might affect them. Until just now, Katie herself had completely forgotten there'd be a hundred new faces in the halls and classrooms and cafeteria. She tipped her head to one side and thought for a moment. "I imagine they'll be regular kids, just like us," she suggested.

"You don't think they'll be different? I mean, being from Stevenson?" asked Eric.

"Nah." Greg shrugged his broad shoulders. "They'll fit right in. Things won't change much."

Molly leaned forward, folding her arms across the top of the front seat. "Maybe things won't change for *us*, but for them. . . ." She paused, wrinkling her freckled nose. "I don't know, I guess it hasn't been that long since I transferred here from Pacific Point. It really turns your life upside down. You have to start over in so many ways. This semester could be kind of rough for the Stevenson kids."

Katie watched Molly as she spoke, and smiled sympathetically. They'd become friends soon after Molly moved to Rose Hill halfway through their junior year. Katie remembered how surprised she'd been when Molly had confided in her about her romance with Ted Mason, Kennedy's star quarterback and all-around popular guy. They had met the previous summer when Molly was living with relatives and working as a lifeguard in Ocean City. Katie had been even more surprised by Molly's reluctance to face Ted again and renew their relationship. It had taken her a while to see that it wasn't that easy for Molly and Ted to just pick up where they'd left off.

She understood where Molly was coming from now. "You're right, Moll," she agreed. "It probably will be tough for them. What do you think we could do to help?"

"Help?" Eric asked, puzzled. "Since when did you two join the Girl Scouts?"

Molly turned to him, her blue eyes serious. "Think about it, Eric. How would you feel if a hundred of *us* were packed off to spend the remainder of our high school days at Stevenson!"

Eric nodded thoughtfully. "You've got a point there."

Greg laughed. "You've *really* got a point there!"

"If you think about it, we kind of have a duty to help the news kids out." Katie quickly adopted Molly's argument. "I mean, not just in order to do a good deed but because it's our school. We're seniors. . . . Well, most of us are" — she kissed Greg lightly on the cheek — "and we know the ropes. Our crowd is used to taking the lead around Kennedy. If we don't make an effort to help the new kids out," she concluded earnestly, "who will?"

"Hear, hear!" Greg cheered as he turned the Mercedes into the Kennedy High parking lot with a flourish.

"What a speech! I'm inspired," Eric exclaimed. He was being sarcastic as he often was, but Katie

12

could tell by his teasing smile that he agreed with her.

"Well, I, for one, am going to spread the word to the whole crowd about giving the transfer students a warm welcome," Molly decided. She fumbled under Greg's seat for her hat and mittens, and then swung the car door open.

Shouldering his backpack, Greg strode around to where Katie was waiting on the other side of the car. He held her hand as they headed across the parking lot with Molly and Eric right behind them. "We are pretty lucky to have each other," he said, bending down to kiss her on the ear.

She peeked up at him. "You and me?" she asked playfully.

"You and me and everyone else in the gang!" he corrected. He gave her a warm, secret smile that made her blush with pleasure. "But especially you and me."

"The crowd really does hold us all together," Katie heard Molly say to Eric. She couldn't help thinking how true that was. A lot of things had changed — like when she broke up with Eric and started seeing Greg — but the friendships lasted and even got stronger with time.

"Hey, speaking of the crowd," she said aloud, checking her watch. They'd reached the front door of the school and were huddling by the flagpole. "We still have a few minutes before the bell. Why don't we check out the quad and see who else comes by? You know, catch up on their

13

vacations and stuff. It's a nice morning, even if it is a little cold. Besides, we haven't sat out there in ages!"

"That's a great idea, Katie," Eric agreed.

"Yeah, let's go," said Molly.

Greg was enthusiastic, too, so instead of going inside they headed around the south side of the building. The quad was a busy place, especially in the spring and fall, and Katie and her friends were regulars there. At the start of the school year, they'd taken over the territory originally staked out by Ted, Phoebe, Chris, Woody, and Peter, last year's top senior crowd. It had been a while since they'd hung out there, though. Actually, it had been a while since the entire group had hung out anywhere, Katie realized suddenly.

As the four rounded the corner, identical frowns crossed each of their faces. Some girls, none of whom Katie recognized, and a few boys in Stevenson varsity jackets had taken over their space.

"Hey, that's our cherry tree!" Katie exclaimed, tossing her red ponytail indignantly.

"And those are our benches!" Eric growled.

They looked at each other, then turned sheepishly toward Greg and Molly. They all burst out laughing. "Listen to us!" Katie said ruefully. "You'd think we owned this place."

"But we do, sort of," Eric said with a grin. "They just don't know it!"

"No, we don't," Molly disagreed, shifting her books from one arm to another. "Our spot on the quad is just one of those things we take for granted. This just goes to show we shouldn't!"

"Molly's right," Greg declared. "What rights do we have over a couple of benches and a patch of grass?"

Katie and Molly giggled, and Eric threw his hands up in defeat. Just then the warning bell rang. "We'd better hurry," Molly said to Eric. Their homerooms were at the opposite end of the building. "I don't want to start off the semester with a tardy."

Katie and Greg waved at them and then turned to each other. Greg leaned down as if to give her a kiss. Katie closed her eyes and puckered up in anticipation. The next thing she knew Greg had wrapped his arms around her and lifted her right off the ground so that her face was level with his. His eyes crinkled in a teasing smile. "That's the problem with having such a shrimp for a girlfriend," he observed. "If we want to see eye to eye, I have to pick you up!"

"Put me down!" Katie demanded, laughing. "You know I'm afraid of heights. And this is almost as scary as being at the top of the Washington Monument!"

"Balance beams notwithstanding, of course," Greg teased and kissed her before setting her gently back on her feet. Then he kissed her again. Reluctantly Katie pulled herself away from the warmth of his arms and lips. "If we don't hurry, we're really going to be late," she reminded him. "Lunch?"

"Lunch," Greg repeated with an affirmative nod. "I'll see you then, same old time, same old place."

"Maybe we should get to the same old place a few minutes early," she called back as they parted to head for their homerooms. "Otherwise we might find somebody's taken over our lunch table, too!"

Greg was laughing as he pushed through the heavy metal door leading into the south wing. Katie watched him disappear inside. She knew she should hurry back to the front entrance and her own homeroom down the hall from the principal's office, but instead, she lingered at the edge of the quad. One of the Stevenson girls was still sitting on what until this morning had been the gang's bench, and Katie couldn't help staring. The girl was flashy and beautiful. Her long, tawny red hair had the kind of windswept look that didn't come from standing in a breeze. Katie guessed she had worked hard to make it look that casual. And the girl's electric-blue minidress visible underneath her unbuttoned coat was very short. It was definitely shorter than anything Laurie Bennington, the glamorous sex symbol of last year's senior class, had ever worn.

But what froze Katie in her tracks, more than the girl's clothes and makeup, was her expression. She was looking around the quad like she'd just bought it and was planning to completely take it over. Something inside Katie bristled. Was this girl an exception, or were all the Stevenson kids like her? Were they all planning to take Kennedy High by storm? Katie wondered. She felt annoyed and offended and also a little silly. As she spun around and began walking rapidly toward homeroom, she couldn't help wondering if the school merger between Kennedy and Stevenson would really be so easy after all.

Chapter 2

Roxanne Easton turned up the shawl collar of her black cashmere coat as a gust of bitter cold January air whipped a strand of auburn hair across her face. She brushed it aside with an impatient gesture.

"You did tell your mom by the flagpole, didn't you?" Frances Baker asked in a hesitant voice. They had stayed after school to meet with their new advisors, and the Kennedy school buses had long since departed.

"Of course." Roxanne waved a gloved hand dismissively. "Don't worry, Frankie, she'll be here. You know she always likes to be fashionably late."

Frankie tucked her chin down into the collar of her shapeless down jacket and nodded. "That's right," she acknowledged. The two girls had been

18

best friends since fifth grade and Frankie was certainly familiar with Mrs. Easton's style. Glamorous and divorced, Roxanne's mother was seen regularly on the arms of the most eligible and influential bachelors in Washington. She was also dedicated to making entrances, and fashionably late was usually an understatement. Frankie sat down at the base of the flagpole and wrapped her arms around her knees, prepared for a long wait. For the millionth time that week she wished she and Rox were still at Stevenson, riding their familiar old school bus home. It was Wednesday, and they'd only been at Kennedy High for three days. But it felt like three weeks, three years even, to Frankie.

A light snow had begun to fall. A few large, fluffy flakes clung to Frankie's long, pale eyelashes. She blinked at Roxanne, who was sitting beside her. "So, Rox," she said, her teeth chattering, "how do you think you're going to like being a junior at Kennedy?"

Rox shrugged elegantly, narrowing her deep green eyes against the snow. "I think I'll like it a lot," she answered, her tone decisive. She laughed. "I know I'll like it!" She turned to Frankie, her eyes gleaming. "Don't *you* think it's fun, being the new girl in town and knowing people are noticing you?"

"But no one notices *me*," Frankie reminded her. "I think it's hard to be new. It's scary."

Roxanne sniffed. "Maybe that's true for you, but I think it's fun." She laughed happily. "Remember the expressions on those four Kennedy kids' faces Monday morning when they saw us sitting on that bench on the quad? It was pretty obvious that they were expecting to have the place to themselves!"

Frankie couldn't feel quite as triumphant as Rox. Her own sensation at that moment had been closer to terror. She shook her head and her straight, fair hair swung across her face like a curtain. "Actually, they looked sort of like they belonged there. That's more than we can say."

Roxanne's smile faded and Frankie saw her jaw tighten. Her expression became stiff and cool. "A lot more than we can say," Roxanne agreed begrudgingly. "Yeah, it's their turf." She beat one gloved fist lightly on her knee. "Just when I'd made Stevenson my turf, wouldn't you know we'd get transferred?"

Frankie heard the edge of frustration in Roxanne's voice. "It'll take a while to fit in here, but it'll happen," she said softly, trying to reassure herself as much as Rox.

"Well, I don't plan to wait," the other girl declared. She tapped the pointy toe of he black boot briskly on the sidewalk. "I'll make it happen now!"

"How?" Frankie asked.

"It's easy!" Roxanne's face lit up once more in a self-confident smile. "I haven't wasted these first few days moping around and worrying about being new, you know." Frankie's insides tightened. Roxanne's words only reminded her that

20

that was exactly how she *had* spent her first few days at Kennedy, and that she'd probably spend a million more that way. "No, I've been busy discovering how things work here," Rox continued. "You know, who's who and what's what. It's actually an interesting scene . . . and much more exciting than Stevenson was. Challenging." She laughed. "And I always like a challenge!"

Frankie blew on her hands to warm them. "What about those kids we saw on the quad?" she asked. "The two girls and the two guys. Have you met them yet?"

"No, but I know who they are. There seems to be a tight crowd of upperclassmen that pretty much runs this place and those kids are part of it." Rox smiled coyly. "One *very* nice boy who sits next to me in homeroom told me all about them. Apparently this one guy, Jonathan Preston, is involved in student government somehow — he's the school social director or something. He sounds like just the sort of person I want to meet. In fact, I plan to pay him a visit very soon," she informed her friend with a smile. "What better way to break into the popular crowd than to start with the school hotshots, right?"

Frankie could only nod. Such a thing would never occur to her, but Roxanne made meeting Jonathan Preston seem like the most natural thing in the world. Kennedy High was like a crossword puzzle, she thought, and the more letters Rox filled in, the faster the puzzle-solving would move. Frankie realized, not for the first time, how lucky she was to have Rox for a best friend. Rox was, and had always been, everything she wasn't — clever, beautiful, magnetic, fun. Sometimes Frankie wondered where she'd be if it weren't for Rox. On her own, she was too quiet and shy to make waves, but as Roxanne Easton's best friend she could be a part of things. Even if it was only a small part of the excitement that surrounded Rox wherever she went.

Frankie realized that her friend was studying her now, her wide-set, almond-shaped eyes speculative. "Have *you* met anyone? What have you learned about Kennedy so far?" Rox quizzed her.

Frankie shrugged her shoulders, hunching further into her coat for warmth. "Not much, I guess," she admitted. "I've been concentrating on my classes more than anything else. Coming from another school midyear is a little confusing. In some subjects I'm way behind and in others I'm way ahead. One thing I'm really psyched about — the Kennedy computer system is fantastic!" Frankie had been in the Computer Club at Stevenson and even though the equipment there was outdated, she'd managed to develop formidable computer skills. "It's about a million times better than the old stuff at Stevenson." Frankie's light brown eyes — they were so light Roxanne often said they were beige to tease her — almost sparkled. "Someone told me there's a fancy new Apple computer in the student government room that anyone can use if they ask. I can't wait to get my hands on it!"

Roxanne didn't comment at her friend's un-characteristically enthusiastic speech. She merely raised her hand to her mouth, delicately disguising a yawn. Frankie's pale cheeks turned pink. Obviously she was boring Rox with all her computer talk. She quickly changed the subject to one that would interest her friend more. "But anyway, Rox. . . ." She hesitated and then asked shyly, "What, uh, what do you think of the Kennedy guys?"

Frankie knew this was a safe subject. Rox didn't really have any interests — she hadn't joined any clubs or been on any teams at Stevenson. But the one thing she was wild about, wilder even than Frankie was about computers, was boys. Even back in grade school Rox had been like a queen bee with a circle of admirers. She had been collecting boys for as long as Frankie could remember. Take Susie O'Malley's fifth-grade birthday party, for instance. It was during the summer and Susie's parents had set up a candy treasure hunt in the backyard. At the end of the hunt Frankie had a bagful of candy, more than anyone, while Rox had only found one lollipop but had stolen the heart — and candy — of every boy at the party. Frankie smiled to herself at the memory.

Meanwhile, Rox was considering Frankie's question seriously. First she smiled. "There are some amazingly good-looking guys at this school," she began. Then her eyebrows wrinkled with concern. "Most of the cool upperclass guys seem to have girlfriends, though. I don't plan to spend my Friday nights sitting home without a date, but it's hard to know who to go after." She paused thoughtfully. "That's another area where I just need to *know* more. Like exactly who's going out with whom and for how long, what the guys like and don't like. . . ."

Roxanne's voice had trailed off and she was pursing her lips in an expression of concentration. Frankie rubbed her hands together. They were starting to tingle a little from the cold. "But Rox, why do you need to know all that?" she wondered, puzzled. "I mean, you can't plan liking someone and having them like you. Love just . . . happens. Like magic." Frankie blushed as she spoke. She didn't really know this was true. She'd never been in love herself, but it sounded right, more right at least than the mechanical process Rox was describing.

Roxanne sniffed. "Forget that," she said curtly. "Love doesn't 'just happen.' It's not some kind of fairy tale. You can control it. It's just a question of determination. You can get what you want if you just go after it."

"Maybe you're right," Frankie allowed, sounding doubtful.

"I know I'm right. I've learned a lot about this sort of thing from my mother, and you have to admit that if anyone knows about men, it's her!" There was a funny, strained note of pride in Rox's voice. Frankie turned to look at her. The mention of Mrs. Easton reminded both girls that they were still sitting in front of Kennedy High, their ride nowhere in sight. Ordinarily Frankie could have waited like this all day, but the snow was starting to fall faster and now her toes as well as her fingers were growing numb.

"Rox, do you think your mom — " she began delicately, not wanting to offend her friend.

"Forgot?" Rox completed the sentence for her. She stood up abruptly and brushed the snow off her coat. Then she sighed. "It sure looks like it."

Frankie slung her backpack over one shoulder. She really wasn't terribly surprised. This wasn't the first time Jodi Easton had forgotten about them. She squinted through the snow and looked out at the early rush-hour traffic. "We can get a bus down the street," she suggested. "Let's go."

Roxanne had become strangely quiet. The two girls walked in silence for a few minutes, their footsteps muffled by the snow. Finally Rox glanced at Frankie. "Sorry, Frankie," she mumbled. "I mean, about my mother blowing us off. It's just, she has such a busy social life, you know." She laughed awkwardly. "Torrey and I are used to this."

Frankie heard the hurt underneath Rox's nonchalance. "Something important must have come up," she assured her friend. "I'm sure she would have been there, otherwise, especially since this is your first week at a new school." Frankie bit her lip after she said this. Roxanne's stony silence made it clear that she'd only made things worse.

They did n't say much during the bus ride.

Frankie was feeling anxious but as soon as they left Rose Hill and entered Carrolton, she began to relax. Familiar home territory — it was such a welcome sight.

The bus stopped in Roxanne's neighborhood first. They said good-bye and Frankie watched Rox walk down the aisle to the front of the bus. She walked like she was on a tightrope, holding her coat so it wouldn't brush against anything. She was also careful not to touch the grubby handrails, Frankie noticed. Frankie knew Roxanne hated public transportation. She couldn't wait to get off the bus and be home herself. Three days at Kennedy High down, Frankie thought, looking glumly out the bus window, and about a million more to go.

The heavy front door of the Easton home closed behind Roxanne with a muffled thud. She ambled down the long hallway toward the kitchen, tracking melting snow across the smooth flagstone floor. "Dumb bowling alley," she said out loud to the hallway. Only the sound of an empty townhouse answered her.

She stopped halfway down the hall. The study door was ajar so she pushed it open and peered inside. The plum-colored brocade curtains and dark paneled walls combined to make the room look even gloomier than the day outside. Once Roxanne's eyes adjusted to the dimness she detected her brother Torrey, who was now a sophomore at Kennedy, asleep on the couch with his

Walkman on. Torrey's sneakered feet were planted firmly on top of one of the couch's velvet-covered arms. Rox shook her head. "Mom's going to kill you," she whispered, stepping back into the hall and closing the door softly behind her.

If she even sees it, that is, Rox added silently to herself. As she poured Diet 7-Up into a wine glass, she glanced at her mother's engagement calendar, which was pinned to the kitchen wall next to the old-fashioned Dutch oven. Her mother was at a cocktail party, and then she'd probably have dinner with a senator or something. Then she'd go to an opera or play and not even get home until after she and Torrey had gone to bed. Well, it wouldn't be anything new.

Roxanne started opening cupboards, just for something to do. In the fourth cupboard she found a can of mixed nuts wedged behind a jar of caviar. She opened the nuts, enjoying the funny pop it always made when you pulled the metal tab and released the vacuum. As she sat down at the glass-topped table in the breakfast nook, a picture that had been stuck to the re-frigerator with a magnet shaped like a miniature stalk of broccoli caught her eye. It was the torn-off cover of the December issue of *Town and Country* magazine. It was a photograph of her mother.

Rox stared at the picture for a while. Then her eyes focused on the blurb in very small print on the bottom right-hand corner. She was a little too far away to read it, but she knew it said,

"Mrs. Jodi Easton, Glamorous Washington, D.C. Hostess," or something like that. Roxanne picked through the nuts until she found a cashew and then she studied the magazine cover again. A beautiful woman with chin-length, white-blonde hair, smooth, lightly tanned skin and ice-blue eyes smiled at her. Rox smiled weakly back. It was nice for her mother to have such a wonderful life, but it wasn't nice to be forgotten after school, especially in front of her best friend.

Rox remembered Frankie's reassuring words about how something important must have come up for her mother. Her toes curled inside her boots. She didn't like to think that Frankie would ever feel sorry for *her*. That kind of role reversal made her very uncomfortable. She supposed it didn't really matter, though, as long as Frankie didn't suspect the truth behind her mother's forgetfulness.

Roxanne knew her mother was busy; so were lots of people's mothers. Hers didn't even have a job, so she couldn't use work as an excuse for not having time for her kids. The truth is, Rox decided, crunching hard on a handful of nuts to keep the tears from starting in her eyes, Mom just forgot. She forgets time and time again, and she forgets because, to her, anything's more important than I am.

Roxanne's eyes were still locked on the photograph of Mrs. Easton on the fridge and now they became determined despite the sparkle of threatening tears. "I'll show you," she whispered, propping her elbows on the table and clasping her hands together. "I'll knock 'em all dead at Kennedy High. I might not get my face on a magazine but I'll get attention — lots of it! I'll have even more guys calling me than you do. Just you wait and see how important I can be!"

Chapter
3

"So, what do you think of the Stevenson kids so far?" asked Katie, hoisting herself onto the top of a desk and pulling an orange from her jacket pocket. She and Greg had dropped by the student government room during lunch to find Eric, Jonathan Preston, and Matt Jacobs already hanging out there listening to the WKND noontime show.

"I haven't met that many of them," Eric remarked. He was reclining on the lumpy flowered couch the Prestons had donated to the room, and now he tipped his head back so he could meet Katie's eyes. She turned her own head so she'd be looking upside down like he was. He laughed. "There are two great guys from Stevenson who've joined the swim team, though. They seem like all-right guys, and they're good swimmers, too. We sure can use them."

"Any gymnasts?" Jonathan turned to look at Katie.

She shook her head and tossed a piece of orange peel into the wastebasket. "No new competition," she informed the group. "Not that I'd expected any."

Matt rubbed his chin thoughtfully. He was one of the few guys Katie knew who sometimes looked as if he actually *needed* to shave. "I don't think I'd even know which kids were from Stevenson if I saw them," he admitted. "I mean, there are a lot of *Kennedy* kids I don't know. But I did meet a couple guys when I was working at the gas station the other day. They had Stevenson letter jackets so I figured it was safe to assume they were new. I asked them how it was going and they were pretty friendly." He grinned. "And boy, were they in one hot car!"

Greg hitched himself onto the desk next to Katie and opened his mouth so she could pop a section of orange into it. He shrugged his broad shoulders. "I feel like I've heard more about the new kids than anything else. I know that an all-city quarterback transferred, but we won't get to see him in action until next fall. And hey," he said, putting an arm around Katie to give her a squeeze, "you guys won't even be *around* any more by then!"

"Pamela told me the editor of the Stevenson

31

newspaper transferred, too," said Matt. His girl-friend was the arts editor of *The Red and the Gold*, the Kennedy High paper. "I suppose that could change some things."

"Maybe." Jonathan tipped his Indiana Jones fedora down over his nose and tilted his chair backward. He shoved his hands in the pockets of his khakis and yawned lazily. "In general, though, I don't notice the Stevenson kids making much of a difference."

Greg threw a piece of orange peel at Jonathan and it bounced off the brim of his hat. "This is still your little empire, huh?" he joked.

Jonathan grinned broadly. "You bet." He slammed his chair back down on all fours and slapped his hands on his knees. "But now," he said purposefully, "since I've got you all here, I'm going to put you to some good use. What do you think about the upcoming Valentine's Day Dance?"

"What's to think about?" Katie asked, swinging her feet lightly against the desk. "A dance is a dance."

Jonathan shook his finger at her. "That's where you're wrong, K.C. I want to make sure that everyone'll go to this one. The newspaper staff suggested a Sweetest Sweethearts contest to boost attendance."

"Sweetest Sweethearts?" Matt repeated, running a hand through his rumpled dark hair and rumpling it even further.

"Yeah, you know. Everybody votes for the, uh, cutest couple." Jonathan shrugged. "It's really not that complicated."

"If you ask me, there's nothing to vote about." Greg winked at the guys. "Everyone knows the sweetest sweethearts are right here." He bent over to kiss Katie on the nose. She rolled her eyes and grinned.

"We all know that," Jonathan agreed, "but just to be democratic, I think a vote is in order. And that's where I need your help. I'm supposed to pass out ballots, but first I have to figure out how to print them up on the computer."

Everyone turned to look with suitable seriousness at the new Apple computer on Jonathan's desk. He made a dramatic production of inserting the disks and turning it on. A multicolored design appeared on the screen. "Fancy software," Greg observed.

"Ain't it, though?" Jonathan beamed proudly. "Only problem is, I don't really know how to use it yet. It's a lot different from the school's regular computers." He glanced around at his friends for suggestions.

"Don't look at me!" Eric put his hand up and shook his head. "I'm allergic to those things."

Katie giggled. "If it could swim, then maybe he'd get near it."

"Here, let me try." Matt stepped forward and took the instruction manual from Jonathan. He opened it to page one. "Hmmm," he said, turning

33

the pages slowly. "Hmmm, hmmm." He raised his eyebrows in puzzlement and smiled slowly. "Well, er, I think I'd better stick to cars."

Resigning himself, Jonathan squared his shoulders in front of the computer and rubbed his hands together. "Well, here goes," he announced. "I've got nothing to lose, except the rest of my lunch hour, I suppose."

Outside in the quad Frankie lowered the wide-brimmed straw sunhat that Roxanne had plumped down on her head. It had a huge pink ribbon around the crown. It made Frankie feel like a jerk to wear it on such a gray, damp day. But Rox had insisted.

"It's perfect for a day like this," Rox said restlessly. "It will make you think that spring will actually arrive some day."

"Right," Frankie answered, finally taking the hat off and sticking it on Rox's beautiful head. The hat had actually kept her hair dry. But standing in the middle of the quad under that big hat with all her new classmates flowing back and forth during lunch hour made Frankie feel like a spectacle. Roxanne loved it, but then Roxanne was like that. She *was* a spectacle. Every boy who passed by, stared. Half of them probably already knew her name and the other half were no doubt trying to get the nerve up to ask her on a date. But Frankie didn't like that kind of attention. She simply wasn't that kind of person.

Of course, in a way, she wanted to be. That was why she hung out with Roxanne. She admired Rox's charm and her wit and the way she could make people notice her. She wasn't sitting around like a lump, complaining about being in a new school. She was doing something, trying to figure out how to make new friends.

"Have you heard about this dance that's coming up?" Roxanne inquired as she smoothed her foot along the wet grass.

Frankie stared, dumbfounded. It somehow seemed weird to think about a school dance. Kennedy still felt too strange and unfamiliar. Dances had been scary enough at Stevenson. But here, where she barely knew anyone? Frankie didn't want to think about it.

"We definitely have to go," Roxanne said emphatically. "In fact, I've already figured out what I'm going to wear."

"What kind of a dance is it?" Frankie wondered.

"Valentine's Day," Roxanne said a little breathily. She was staring out across the grass, as if she had envisioned some perfectly wonderful Kennedy boy walking up to her and asking her to dance. That was the thing about Roxanne, though; she didn't really even have to imagine. It was sure to happen. She snapped out of her reverie and frowned at Frankie. "But I hear they've chosen a really dumb theme."

"What's that?"

"Sweetest Sweethearts."

Frankie looked puzzled. Sweetest Sweethearts didn't sound so dumb to her.

"It's a terrible theme," Roxanne explained as if she could read Frankie's thoughts. "It was probably deliberately chosen to keep us Stevenson people out."

Frankie looked shocked. "Why?"

"Don't you see?" Roxanne shot back. "They're going to have a contest! The Sweetest Sweethearts. That means the couple that's most popular will be the winner. And as far as I can tell, Kennedy High is full of couples."

Frankie nodded, beginning to get it now. "And you mean that because there aren't very many couples from Stevenson, and lots of us will be coming without dates, we'll be left out."

Roxanne smiled and nodded, although it was a grim kind of smile.

"That's not really true, though," Frankie reasoned. "I mean, a lot of Kennedy kids have to be going alone, too. Not *everyone* at Kennedy is part of a couple. And there are some couples who transferred from Steven — "

Roxanne glared. It was her look that meant, Just shut up Frankie, because smart as you are, you do not know nearly as much about this as I do. Frankie held her tongue.

"It's terrible the way we're being excluded," Roxanne huffed. "I mean, I'd like to have a chance to meet lots of Kennedy guys at the dance. But how can I do that if they all come as couples so they can compete in some dumb contest?"

Frankie backed up to avoid a giggly group of freshman girls coming over with their lunches. Roxanne whipped out her Vent brush. The little freshmen gaped as Roxanne's hair spilled over one shoulder as she brushed it. The younger girls scattered. Roxanne could make her presence known just by brushing her hair.

"You know," Frankie said timidly, "it's too bad it wasn't more of a Stevenson/Kennedy mixer. If only we could find a way to match Stevenson and Kennedy people up somehow."

Roxanne frowned, "Yeah, but how?"

"Well, I d-don't know," Frankie stammered. "Maybe like those computer dating services or something. They have the kind they advertise on cable TV and in the personal ads in magazines and stuff."

Roxanne rolled her eyes. "Computer dating services? Oh, Frankie, please."

"I actually wrote up this silly program once on my Apple at home that would match up couples." Frankie was trying to make light of her idea and save face. "It asked for all the information to lead to the perfect match . . . looks, personality, intelligence. It was pretty dumb."

"And who did it match you up with at Stevenson?" Roxanne asked. "That nerd Jacob Marzelman who was in your physics class?"

"Rox, don't be mean." Frankie sulked for a moment. "I never asked anybody at Stevenson to fill it out. I didn't think anybody would be interested. Besides, it was meant to match up strangers. It was just a joke."

Suddenly Roxanne froze dead still. She turned around and looked at her friend. She extended her arms and gripped Frankie by the shoulders. "Did you say it was designed to match up *strangers?*"

"Yes. All you have to do is make up questions to find out important things about a person, and then create a program to match — "

Roxanne held up a hand and Frankie stopped talking. "Do you think you could do the same thing on the computer they have here at school?"

Frankie nodded. "I don't see why not. There's an Apple in the student government room." She stared at Roxanne, trying to figure out why Rox was so excited all of a sudden, and then it struck her. "Rox, do you think we could. . . ."

"It's a great idea," Roxanne breathed, "an absolutely stunningly great idea." She grabbed Frankie's hand. "I was just teasing about Jacob. You know that, don't you?" Frankie nodded. "You're a genius, Frankie. This is just what we need."

"Do you really think it's a good idea. . . ?"

Even before Frankie could finish her sentence, Roxanne was pulling her down the hall into the building.

Just as Jonathan was about to give up on the computer, the door swung open. The girls marched in, new faces to the five in the student government room. The guys all jumped to their feet, and even Katie sat up straighter. One of them was the beautiful auburn-haired girl she'd noticed the other morning on the quad.

"Hello, boys," Roxanne purred in a low, warm voice. "I'm Roxanne Easton and I'm new, from Stevenson. This is my friend, Frankie Baker."

Jonathan strode forward, too eagerly, Katie thought. She, meanwhile, was gritting her teeth at the obvious slight intended in the new girl's "Hello, *boys*" greeting. Jonathan held out his hand to shake Roxanne's with as much enthusiasm as if he were meeting the President. "Nice to meet you, Roxanne," he declared sincerely. "Hi, Frankie," he added, not quite as ambitiously.

Roxanne slipped a black leather bag off her shoulder and draped it casually across the back of the chair Jonathan had been sitting in. To Katie, the gesture smacked of ownership, and she clenched her teeth again. A moment ago she'd been on the verge of taking off — she had some books to renew at the library — but instead, she crossed her arms and settled herself into her seat. She wasn't going to miss this scene for the world.

After everyone was introduced, there was a long, quiet moment during which Roxanne gazed around her at the four attentive boys. It was clear to Katie that they were waiting breathlessly for her next word. Roxanne lowered her long mascaraed eyelashes. Her full lips curved in a provocative smile. "As I said, I'm new here," she began. "And I'd really like to meet people and get involved in Kennedy activities." Now she opened her eyes wide, her expression sweet and helpless. "Did I come to the right place?"

"Did you ever!" Jonathan swept his hat off his head and bowed. Katie bit back a giggle. "This is where the action is, and of course we'd love to make you part of it. Why don't you sit down?" He waved his hat toward the couch. Before Roxanne had taken a single step, Eric practically leap-frogged over Matt in order to fluff up the cushions while Greg hurried to adjust the desk lamp on the nearby table so it wouldn't shine in Roxanne's eyes. When Roxanne sat down, her clingy purple sweater-dress slid up a few inches above her black-stockinged knees. She crossed her ankles gracefully. Katie shot a sharp-eyed look at Greg. His eyes weren't popping out of his head as much as Jonathan's, Matt's, and Eric's were, but they were popping nonetheless.

Meanwhile, Frankie had taken a seat in a chair not far from Katie, completely unnoticed. Katie's sympathy went out to the other girl. She'd only just met her, but she could imagine what it must be like to be Roxanne Easton's friend.

Roxanne tossed her thick, shiny mane of hair to one side and patted the space on the couch beside her. She looked at Jonathan expectantly. "As a student government official you must be *very* busy," she said. "What projects are you working on now?"

Jonathan sat down and began explaining the

40

need to get kids to go to the Valentine's Day Dance, especially since the ticket sale proceeds would go to the student activities fund. He didn't once look at Frankie, but directed all his remarks to Rox, who was an admiring audience.

"A Sweetest Sweethearts contest!" Rox exclaimed. "What a fabulous idea. Don't you think so, Frankie?"

Frankie started forward in her chair, looking a little bit surprised that someone was asking her opinion. "Mmm-hmmm," she agreed softly.

"The student government at Stevenson never had such good ideas," Rox assured Jonathan and the others, forgetting the fact that twenty minutes before she had told Frankie it was the dumbest idea in the world. "I can tell I'm going to like Kennedy about a million times more. It's all so much more . . . *stimulating*." She clasped her hands together and smiled, her green eyes sparkling with enthusiasm.

Jonathan glowed with pride. "We'll make sure you like it better," he said with a definite nod. "But as for the Valentine's Day Dance, we might have a great idea, but we can't get it off the ground. We can't figure out how to print up the contest ballots." He shook his head. "What's the point in having a brand-new computer if you can't figure out how to use it?"

Rox stood up and strolled across the room. The eyes of all four boys followed her every move. Katie watched them watch Roxanne and wanted to be sick. "This old thing?" Rox asked, tapping the Apple with one long fingernail. "Why, it's a piece of cake!" She waved to Frankie, who hurried over to join her. "I'm sure we can put together a ballot for you in no time. What do you want it to say?"

As Frankie took a seat in front of the computer, Jonathan ticked off on his fingers the information that should be included. Frankie typed rapidly and in few minutes she had designed a ballot, which was neatly displayed on the screen. In another moment it was running off on the printer.

Jonathan tore off the form and nodded. "This is exactly what I had in mind!" he exclaimed, glancing briefly at Frankie before turning his attention to Roxanne again. "I'm sure glad you two stopped by the office!"

"Roxanne, you must have been involved in student government at Stevenson. Have you thought about running for student body president yourself?" Greg asked honestly.

"Well, she sure was all caught up in student *politics*, anyway," Frankie muttered under her breath.

Rox waved Greg away, blushing but looking pleased. "You're such a tease. All I want to do is help."

"Well, you sure did," Eric said, taking the sample ballot from Jonathan and reading it carefully.

Roxanne had been standing next to Jonathan, one hand resting on top of the computer and the other lightly touching his sleeve. Now she interrupted the group's praises, her eyes lit up with inspiration. "This computer just got me thinking," she said. "I have the greatest idea!" She paused long enough to make sure she had everyone's attention. Even Katie couldn't help leaning forward in anticipation. "What if," Roxanne continued breathlessly, "we ran a computer Valentine service! Kids could fill out questionnaires and the computer would match people up. It could even arrange a time and a place for a romantic rendezvous at the dance!"

Roxanne's scheme was greeted with enthusiastic whoops by the guys. Katie had to admit to herself that it sounded like a lot of fun. Coupled with the Sweetest Sweethearts contest it was sure to draw more Kennedy — and Stevenson — students to the Valentine's Day Dance then ever before.

Roxanne and the four boys got involved in an animated discussion. Frankie, still seated at the computer, simply smiled. Katie glared sourly. After a few minutes it was decided that Rox and Jonathan would work up the questions. Frankie would program the computer to make the matches and then enter the information from the questionnaires. The room was buzzing with enthusiasm when they heard Brian Pierson signal the end of his noontime radio show. That meant the end of lunch, too. Roxanne retrieved her shoulderbag and turned to leave, and Frankie quickly headed to her side. "It was fun meeting

43

all of you," Rox said sincerely. "I'm really looking forward to helping with the dance!"

"It's going to be wild, thanks to you," Jonathan
assured her. What about Frankie? Katie wanted
to interject.

"Hey, Rox, speaking of school activities, do
you ski?" asked Eric.

Roxanne smiled and gestured with her hand to
indicate a little. "Why?"

"Kennedy High is sponsoring a ski trip in a
couple of weeks," he explained. "It's so popular,
there are only a few seats left on the second bus."

"You should definitely think about going,"
added Matt. "It'll be a great way to meet people."

Roxanne tipped her head to one side so that
her perfectly spiky bangs fell across her eyes.
"Gee, thanks for asking me. I'd love to go."

Greg apparently glimpsed Frankie out of the
corner of his eye and realized they hadn't included her. "You'll come, too, won't you,
Frankie?" he said politely, his smile friendly.

Frankie smiled shyly back but kept her eyes
on the ground. She shuffled her feet and edged
a little closer to the door. "I don't think so," she
said in a small voice. "Thanks anyway, though."

Eric, Matt, and Jonathan were still glued to
Roxanne and, by extension, Frankie. "What class
do you have next?" Matt asked solicitously. Rox
and Frankie both had English with Mr. Barclay,
and coincidentally all three boys were going the
same way. They offered to escort the girls to class.

As Greg reached under the desk where he'd

44

stashed his books, he spotted Katie still sitting in the corner, a decided pout on her pretty face. "Hey, what's the matter?" He crossed the room to stand in front of her, putting a hand on each of her shoulders. When he leaned forward to kiss her, Katie turned her face away, her frown only deepening. "What? Cat got your tongue?"

Greg nuzzled her neck and Katie giggled in spite of herself. In a manner of speaking! she thought. Aloud she said, "Have you ever known me to be at a loss for words?"

"No, I've got to admit I haven't." He tugged on her ponytail affectionately. "So why the long face?"

Katie shrugged. "I don't know. It was just a little nauseating how you guys fell all over that Roxanne person." She said the name with distaste. "You'd think none of you had ever seen a girl before! How do you suppose Pamela would've felt if she'd seen Matt gushing over a total stranger!" Katie gave Greg a pointed look. Matt wasn't the only one of the boys with a girlfriend. "And the way she pushes poor Frankie around," she continued, wrinkling her nose. "It's absolutely appalling!"

Greg burst out laughing. "I'd say, poor Rox! You just tore her apart pretty completely. I thought we agreed to go out of our way to help out the new kids."

Katie snorted. "Helping out is one thing. Drooling is another!"

"I know what this is all about." Greg held her

eyes, his own eyes crinkling mischievously. "Could it be that Katie Crawford assumed she'd be all alone in the spotlight this spring with her gymnastics title? But now it looks like Roxanne Easton may be a little competition?"

Katie blushed. "Don't be ridiculous!" she said with an indignant toss of her head.

"Don't be ridiculous!" he mimicked teasingly, grabbing Katie around the waist to tickle her.

"Get your hands off me!" she shrieked through her laughter. "I'm mad at you! You insulted me."

"Don't *you* be ridiculous," Greg ordered. "I'll only stop tickling you if you admit that you're silly to be jealous of Roxanne Easton and that you shouldn't be so competitive because it's not good for your blood pressure and that you know the last thing you should ever doubt is the way I feel for you."

Katie was giggling helplessly. "I admit it, I admit it!" she gasped. She could never stay mad at Greg for long, and she knew there was no reason to be angry now.

Greg threw his arms around her and hugged her tightly. "I knew you'd wise up."

Katie frowned again. "But Greg, she — "

"That's enough, K.C." His voice was tender, and he kissed her before she could say another word. Katie wrapped her arms around his neck and kissed him back. They were still tangled up together when the bell rang. Reluctantly Greg pulled away from Katie. "Time to go to class."

He sighed and pulled her close again, rubbing his cheek against Katie's soft hair.

"Wouldn't you rather lock the door and hide out here for the rest of the afternoon?" Katie suggested, raising her eyebrows at him meaningfully.

"Naw. To tell the truth, I'd rather chase Roxanne Easton down the hall," he teased.

Katie punched him lightly on the arm. "You bum!" He pulled her to her feet. As they headed for the door, Katie noticed the computer was still on. She made a move to flip off the switch but Greg grabbed her hand. "You don't just turn these babies off," he instructed her. "You have to hit a few keys first."

"Which ones?" Katie looked from the screen where the Sweetest Sweethearts ballot was still displayed to the keyboard, and back again.

"Um. . . ." Greg did the same, and then positioned his hands over the keys and closed his eyes. "These!" he said, typing randomly for a few seconds. Katie peered over his shoulder.

"Nothing happened," she observed.

Suddenly the printer beeped and blinked. An instant later it started printing and churning out Sweetest Sweethearts ballots faster than Greg and Katie could catch them. "Step right up and cast your vote for the Sweetest Sweethearts!" Greg howled.

Katie was laughing so hard her ribs ached. She grabbed an armful of ballots and threw them at

Greg. "Take that, Greg Montgomery!" she shouted. "I bet they're all votes for Roxanne Easton!"

Greg lunged for Katie, managing to grab her arm just as he stepped on a ballot and his foot slipped out from under him. They slid to the floor together in a heap of paper and laughter. "Don't say I never swept you off your feet," Greg panted.

Katie giggled. "You sure know how to show a girl you like her!"

"I'd go a lot further than this to show this girl I'm crazy about her," Greg told Katie. The paper ballots were still showering down on them as they kissed again.

Chapter 4

Holly Daniels shaded her eyes against the bright afternoon sun so she could see Diana Einerson. Diana was describing the dress she'd bought to wear to the symphony with her boyfriend, Jeremy Stone. ". . . and it goes down to about here with a flared hem and a dropped waist that kind of skims over my hips. And the sleeves end about here and the neckline kind of goes like this. . . ." Diana stopped gesturing. "Holly? Yo, Holly!"

Holly blinked her hazel eyes twice. "Sorry, Di! I'm listening, I really am. I was just so . . . *enraptured* by the thought of your new dress I lost touch with reality for a minute." She grinned impishly and her friend groaned. "No, really, it sounds gorgeous," Holly assured Diana. Her smile faded slightly. "But my mind *is* elsewhere."

"It couldn't be at the library already." Diana and Holly had bumped into each other in the hall after school, and Diana was walking Holly to the library before she headed for the sub shop.

"No." Holly shook her head sorrowfully. "I haven't even thought about that dumb European history paper! I don't know who I'm fooling by going to the library anyhow. There's no way I'll get anything done."

"How come?" Diana pushed a strand of long blonde hair out of her eyes.

"Same old reason," Holly answered. "What always distracts me? I miss Bart."

"Oh," Diana said simply, but Holly knew the one word carried all the sympathy and understanding in the world. Holly's boyfriend, Bart Einerson, also happened to be her best friend Diana's older brother. Sometimes that could be awkward — Holly thought back a year to when things weren't going well between her and Bart. She'd confided somewhat hastily in Diana, which only forced Diana to jump to her brother's defense. But for the most part, Diana was caring and very fair, and sometimes it made Holly feel better to commiserate with someone who missed Bart almost as much as she did. Today, though, Diana's friendly smile and the freckles on her nose only reminded Holly of Bart and how quickly the trip to Montana over the Christmas holidays had passed. Bart was away at college in Montana, and at this point, nothing but vacation would bring him any closer.

The two girls reached the library, but instead of going in, they opened a door that led outside and sat out on the broad white stone steps. Diana seemed to know that Holly needed to talk. "Bart misses you, too," she said. She slipped her light brown suede jacket off her shoulders and tilted her face toward the sun. It was a freaky day, so sunny and warm that it felt like spring. "Mom called him at school last night and I hopped on the phone, too." Diana laughed. "He actually *told* me he missed you. He's definitely getting soft and sentimental in his old age!"

Holly laughed, too, but there was a little catch in her voice. Resting her elbows on her knees and her chin in her hands, she turned to Diana. "I don't think he's changed that much," she said with a long, sad sigh. "He's probably the same old Bart."

"Yeah, I guess he is," Diana agreed. She patted Holly's shoulder. "You must really be blue, Holl, if you're pining nostalgically for the same old girl-chasing Bart!"

Holly nodded, one brown curl falling over her eye. She puffed a breath upward to blow it aside. "True," she admitted. "*Last* winter Bart and I almost broke up because of the way he flirts with every girl he meets. But now I even miss his flirting!" Both girls burst out laughing. "Seriously, Di, now I could deal with it. If he were home, I wouldn't mind if he had ten blonde bombshells hovering around him every minute. I'd know it didn't mean anything, that it wouldn't change the fact that I'm the one he cares about. Instead, here it is, almost another Valentine's Day and we're not together. We won't be for a long time." She looked over at Diana. "It's hard to have to listen to everybody planning the computer Valentine service and the Sweetest Sweethearts Contest when I don't have anything to look forward to. I just feel . . . *lonely*."

"I know." Diana's blonde eyebrows were knit with concern. "I mean, I don't *know*. I'm lucky that Jeremy and I are in the same class. But I can imagine how it would be if we were separated."

"It's rotten." Holly kicked the rubber toe of her pink sneaker against the cement step. "It was so great to see him over Christmas vacation, but in a way that only made it harder. It was such a short visit. Oh, Di, he's so far away."

Diana picked at a loose thread on the lace border of the white petticoat she was wearing underneath her full blue chambray skirt. "You're not getting discouraged, are you, Holly? I mean, you still think things can work out for you two?"

"Yeah, I do." The frown left Holly's pretty face and she smiled hopefully. "A year from now maybe I'll be a student at the University of Montana, too, doing premed! That's what I'm working for. If I get that scholarship, I'm all set!" Holly looked at her watch. "Which is why I should have been in the library half an hour ago!"

"You can do it," Diana encouraged her. "I

know it. Hey!" Diana's eyes lit up. "My mom is going to put together a care package to send to Bart in the next few days. Why don't you write a special pre-Valentine's Day letter to add to it? It would be a really nice surprise for him."

Holly nodded as she gathered her books together and climbed the last few steps to the library door. "I'll write one right now!" she declared, her eyes sparkling with inspiration. "European history can wait."

Diana hopped down two steps, heading back toward the road. "Well, I'll leave you to it. I'm off to the sub shop — Jeremy's waiting for me. The whole gang'll probably be there. Are you sure you don't want to come?"

"No, thanks. Now I have *two* projects to work on! I'll be here all afternoon."

"Okay, but I tell you what — I'll stop back here on my way home. You can give me the letter then."

"Great!" Holly waved good-bye to Diana and turned to open the heavy glass door of the library. Then she turned back again. "Hey, Di!" she called after her friend.

Diana spun around on one cowboy-booted heel, her blonde hair swinging in a silken arc. "What?"

"Thanks for cheering me up," Holly said. "I feel a lot better."

"Hey, no problem!" Diana shrugged, smiling. "What are friends for?" Her smile broadened into a grin. "Besides, I have an added interest in keeping you and your boyfriend happy. After all, he is my brother!"

Once inside the library, Holly headed straight for the far wall. She chose her favorite seat, at one of the carrels along the full-length windows overlooking the lawn. This way if she got tired of her work, she could escape for a minute and watch the passersby. Holly loved to study the little saplings that lined the sidewalk for signs of buds. Bart had spent a lot of time outdoors when he lived in Montana, before his family moved to Rose Hill, and he had taught her to notice things like that. Now she made sure to watch the way the branches of trees changed color in late winter as they got ready to burst into leaf. Bart had said. . . . Holly cut her thought short with a determined sigh. She didn't have time to reminisce if she wanted to write a letter to Bart *and* get a good start on her history paper.

Holly piled her books on the corner of the desk — *Biography of a Revolutionary, Perspectives on the French Revolution, The Reign of Louis XVI and Marie Antoinette* — in alphabetical order. Then she restacked them with the biggest book on the bottom and the smallest one on top. She didn't know where to start. Her teacher had assigned one of those topics that you could write about a hundred different ways: the French Revolution. Maybe she'd write to Bart first.

Holly pulled out a clean piece of notebook paper and smoothed it out on the desk. *Dear*

Bart, she wrote carefully. She wiggled forward on her chair, chewing on the end of her pen. *Dear Bart . . . what*? She leaned back again and stretched, gazing around her for inspiration. Then it hit her. In addition to telling Bart how much she missed him and wished they could be together this Valentine's Day, she could imagine the scene next year on Valentine's Day when they *would* be together, in Montana!

Holly's eyes became dreamy as she ran over the imaginary details in her mind: the horseback ride on the snowy range, dinner in a candlelit cabin. . . . Then she shook her head, realizing she'd been staring blankly at the profile of an unfamiliar boy a few tables away at the microfilm projector. A half smile touched her lips. Something about him reminded her of Bart. Not his coloring — Bart was dark and this boy had blond hair — but his build and athletic way of moving. Holly forgot about writing her letter and watched the boy instead. He was trying to set up the microfilm on the machine but was failing miserably. First he couldn't find the light switch, then he seemed to have trouble figuring out how to feed the spool. He was all big hands and muscular arms, and he looked to Holly as if he'd be a lot more comfortable handling a football than a tiny roll of film. Finally, after a few more fumbles, the film spilled out of his hands and rolled onto the floor. Holly started to giggle, but to her surprise the boy crossed his arms on the desktop and buried his head in them. He wasn't laughing at himself but instead, looked utterly defeated and discouraged.

Holly stared at his bent back and the word STEVENSON stared back at her. Of course, she thought, surprised, he's one of the new students. A warm rush of sympathy flooded through her. She remembered the talk with her friends a week ago when they'd all agreed to be extra-friendly to the Stevenson kids. Well, here was her chance. This guy certainly looked as if he could use a friend.

Holly pushed back her chair and stood up, smoothing her hands down the front of her lemon-yellow knit dress. A few steps later, she was standing next to the boy at the microfilm projector. Just as she leaned forward to speak to him, he sat up straight. Their eyes met and he looked startled. Holly hurried to introduce herself. "Hi," she said, gesturing with a smile at the projector. "I noticed you were having a little trouble with this miracle of modern technology. I'm Holly Daniels. I'm a senior."

The boy's glum expression lifted and he returned her smile shyly. "I'm Zachary McGraw. Um, I'm a junior and I just transferred from Stevenson." He glanced at what were clearly still unfamiliar surroundings and then nodded at the uncooperative microfilm machine. "I'm new at this," he explained.

Holly laughed. "I figured that! Want some help?"

This time Zachary's smile was big and bright.

"I guess it's pretty obvious, huh?" he said good-naturedly. "I would really appreciate your help. I'll never catch up in this government class at the rate I'm going."

"This machine's pretty easy, really." Holly pulled up a chair and reached to take the film from him. As she did, their eyes met and they smiled at each other again. Zachary McGraw, she thought, and then realized why the name seemed familiar. Zachary McGraw was the all-city quarterback all the Kennedy football players had been talking about! And here she was, about to give him a lesson in using a microfilm machine.

From everything Holly had heard, Zachary was an ultrasensational athlete. Now she could see for herself that he was gorgeous to boot. In her experience, this was a dangerous combination. She found herself feeling more than a little taken aback. She would have expected a celebrated jock, especially one as good-looking as Zachary, to come across as conceited or at least bold and flirtatious like Bart. But this boy seemed just the opposite.

Holly forced her attention back to the task at hand. Zachary was watching her attentively. "Like I was saying," she continued, hoping he hadn't picked up on her surprise, "this is simple. You just take the film and thread it through here, making sure you line it up correctly. Then it goes on the other spool like this. Oh, and first you switch the light on! Then you just turn this knob to get to the frame you want." Zachary nodded but Holly caught his doubtful expression. She patiently ran through her explanation again, and this time Zachary nodded that he understood. Now she watched him as he easily located the newspaper article he was looking for.

"Fantastic!" he exclaimed. "You're right, this *is* easy." He turned to face her, running a hand carelessly through his hair and making it stand up on top. "Holly, thanks. You really saved the day for me."

Holly lifted her slim shoulders and smiled. "No problem. I remember the first time I tried to research a paper here. I didn't know microfilm from a microwave!" Zachary laughed heartily. "Anyway," she added, "it's tough to be new, I know."

Zachary's blue eyes held hers. "It is kind of tough being new here, but meeting someone as friendly as you has made it a lot easier already," he said sincerely.

Holly felt herself blush. She turned toward the projector screen so Zachary wouldn't notice. There was no reason why a simple, harmless compliment should have such an effect on her.

"Yep," Zachary was saying, "since I've talked to you, it's a whole new ballgame! I think I stand a chance in this library and on my government paper, after all."

Holly put her hands to her face, which still felt a little warm beneath her cool fingers. She looked back at Zachary. "You've mastered the microfilm machine, but what about the rest of this place?" she asked, doing her best to sound casual.

Zachary wrinkled his thick eyebrows and smiled sheepishly. "I don't suppose you have the time to give me a real tour?" he asked, his voice hopeful.

Holly laughed. He was such a nice guy that she could hardly refuse. She grabbed his arm and they both stood up and headed over to the card catalog section. "I'm sure you know about the Dewey Decimal System and all that," Holly whispered. "So you just have to learn what numbers are located where. There are three floors and the stacks get kind of confusing. And there are other ways to get to periodicals besides the microfilm. Over here are bound copies of about a million magazines and journals, and up there. . . ."

Holly and Zachary ended up spending almost an hour discussing the ins and outs of the Kennedy library. Or rather, they spent about ten minutes discussing the ins and outs of the library and the rest of the time discussing the ins and outs of Kennedy High in general. Holly was more and more impressed by Zachary. He was friendly and curious, but at the same time a little bit shy and very polite. He greeted every new bit of new information Holly told him, every helpful hint, with a grin of appreciation. For Holly, who had never thought of herself as knowing and experienced, it was fun to suddenly be in the position of local expert.

The two were sitting by the microfilm projector again whispering about which English teachers to avoid and why second shift lunch was better than first, when Holly glanced up and saw Diana stroll into the library. She looked down at her watch. Five o'clock! Where had the time gone? Zachary caught her expression and got slowly to his feet as Holly jumped to hers. "That's my ride," Holly explained, waving vaguely in the direction of the library entrance. "I've gotta run."

Zachary pushed his hands into the pockets of his jeans and nodded, a shock of unruly blond hair falling over his forehead. "Well, Holly, uh, I'm really glad I met you."

"Me, too!" Holly said with genuine feeling. They stood there for a moment smiling at each other and then Holly dropped her gaze and half turned away. "I'll see you around."

"Sure hope so!" Zachary laughed. "Thanks again for helping me out."

"Any time." Holly gathered her books together quickly and trotted toward the front of the library to find Diana. For some reason she didn't want her friend to see her with Zachary. She wasn't doing anything wrong by talking to him, but. . . . Holly knew Diana would approve completely of her playing tour guide for one of the new Stevenson students. Still. . . .

Holly looked over her shoulder just before she joined Diana. Zachary was watching her from the far table. She waved discreetly and he waved back. His friendly smile warmed her from across the cold, crowded library.

"Ready, Holly?" Diana was asking. "Jeremy's waiting in the car."

"Uh, sure. Let's go!"

Holly pushed the door open. Diana stepped through and then stopped and turned to Holly expectantly. "So, where is it?"

Holly looked confused. "Where is what?"

"Everyone wondered why you weren't at the sub shop and I told them you were busy composing the greatest love letter ever," Diana said teasingly. "Let's have it!"

Holly clapped a hand over her mouth. She realized now that one of the pieces of paper she'd shoved into the pages of the book about Louis XVI and Marie Antoinette was a blank sheet with only two words on it: *Dear Bart.*

"Oh, Diana," she exclaimed. "Would you believe I didn't even — I didn't finish it yet! I felt kind of obligated to spend a few minutes on my history. I'll bring it over to your house tonight, okay?"

"Fine with me!" she replied and Holly breathed a secret sigh of relief. Luckily, Diana was very easygoing.

When they reached Diana's white convertible Mustang, Jeremy was hanging out the window on the passenger side with his camcorder aimed at them. "Say cheese!" he hollered. Diana squealed and held her hands up to her face. "Just kidding," he assured her in his English accent, which had faded a little bit during the time he'd been living in the U.S. "Look, no film! Hi, Holl."

"Hi, Jer." Holly settled herself into the backseat and looked out the window at the library building while Diana and Jeremy debated whether or not to put the car top down. Jeremy observed that it was nearly as warm as spring, and Jonathan drove his car with the top down *all the time*. Diana pointed out that even though it was nearly as warm as spring, it was still only January. Holly didn't really hear them, though. She was wondering how she could have let herself be so distracted by Zachary McGraw when she should have been devoting all her thoughts to Bart and the special letter she was going to write him. She pressed her nose to the glass of the window, puzzled. Of course, Zachary was very cute and he was a star athlete and all that jazz. But those sort of credentials had never carried much weight with her. Besides, she knew they had nothing to do with why the new boy had made such an impression on her.

As Diana pulled away from the curb, having won out in the car top issue, Holly realized what it was about Zachary that attracted her. She'd enjoyed his company but it was more than that. Zachary had made her feel something that Bart had never made her feel in all their time together: *needed*.

Chapter
5

Frankie Baker held a huge stack of books against her chest. Physics text. Notebook. Three computer manuals. Algebra/Trigonometry — that one was really fat and heavy. Plus four sci-fi novels from the Kennedy library. She wobbled under the weight, barely making her way down the crowded hallway.

"Room four twenty-three. East Corridor," she muttered, reminding herself where to go for her next class. Then she looked around to make sure that no one had seen her. It was weird enough being the smartest person — not just girl but person — in all her math and computer courses. All she needed was to have people think she talked to herself, like those geeky guys who stayed after school every day in the physics lab.

Frankie flattened her slender body against the

wall and let the other Kennedy students rush past. She suddenly couldn't remember which direction she was supposed to head in. But everybody else looked so sure, so rowdy and confident, that to ask for directions — even though she was new — seemed unthinkable.

She'd been at Kennedy for a couple of weeks now but without Roxanne, she still didn't know her way around. It was funny how it worked. Roxanne had led the way in everything since they were kids — back in the fifth grade when they shared a car pool. Even though Frankie knew she was much smarter, Rox always seemed quicker to react, to find her way, to get attention. And as much as Frankie sometimes resented the way Rox bossed her around, she often felt lost without her.

Frankie backed up even further and let the other students pass. She felt almost invisible, part of the wall. That was the way she saw herself when she looked in the mirror. Blended. All one color. Pale skin. Beige eyes, like Rox said. Straw-colored hair. Sometimes when she stared at herself, she saw little more than a pale, freckled blur.

In contrast, Rox was all color and flash. Everyone noticed Rox, even gave her credit for things that weren't her doing. Like in sixth grade when Frankie had planned the entire elementary school science fair. Rox thought a science fair was the height of nerd-dom and didn't want to talk about it. But then when they placed in the state finals and the whole class got a special tour of the Smithsonian, suddenly it was Rox who'd made the whole thing happen. But Frankie knew that's how it was when your best friend was a dazzler like Rox, and you were just . . . Frankie.

"FRANKO!"

A deep, confident voice was suddenly calling from the other end of the corridor. The sound of it jolted Frankie out of her thoughts. She stiffened and looked up.

"Hey, Frank! Is that you, Franko?"

Frankie's heart was jumping over hurdles. There was only one boy who called her Franko — a childhood name — after Franko American Spaghetti. He was a boy she'd known as long as she'd known Rox — and he was a boy she'd loved as long as she could remember. Football star, Zachary McGraw.

"Franko," Zachary grinned, easing his way over. His wide shoulders split an even passageway through the crowd.

Frankie, suddenly aware that she was smiling like an idiot, looked down. As she did, some overactive freshman bumped her from behind. Her books scattered, and Frankie fell to her knees. "Oh, no," she gasped, trying to gather up her books again.

Zack eased down gracefully and helped her. As he picked up each book, he examined the title and shook his head. "Brainy Franko."

Frankie shrank a little and grabbed her books back, stacking them on the floor beside her. "Thanks," she said, finally looking into Zack's face. His eyes were the clearest blue and his hair was freshly cut. When he smiled, his cheeks folded into two identical dimples. "How do you like our new school?"

"Okay," Zack answered easily. "You know me. I'm never too into things until football season starts." He looked at his Stevenson letter jacket, then back at her. "I never see you around."

Frankie shrugged, not sure how to respond. She took all the hardest subjects. Since Zack wasn't a very good student, they hadn't been in classes together since grade school. But at Stevenson she'd memorized his schedule. She'd figured out how to "accidentally" run into him outside his general math class, to "coincidentally" pass his locker, to cross paths with him before he went to football practice. But since the transfer she hadn't known where to look for him. She'd missed him like crazy. "I know."

"I've missed you," he said carelessly.

Frankie beamed. For a short second she let herself believe that he really meant something. But when she looked in his face again, she knew otherwise. His expression was polite and cool. To Zack, she was just brainy Franko. He'd never miss her the way she'd missed him. "It's weird being in a new school, isn't it?"

Zack nodded. "I think we're all having a hard time getting used to it."

"Everybody except Rox," Frankie blurted. "She's into everything right away."

Zack picked up her books as Frankie stood

up. He rolled his eyes. "That figures," he grumbled. He and Rox didn't like each other, although Frankie had never been sure exactly why. She wasn't sure she wanted to know.

Zack started to walk. "We'd better get to class. Where are you headed?" He held her books securely under one strong arm. "Maybe I'd better help you carry these."

Frankie led the way to her class. Suddenly the direction was as clear as anything. It was always like that when she was near Zack. Great clarity mixed with breathless confusion. "If you ever need any help," she hesitated, not wanting to leave him so soon, "with math or anything, you know I'd be glad to."

He carefully handed back her books and smiled. When she was loaded up again he playfully chucked her chin with his fist. "Good old Franko," he teased, "always looking out for me."

Frankie blushed. She wondered if she'd said the wrong thing. Sometimes she got the feeling that Zack was embarrassed about not being a better student. She hoped that he didn't think she was making fun of him. "I just meant, if you wanted to. Not that you need it or anything."

"Right." He started to go, breaking into a jog. "See you soon, I hope, Franko!"

"Zack," Frankie called after him. "They have this Apple — this computer — in the student government room. I guess I'll be in there sometimes, working on it." Instantly she wished that she could have said, I'll be at cheerleading practice or play rehearsal or something more exotic. "So if you need me," she added in a tiny voice — or you just want to see me, she prayed silently.

"I can find you there." He smiled.

"Yes. You can find me there."

"Okay." He was running now. "Gotta go. 'Bye, Franko!"

" 'Bye," Frankie whispered. She watched him go and, with a burning heart, headed into class.

That afternoon, as soon as the last bell rang, Katie bolted out of class and raced across campus. Since that day when Greg and the others had hung on Roxanne's every word, she'd been feeling edgy, uncertain. Even though she and Greg had laughed over it, every time Katie saw Roxanne, her insides curdled. Breaking into a full run, Katie passed the student government room and the boys' gym. She didn't want to see Greg right now. Finally, she breezed into the locker room, changed, and rushed out onto the gym floor.

At last she felt at ease. Katie loved the Kennedy gym. The echo. The thump of bare feet against the gymnastic mats. The smell of chalk and wood and even sweat. The murmur of voices, punctuated by a few laughs and the blast of Coach Muldoon's whistle. This was her favorite place in Kennedy High, and she felt incredibly lucky to spend the last two hours of every school day in it.

"Hey, K.C.!"

Katie looked up at the sound of her coach's voice. Ms. Muldoon, the slender, young gymnastics teacher, was standing over her, smiling. "I'm almost warmed up," Katie informed her. She was in a full split, easily stretching with her chin resting on the gray floor mat.

"How do you feel?" Coach Muldoon asked.

"Great."

"Are you totally warmed up?"

Katie nodded.

"You sure?"

"Yes!"

"Okay." Ms. Muldoon gave her a funny smile. "On your feet, then. I bet you can't do a cartwheel into a double flip."

Katie jumped up and grinned at her coach. This was an old game between Katie and her teacher. Ms. Muldoon knew that Katie could never resist a challenge or dare of any sort. Katie immediately went along. "Says who?"

Ms. Muldoon looked back at the other girls on the team. They were finishing with their own warmups and starting to watch Katie. "Says me."

Katie put her hands on her hips. She wore a long-sleeved V-neck leotard. Her legs were bare and there were dabs of chalk on her palms. She gestured for her teammates to clear the mats at the center of the gym floor.

As Katie walked out, Coach Muldoon added, "With a perfect landing."

"Just put the ten up there right now," Katie answered over her shoulder.

Ms. Muldoon laughed.

Katie approached the corner of the mat, then stopped and took a deep breath. She went over the move in her mind, seeing herself execute it perfectly. She felt her strong legs relax. She cleared her brain of everything else — Greg, the silly argument over Roxanne Easton and the Valentine's Day Dance. She leaned forward, pressed into the floor with the balls of her feet, and took off.

She flew, fearlessly throwing her head down, skimming the mat with her palms, her legs stretching into the air like a pair of scissors. Over she went and then pushed off again with her thighs, her arms tucked in now, her stomach tight. Fast and small. Over once. Again. Then she was landing, trying to think of her feet being like anchors, her body all in one piece like a rod of steel. Thunk. She stopped, very still. Her arms stretched way over her head, she tipped her face up and grinned.

"TEN!" screamed her teammates as they cheered and applauded.

Katie did a mock bow, bending at the waist and making a serious face. But when she stood up again she saw a tall boy leaning in the doorway. He was watching her, too, smiling, and holding up his hands. Ten fingers. It was Greg.

Katie was filled with warmth. Greg often stopped by to watch her practice for a minute or two on his way to crew workout or some other after school activity. She was suddenly very glad he was there, that he'd seen her perform. He waved, blew her a kiss, and made a funny rowing gesture indicating that he was on his way to practice himself. Only instead of heading for the river, because it was nearly frozen over, Greg was off to the weight room. Katie flexed a muscle until he laughed, and then she waved good-bye.

"On that inspiring note, I want you to divide up and work on your main events," Coach was ordering.

Katie stayed on the mat, smiling as the other girls filled in around her. They all made sure to give her the most room, the right of way, the prime place on the mat. After all, she was the team star. Katie shook her head and her pigtails brushed her cheeks. Greg could tease her all he liked about being too competitive. But no matter what he said, she knew that being a competitor was the core of her being. Her desire to win was her biggest strength. It was probably what Greg had seen in her in the first place. Katie let out a deep, happy sigh and started to work on her floor routine. She knew now that it was silly to worry about Roxanne Easton or anybody else from Stevenson High.

Chapter
6

Jonathan bustled around the student government room trying to make it presentable. He'd never noticed before how messy and shabby everything was. And that couch! He grimaced. It was truly hideous. Actually, everything was. Maybe he and the other kids should pitch in for something to put on the walls instead of all those juvenile rock star posters. A potted plant or two wouldn't hurt, either. Oh, well, he thought as he grabbed up an armful of scattered newspapers and computer printouts and shoved them into the top drawer of the big metal desk, *It's too late to do anything before Roxanne* — Jonathan stopped himself in midthought. *Before Roxanne gets here,* he'd started to think. He snorted. He wasn't about to admit to himself that he was making a fuss over a girl he'd only met once. No, the student government room needed revamping for its own sake. It was just too late to do anything about it right now, that was all. That was what he *meant* to think, anyway.

The sound of the doorknob turning caused Jonathan to jump to attention. As he rushed over to open it, Jonathan kicked his fedora, which was lying in the middle of the floor, under the table. Roxanne pushed the door the same moment that he pulled it. She almost fell into the room. "Hey, Rox!" Jonathan greeted her enthusiastically. "Thanks a lot for staying after school to help out with this. Here, let me take your coat." Roxanne stood still while Jonathan, being very deferential, lifted the coat from her shoulders and then draped it carefully over the back of the desk chair.

"I'm happy to," she assured him as he turned to face her again. Jonathan stopped in his tracks. If anything, Roxanne looked more fantastic than she had the other day when he met her. Wearing slim-cut, white wool trousers and a fuzzy emerald-green sweater that matched her eyes, she was curvy and cuddly and altogether breathtaking.

He swallowed hard. He couldn't just stand here staring at her speechlessly all afternoon. "Uh, why don't we sit down?" he mumbled, waving at the couch and following Roxanne as she walked over to it. She sat on one side but when he sat on the other, she moved over a little bit to narrow the space between them. Jonathan gulped again. Roxanne beamed.

"It's so nice of you to let me take part in your

Valentine's Day Dance project. I mean, me being new and all." Her green eyes were wide and serious. "Meeting you and getting involved this way makes me feel at home here, or at least more at home than before."

Jonathan felt a stir of protectiveness. Rox wasn't complaining, but her words made him realize it must be pretty difficult being one of the new Stevenson students. He nodded understandingly. "We want you to feel at home — I mean hey, this *is* your home now!" He smiled. "And you'd better come hang out in here anytime you feel like it."

Roxanne put a hand on Jonathan's knee and leaned forward. "That means a lot to me," she said softly. "Thanks."

"Sure. And anyway, this computer Valentine service was your great idea!" He put a hand on hers and squeezed it lightly.

Roxanne's eyes brightened. "So, let's get down to business, okay?" She crossed her legs and then bent down to pull a new spiral notebook from her shoulderbag. When she sat up she had a pen in one hand and there was an alert expression on her pretty face. "I've made up some test questions. Did you have a chance to come up with any?"

"No," Jonathan admitted. He flashed her a devilish grin. "I thought about it a little but I didn't get past 'What color hair do you prefer?' and 'Do you like 'em tall or short?' "

Rox laughed. She shook her pen at Jonathan.

"Now, Jonathan, you know those aren't the things that matter most. If we want our computer to match people up with someone who they'll really have a lot in common with, if we want to make some magic here, we have to probe a little deeper than that!"

"You're right," Jonathan conceded.

"What I had in mind for this afternoon" — Roxanne flipped open her notebook, and Jonathan glimpsed a full page of neatly numbered items — "is, I'll ask you the test questions, and you'll tell me what you think of each one. You know, whether you feel your answer to it would reveal something that would help the computer match you up with your dream girl."

Jonathan laughed. "If you think the computer could do that, you're on!"

Roxanne's smile was self-assured. "We'll see. Are you ready to start?"

Jonathan leaned back on the couch and put his hands behind his head. He winked at Roxanne. "Shoot!"

"Okay." She chewed delicately on the end of her pen and studied her list of questions. "First, we ask for name and class year, of course. And I say we leave out any questions about looks." She lifted her eyes to him. "I mean, that's not what really matters about a person, is it?"

"You're right," Jonathan agreed wholeheartedly. But when someone's as beautiful as you are, he added silently to himself, it's hardly a drawback.

75

Rox held her pen out toward Jonathan, pretending it was a microphone. "So, Mr. X, here's question number one: Name three of your favorite things."

"Raindrops on roses and whiskers on kittens," Jonathan began, grinning. "Just kidding! My three favorite things, huh? Well, that's pretty easy. Mystery novels — my mom writes them, did I tell you that? — and . . . kooky clothes and . . . my Fifty-seven Chevy, Big Pink."

Roxanne giggled. "That *is* a wonderful car. I've seen it in the parking lot. Do you think there's a chance I could ever have a ride in it?" she asked hopefully.

Jonathan smiled, gratified. "Just name the day! Big Pink and I would love to take you for a spin."

"Great! Hey, wait, about the mystery novels," she said. "Your mother isn't by any chance *the* Angela Preston?" Roxanne's expression was awed.

" 'Fraid so."

She clasped her hands together. "Oh, I just love her books!" she exclaimed. "I'm absolutely wild about them. They are so entertaining and *so* intellectually stimulating."

Jonathan shrugged. "They're okay," he admitted, looking pleased. "I'm glad you like them."

"Well, I really do. Anyway, on to the next question." Roxanne referred to her notebook.

"What are your three *least* favorite things?"

"That's easy, too." Jonathan only had to think for a second. "Traveling, poverty, and the ballet."

"What an interesting combination of things," she observed. "Why do you particularly dislike those three?"

Jonathan leaned forward with his elbows on his knees. He shook a strand of iron-straight blond hair out of his eyes. "I'm not really sure." He hesitated. "Traveling is . . . I don't know, it's just not my bag."

"I know how you feel." Rox nodded, her own hair falling loosely over her shoulders. "It's nice to be, well, rooted somewhere. Um. . . ." She waited for Jonathan to resume his reflections.

"Yeah, that's true. Travel can be very educational, but at the same time, it can't help being an impersonal, dislocating process. I guess I think people should just stay where they are." Rox nodded again, clearly in complete sympathy, although she couldn't know that Jonathan was thinking about a specific situation. His former girlfriend, Fiona Stone, a dancer from England, had only recently returned there to study ballet professionally. Their breakup had been painful — and very final. The Atlantic Ocean lying between them made certain of that. "As for poverty," Jonathan continued, "I think it's a crime. I hope in our lifetime it can be eliminated altogether." His gray eyes flashed. "Big changes'll have to be made, but there are little things we can do to help right now. Like raising money for the homeless, for instance. We had a drive to do that last winter."

"I read about it in the *Rose Hill Bulletin*," Roxanne told him. "I remember thinking I really admired the people who were behind it." She smiled shyly. "I hope you'll do something like that again soon so I can help."

Jonathan was warming up under Roxanne's praise. He lifted an arm to rest it along the top of the sofa back behind her shoulders. "I'm sure there will be. There are so many important causes," he concluded. "We're always working on something."

"And ballet?" Rox referred to Jonathan's third dislike.

He arched his eyebrows. "Ballet is . . . *ballet*. Need I say more?"

They both burst out laughing. "I feel *exactly* the same way!" Roxanne wrinkled her pert nose. "I never could stand it." She smiled at Jonathan, her eyes sparkling. "Well, you're just about halfway through my sample questionnaire. Do you want to keep going?"

"You bet! This is a blast."

"Question number three, then: What do you look for in a boy or girl? Name three qualities."

Jonathan closed his eyes to concentrate. Roxanne watched him closely, her own eyes narrowed. "Three qualities I look for in a girl are . . . honesty, a sense o fhumor, and she has to be someone who cares about something other than herself. You know, her community or her school, that sort of thing."

Rox sat up straighter and pushed her long hair back from her shoulders. She smiled encouragingly at Jonathan. "Last serious question: In your mind, what three things make a successful friendship or romance?"

"Now that's a good one!" Jonathan laughed, a little bitterly. He certainly knew what contributed to an unsuccessful relationship. All he had to do was look at his experience with Fiona. "I think it's really important to have a lot in common with the person, the same background, interests, that kind of stuff. At the same time, you have to be independent. And most of all you've got to want to make the other person happy, make them feel good about themselves." There, he thought, everything that was wrong with my relationship with Fiona — in a nutshell.

He jumped. Rox was waving her hand in front of his face. "Hey, Jonathan!" she said, teasing him. "My questions were meant to be thought-provoking, but I didn't mean to launch you into outer space!"

Jonathan grinned and rolled his eyes comically. "Whoa! What a ride!" He looked at her seriously. "But honestly, Rox, those are really good questions."

"I thought so," she agreed with a frank smile. "I'm especially proud of that last one. Too often a relationship doesn't work out because the two people have such different expectations. Don't you think so?"

Jonathan nodded slowly. "You kinda read my mind, Rox," he confessed. "I know we're going over these questions to test them out for the computer Valentine service, but I'm actually finding out a few things about myself. Putting things in perspective, you know? The last girl I went out with — " He stopped and frowned, then laughed wryly. "You really don't want to hear all this."

"No, go on. I'm interested, really." Her low voice was soft and coaxing. Jonathan relaxed. Before he knew exactly what he was saying, he found himself pouring out to her the story of his break up with Fiona. Rox didn't comment or intrude, but her eyes were warm and understanding. Jonathan could tell she knew where he was coming from. When he stopped talking, Roxanne sat silently for a moment. Then she tilted her head to one side. "Are you sorry it's over?" she probed delicately.

"Nope." Jonathan was firm. "It might sound like a cop-out but I really think it's for the best. Next time I should look for a girl who doesn't live on another continent and whose interests are more in line with my own." He grinned crookedly. "A British ballerina and an American social worker — maybe we were mismatched from the start!"

"Well, as you said, you learned something for

next time," Rox reminded him. "And I don't think it's a cop-out to feel that way," she added. "It's just sensible."

"You got it. Now, back to business. Is that the end of the questionnaire?"

Rox snapped her notebook shut briskly. "The last question is going to be 'Who would you most like to be matched with?' and you can actually write down that person's name. You're only guaranteed the match if both people write down each other, though."

"Great idea!" Jonathan's hand slid from the back of the couch to Roxanne's shoulder to give it an enthusiastic squeeze.

"Tell me," she continued, hesitating slightly. "What would you think about asking people who are new from Stevenson if they'd like to be matched with someone from Kennedy and vice versa? Maybe that would encourage a little mingling. What do you think?"

Roxanne looked at Jonathan for approval, a shy, sweet smile curving her lips. I think when you smile that way, your cute, pointy chin and those wide green eyes make your face sort of look like a Valentine, he said to himself. Then he felt his cheeks grow warm. Ugh! How corny can I get? "Roxanne," he said out loud, "that's your best idea yet. That could be just what we need to smooth out this 'transfer transition'!"

"I'd like it to do that," she confessed, tapping the heel of one emerald-green pump against the linoleum floor. "I think it would be the best thing for the students and for Kennedy, too. I've only been here a couple of weeks, but already I really care for this school." Her eyes were glowing with sincerity. "I'd like to help it be as strong as it can be."

"Well, you know how I feel about that." Jonathan gestured around the student government room with a look of proud ownership. "It's my top priority."

"I hope it's become mine, too." Rox looked at her gold watch. The tiny diamonds that circled the face glinted in the light. She changed the subject. "Jonathan, didn't you say something about a pick-up basketball game at three-thirty?"

Jonathan jumped to his feet. "I almost forgot about that! Thanks for reminding me. But hey, I don't want to cut our brainstorming session short. . . ."

Roxanne held up her hands. "Don't worry, I think the questionnaire's all set. All we need to do is print them out and make sure everybody at Kennedy High gets one!"

Jonathan saluted her. "Way to go, Rox! This is going to be some Valentine's Day Dance."

They walked together to the door of the student government room. Roxanne halted halfway and bent over to retrieve Jonathan's fedora from underneath the desk. She perched it rakishly on her own head and flashed Jonathan a winning smile. "I love this hat. Did I tell you I have one sort of like it?" she asked.

"No, really?"

"Yep. I'm wild about fun hats. You can feel kind of crazy when you're wearing one, you know?"

"Sure." Jonathan lifted the fedora from Roxanne's head and settled it on his own. "I guess that's why I wear ol' Indiana Jones here," he said, tapping the hat. He opened the door and ushered Roxanne through it, then locked it behind them. "Can I walk you to your car or wherever before I head for the gym?"

"No, you go ahead. You're late already!" She shifted her coat from one arm to another, suddenly looking a little shy. "This was fun, Jonathan. I . . . I'm really glad I got to spend some time with you. I've already made some new friends here, and of course, I have all my old Stevenson friends. . . ." She pushed a wisp of hair from her eyes and smiled. "But it's so rare that I can really *talk* to someone."

Jonathan looked down at her. She was tall, but he still had almost half a foot over her. He smiled back. "Me, too," he admitted. "You know, I think we feel the same way about a lot of things."

"So do I," Roxanne agreed. "So do I."

"We'll have to get together again soon," he suggested. "Maybe even tomorrow, to print out the questionnaires!"

"Right! See ya, Jonathan."

" 'Bye, Roxanne." She turned to go, and Jonathan watched her all the way to the end of the hall. Her strides were long and graceful and the glossy, tawny hair falling almost to her waist swung softly as she walked. Roxanne is really something else, he thought with admiration. Bright, pretty, fun, committed, sensitive. He laughed to himself. *And* she has the incredible good taste to share a lot of my opinions!

Jonathan broke into a trot as he neared the locker room. The guys were going to razz him for holding up the game, but he didn't care. He was too caught up in daydreaming about Roxanne Easton. It had been a long time since he'd met a girl he liked as much. She sure was different from Fiona, too! Fiona was sharp and beautiful and he'd loved her a lot, but their conversations were always so full of controversy. Even the affectionate ones. Roxanne, on the other hand, was so responsive and appreciative. . . . Jonathan sprinted the last twenty yards down the hall, fueled by a rush of adrenaline. He couldn't wait to fill out a computer Valentine questionnaire himself. He knew exactly who he was going to request as a partner.

Roxanne smiled to herself as she walked away from Jonathan after their meeting. She could feel his eyes hot on her back. It was a good feeling. She wanted him to admire her and she could tell he did. And she couldn't help gloating as she remembered the way her test questions had drawn such personal, *pertinent* information out of him. The things you could discover by asking a few silly questions! She could sit down right now and draw a picture of Jonathan Preston's dream girl.

She was Miss Community Service and School Spirit, she liked funky fashions and mystery novels but hated traveling and ballet.

But, Rox thought as she stepped outside, slipping her coat on as she went, I can do even more than draw a picture of Jonathan's dream girl. I can be Jonathan's dream girl.

As she crossed the parking lot to her mother's black BMW — she'd had the sense today to talk her mother into letting her take the car rather than relying on her Mom to pick her up — Roxanne congratulated herself. It was a brilliant plan. All she had to do was get Frankie, who was in charge of entering the information from the questionnaires into the computer, to show her the ones from the Kennedy guys she was interested in. Then she'd know everything she needed to make them think she was the perfect girl for each of them. She slid easily into the driver's seat and glanced into the rearview mirror as she backed out of the parking space. She winked at her reflection. Jonathan Preston was only the first.

Chapter 7

"Fill it with unleaded, please."

"You got it." Matt twisted off the Toyota's gas cap and reached for the pump with one hand, pushing his hair off his forehead with the other. It was a cold day but he was warm in his heavy mechanic's coveralls. He was only working at his uncle's gas station one afternoon this week, but it was the busiest he'd ever seen it. It seemed like everyone in Rose Hill was bringing the family car in for a lube, not to mention the standard fill-it-up-and-check-the-oil jobs. And he still hadn't gotten around to looking at that Buick with the faulty transmission. . . .

Matt handed the driver of the Toyota her change. He was turning to head into the office when another car pulled in and stopped a few feet away. Pamela Green rolled down the window and flashed him a bright smile. "Five-dollars worth of regular, please!"

Matt groaned. "Not you, too!" he exclaimed in mock desperation.

"Only teasing," she assured him. "Actually, I'm on my way to the art supply store. Then it's off to Garfield House for my class, and then home where, hopefully, I'll get some sketching of my own done before dinner. After that — "

Matt waved both hands to cut her off. "That's enough! I'm getting more exhausted by the minute just listening to you. And I thought I was having a crazy day!"

Matt was familiar with Pamela's busy, art-oriented life-style. He'd met her a year ago when she was teaching art to some of the runaway kids at Garfield, a halfway house, while he ran an auto mechanics class. He remembered how intimidated he was at first by her background. Not only was Pamela an artist, but so where her brother, Evan, and her mother. Her mother lived and painted most of the year in a small town in New Mexico. Evan had recently finished art school and was having his work shown in local galleries. Mr. Green, meanwhile, owned a graphics design firm in D.C. Matt had never been very comfortable with what he loosely defined as "culture." Initially, he had assumed Pamela would look down on him and his own interest in cars. But along with his growing love for her had come a growing self-respect, and a stronger sense of the worth of his own particular talents.

Now Matt clasped his hands onto the roof of Pamela's car and leaned down to kiss her through the open window. "Can you hop out and visit for a while?" he asked in a low, hopeful voice. He reached down to push a wisp of soft blonde hair away from her eyes. Pamela took his hand and held it to her cheek, rubbing her own fingers softly across Matt's rough skin.

"I'd love to, but I really don't have time," she said regretfully. She narrowed her eyes against the sun. "I only came by to say hi and grab a soda."

"I'll get you one. Diet Sprite?"

"Yeah, thanks."

Matt swallowed his disappointment as he loped over to the soda machine, slipped in a few coins, and punched the Diet Sprite button. Pamela's busy schedule was nothing new. And he was working, too. He really didn't have the time to fool around, either. But he could have arranged for a short break if she wanted him to. She didn't have time this afternoon, though. She never had time when she came by the station. She was always on her way somewhere, if she even stopped by at all. Deep inside, Matt understood that Pamela simply didn't *like* the gas station. Not that he could blame her entirely. It wasn't exactly number one on his list of places to spend his free time, either. But it was where he worked. It was part of his life, and while he knew Pamela was proud of his mechanical skills, he also knew she preferred to admire them from a safe distance. All he had to do was mention that he'd found another old car to fix up and ask if she wanted a ride and she was history.

The cold can of soda tumbled out of the machine and Matt bent down to grab it. He flipped the top open before handing it to Pamela. "Give me a call tonight?" he suggested, raising one dark eyebrow and giving her a half smile.

"Of course!" Pamela licked her thumb and reached up to rub a smudge of grease off Matt's cheek. "Right after dinner?"

"Actually, I'm working until eight tonight. Any time after that, though."

"You got it." She tipped her head to one side, her blonde bangs brushing her long eyelashes. "Better yet, why don't you stop by on your way home?"

Matt's smile widened to a grin. "Good idea. I don't suppose there'd be any chance your dad'll be working late at the office?"

"Um. . . ." Pamela winked. "Maybe."

"I'll see you later, then!" Matt waved as she shifted the car into reverse and backed slowly around the pumps. He watched as she rolled up to the roadside, her blinker on, and sat waiting for a nice long open stretch to pull into.

He smiled to himself. Pamela was such a cautious, conscientious driver. Whenever she was behind the wheel she acted as if she were taking a Driver's Ed test. Putting on her turn signal even when nobody was behind her, tapping her brakes when the stop sign was still a hundred yards away, leaving the correct number of car lengths between her and the car ahead of her on the freeway, her hands always firmly gripped the wheel at three o'clock and nine o'clock, the safety position.

For a split second, Matt's vision fogged up a little. The car was gone and now he was picturing a beautiful girl. She looked a lot like Pamela, with the same sweet smile and sunny shoulder-length hair. But her hair was tawny and windswept, almost tangled-looking, and her smile was sexier and wilder than it was sweet. She beckoned to him, her eyes inviting, as she stepped into her cherry-red Corvette and then whipped out onto the road, gravel flying. Matt was ready to follow her — he had to follow her. She wasn't Pamela, or at least he didn't think so. Who was she then?

The brisk, insistent beep of a car horn brought Matt back down to earth. The driver of the black Porsche glowered impatiently at him as he strode toward the gas pump. "I'm coming, I'm coming," he muttered under his breath. Then he stopped, his hand on the gas cap. Matt shook his head to clear it. There was no reason to be irritated. Waiting on customers was his job and he'd been asleep at the switch. He decided to wash the guy's windshield and check his oil to make up for it.

It was hard to concentrate on such duties, though. Matt's mind was definitely still somewhere else. He was cruising down a twisting, sun-dappled back road, the windows wide open to the fresh country air, feeling free and laughing with a girl in a red Corvette.

Pamela blew the soap suds off the dial of her Swatch and checked it: seven forty-five. She sank her hands back down into the dishwater to retrieve the last slippery spoon. There was just enough time to finish the supper dishes and then run upstairs to change. She was still wearing her paint-spattered smock — not too glamorous. Although, she thought, rinsing off her hands with a sigh, Matt wouldn't exactly be dressed to kill. After five hours at the gas station his coveralls would be grease-stained and grubby. Pamela yanked a terry cloth towel from a hook next to the window and rubbed her hands dry. She supposed it didn't really make a difference what Matt wore. He wouldn't be Matt if he showed up in a suit. And after all, it was Matt she loved — rumpled, rough-edged Matt Jacobs, coveralls and everything.

Angie, Pamela's small white dog, followed her upstairs. After she'd changed into her favorite loose, faded Laura Ashley jumper, Pamela wandered up to her father's studio where she had her own worktable in one corner. Matt would know where to find her; he'd let himself in the side door if he got there early and she wasn't downstairs.

Pamela crossed the floor to lean over her father's shoulder. He was sketching in pen and ink. "You sure didn't waste a minute, Dad," she observed indulgently. "You polished off that hot fudge sundae and abandoned me before I'd even gotten past the whipped cream!"

Mr. Green turned his head to smile mischievously into his daughter's eyes. "I had to gobble it down because it was so good."

Pamela rested her chin on his shoulder for a moment. "That's okay. I figured you had something bigger on your mind than ice cream."

Her father pushed a hand through his short salt-and-pepper hair. "Designs for a new client." He nodded at the scattered drawings. "An up-and-coming political consulting firm. It's just letterhead and basic packaging, but I wanted to work on it myself. It could lead to a lot more if they like it."

Pamela nodded. Even though her father had a small talented staff, he kept an eye on every project and often came up with the design concepts himself. Now she reached forward to point to one of the scrawled-upon sheets. "I kind of like this one, where you made the logo vertical."

"Bingo!" Her father smiled. "That's the one I like, too. And I think the firm will agree, but I want to work out a few other proposals to offer them as well."

Pamela went over and settled onto the stool at her own desk. She picked up a watercolor brush and ran the soft bristles along her cheek. "I'll leave you alone, then," she said. "I just came up here to kill five minutes."

"You're not going to draw?"

"Nope. Matt's on his way over."

Mr. Green stuck his pen behind his ear and glanced over his shoulder at his daughter. "Oh, are you two going out somewhere?"

She shook her head. "No," she answered without much animation. "I think we'll just hang out here. Since it's a school night and all."

"Hmmm. Well, it'll be nice to see him," Mr. Green said. "Come to think of it, Matt hasn't been around too much lately, has he?"

Pamela shook her head again. "He's pretty busy. You know, cars, cars, and more cars." She tried not to sound too bored or resentful.

Her father's gray eyes crinkled as he laughed. "That's really his thing, isn't it?"

"You bet."

"What about the sculpting?" Pamela's father was talking about the model of a futuristic automobile that Matt had made last year and Jonathan had entered in the student art show at school. Mr. Green had admired it, and encouraged Matt to develop what looked to him like a promising flair for industrial design.

Pamela pushed her hair back behind her ears and shrugged. "I don't think he's been doing much of it lately. It's just fun to him." She smiled ruefully. "He doesn't want to be considered an artist!"

"But isn't art fun for you, too?" her father countered. "Isn't that something you two have in common?"

"Yeah, but for me it's *serious* fun," she emphasized.

For a second her father looked startled and then he laughed heartily. "You know, when you said that, Pammie, you sounded exactly like your mother. It's uncanny."

Pamela frowned. "What's wrong with that?" she asked, suspicious.

Mr. Green raised his hands in protest. "Absolutely nothing! I love and respect your mother. In fact, there's no one I admire more. But if there's one word that describes her, it's 'serious.' " There was a wistful note in his voice that Pamela had heard before, a note that usually crept in when he spoke about his wife. He missed her when she was off painting. "Your mother's seriousness has made her a great artist," he continued, "but it has also caused her to periodically abandon the security of a traditional life-style, home, and family." Pamela was about to argue but he held up a hand again. "She still has us and we still have her and that's what really matters, I know. The unconventionality is secondary."

Pamela nodded with conviction. "I wouldn't trade her for any other mom in the world, traditional or not," she declared, her eyes glowing.

Her father's smile was sympathetic and more than a little proud. "I'm glad you feel that way. We're a lucky family to care so much about each other." He pushed his sketches into a neat pile on one side of the table. "That's funny," he observed. "We started talking about Matt and ended up talking about Mom. How did that happen?"

Pamela shrugged, hopping off her stool. "I don't know." She smoothed her hands down the pleats on the front of her jumper. "And speaking of Matt, I think I hear his car in the driveway. I'm going downstairs to meet him."

Her father winked. "Tell him I say hi and that I think he needs a new muffler."

"Sure. See you later." Pamela closed the studio door softly behind her. She raked her hands through her hair and straightened the bangs across her forehead as she headed back down the stairs to the kitchen. Talking with her dad had really started her thinking, not just about Matt and their relationship but about her background and herself. Sometimes she felt as if being an artist made her different from other people. Maybe not as radically different as her mother — Pamela had no desire to seclude herself in a tiny town in New Mexico where the nearest supermarket was fifty miles away — but still different. Then at other times, she wanted nothing more than to blend in with the crowd and be just like them. She wanted to meet Matt at the gas station, hang out at the sub shop, and be . . . average.

As for Matt, it was no secret to either of them that they didn't have many common interests. That had been all too obvious right from the very beginning. But they did love each other. Their relationship had faced challenges, like this past summer when they'd had brief romantic flings with other people, but it had always come back to the same thing: love. The trick, Pamela decided, was to have something in common that ran deeper than their "interests." An attitude maybe? A philosophy of life? Did she and Matt share that?

She was still puzzling this over as she opened the back door. Matt crossed the driveway, his breath coming out frosty in the cold night air. The collar of his coveralls was turned up against the chill. When he kissed her, Pamela forgot her questions and her concerns in the warm, reassuring strength of his arms. Maybe love really was all that mattered.

Chapter
8

Roxanne tapped the toe of her Italian pump impatiently. The final bell had just rung and she knew Frankie was planning to spend the afternoon in the student government room entering Valentine questionnaires into the computer. Rox wanted to make sure she was there to help Frankie get started. There were a few forms she needed to see, in the worst way, for herself.

The computer Valentine service had taken Kennedy High by storm. It looked like it was going to be an even bigger hit than Jonathan and the others had expected. And Rox certainly didn't mind letting everybody — her new Kennedy acquaintances and her old Stevenson friends alike — know ever so subtly that the whole thing had been her idea.

She peered down the hallway at the thinning

stream of students who were loading up book-bags and backpacks before rushing out to waiting school buses and cars. If only she could get in to the student government room! But Jonathan had only had one spare key and he'd entrusted it to Frankie. Rox closed her eyes. She could picture the tall stack of questionnaires on the desk, and a few dozen more forms scattered on the floor after being shoved under the door. One of them might be Matt's or Eric's or Greg's. . . . She smiled secretly in anticipation. She was really too curious for words.

Just then, Frankie rounded the corner and came up behind her. Frankie tapped her friend on the shoulder and Rox jumped about a foot. "Frankie," Rox exclaimed, her hand flying to her pink cashmere sweater in surprise.

Frankie giggled at Roxanne's startled expression. "Sorry to scare you!" She paused, a little out of breath from hurrying all the way from her locker, then asked, "What are you doing here, anyway?"

Rox had dropped the notebook and pen she'd been holding when Frankie surprised her, and now she bent over to retrieve them. When she straightened up again she was smiling brightly. "I wanted to see if you needed any help with the computer Valentine forms before I headed home. I know about a million have come in and that's a lot of work for one person!"

Frankie gave Rox a grateful look as she fumbled in her coat pocket for the key to the student government room. "That's really nice of you, Rox." She found the key and fitted it into the lock, then swung the door open and switched on the overhead light. "But I don't really think there's much you could do. There's only one terminal in here," she pointed out. "And anyway, it's just typing."

Rox was hardly listening to Frankie. She had bent over swiftly to scoop up the piles of forms that were lying on the floor just inside the door. As she shuffled them into an orderly pile to hand to Frankie, she glanced at the names of the students who'd filled them out. There was a Tom, a Bill, an Amy, a Steve, a Joel, even an Oscar. No Matts or Erics or Gregs here, she thought, disappointed. Her eyes darted to the forms already stacked on the desk. Hmmm. . . .

Frankie took the questionnaires and placed them next to the others. Rox moved to stand beside her as she settled herself in front of the computer and turned it on, then typed in the commands to start the program. Rox watched carefully. When the screen suddenly went blank except for a number of small, bright arrows, she raised one neatly plucked eyebrow. "There's nothing there!" Roxanne pointed out, puzzled. "What happened?"

"For every entry there are fourteen fields, one that correlates to each of the categories of information that can be pulled off the forms," Frankie explained. "First I'll enter the person's name. Then, by pressing the tab key, I move to the next field and enter the next item — class year. See how it works?"

Rox shrugged and nodded. "That seems straightforward enough," she remarked.

"It is," Frankie agreed. "The hard part was designing a program that would sift through all the information and match people up. But I did it!" Frankie's light brown eyes glowed. "The computer will match interests and set up only one Valentine's Day Dance rendezvous per person. And of course if two people put each other down they'll get matched automatically."

Rox leaned closer to study the computer, amazed. It can really do all that! she thought. Incredible. She rubbed her hands together, thinking quickly. "That's a lot of stuff to enter into the computer," she began, briskly patting the stack of forms for emphasis. "I bet it would go much faster if I read the forms out loud to you while you typed. I really wouldn't mind giving up part of my afternoon to do that, either," she said, adopting a loyal and unselfish expression. "Seriously!"

"But Rox, you know the forms are supposed to be confidential." Frankie sounded a little anxious. "We agreed on that at the beginning, and I've promised Jonathan nobody'll see them but me. Those are the *rules*."

Roxanne tossed her head. "Oh, pooh on rules!" She picked up the top form and glanced at it in a casual but determined way. "It's not like I'm a *stranger* reading these. I mean, after all, I did *create* the entire scheme!"

Frankie reached back with one hand to tug nervously at her thin blonde braid. With her other hand she took the form from Roxanne. "I know," she said timidly, "but I promised Jonathan. He might get mad —— "

Rox snatched the form back. "Don't be ridiculous!" she snapped. Frankie flushed, and turned away. Rox observed this and relented a little. "I'm sorry, Frankie," she said, her voice softer but still firm. "You're absolutely right. We said we'd keep everything confidential and it would be wrong to do anything else. You really should work on this by yourself."

Frankie heaved a huge sigh of relief, "I'm so glad you understand, Rox," she confessed.

Roxanne had turned to pace across the room. Now she paced back to Frankie's side. "I won't read the forms to you, Frankie, but there's no harm in my just flipping through them, is there?" Her expression had become playful. "Just a quick peek? None of these precious secrets will pass my lips, I swear!"

"Well. . . ." Frankie still looked doubtful and worried.

"Really, I just want to glance at a few," Rox assured her. "To see the different interests people have listed. They might give me, uh, some ideas about activities I — we — could get involved in ourselves now that we're at Kennedy."

As an excuse for snooping, Rox knew this one was pretty lame. She did her best to look absolutely calm and sure of herself, waiting hopefully. Finally Frankie relented with a sigh and a shrug. "Sure, go ahead. As long as you promise — "

Roxanne pulled an imaginary zipper across her triumphant smile. "My lips are sealed!"

Frankie began entering the information from the forms that had just come in, the ones Rox had already scanned. Meanwhile, Roxanne made herself comfortable on the sofa and delved eagerly into the rest of them. After flipping rapidly through the first dozen or so, she still had yet to sight a familiar name. Rox began to worry a little. What if none of the guys she was interested in had submitted a form? After all, the deadline was still a week away. Then she stopped short. Her eyes lit up. *Matt Jacobs* was scrawled in very sloppy, very male handwriting across the top of a form that looked as if it had been carried around in someone's back pocket for days.

Rox bit her pink-frosted lip and read. *Cars . . . travel . . . freedom. . . .* The list went on and on. "Very interesting," she whispered to herself. "Very, very interesting!" She started flipping through the pile again. More strangers and then GREG MONTGOMERY in bold, block letters. CREW, POLITICS, CARTOONS, COMPETITION — he was easy. It was too much to hope that Eric Shriver's form could be in the pile, too, but there it was, as big as life. Rox read quickly. *He* was a laid-back, fun-loving swimmer, and his form gave away a few other things she might not have guessed just by looking at him.

Roxanne was so absorbed in the treasure trove she'd found that she didn't notice that the door had opened and Jonathan had come in. She looked up suddenly to find him standing a few inches away and smiling down at her. "What have you got there?" he asked in a friendly, unsuspecting voice.

For a brief second Roxanne considered trying to hide the forms under the couch cushion. Instead, she smiled back up at Jonathan with all her might, straightening her back into a more official posture. "These are the computer Valentine forms," she announced. "I'm just . . . alphabetizing them for Frankie."

Frankie's back stiffened slightly at Roxanne's words, but Jonathan didn't notice. He couldn't take his eyes off Rox. "Great!" he enthused. "More hands make the work go faster, I always say."

Roxanne rose quickly to her feet. "I agree. And I'm all finished so — "

"Here, let me take those," he offered.

"No!" Roxanne swallowed hard and then repeated herself in a lower, more controlled voice. "No, that's okay. I've got it." The last thing she needed was for Jonathan to see that according to her alphabet, "*W*" came before "*B*" and "*L*" came after "*T*."

She stacked the forms back on the desk where Frankie was still working wordlessly. A small "thanks" was all Frankie said. Rox turned back to Jonathan. He was watching her with a mixture of expectations and admiration, and she realized she didn't have to worry about him suspecting her of any wrong-doing. No, she definitely had him eating out of the palm of her hand. Rox allowed herself a quick self-satisfied smile. She could be picking his pocket and he wouldn't catch on!

Now Rox noticed that Jonathan also had an armload of papers. "What are *those*?" she asked, curious.

"All the Sweetest Sweetheart ballots you could ever hope to see!" He strode over to the other desk and put down the stack with a brisk slap. "I just picked them up at the radio station. We're collecting them there so they won't get mixed in with these others. Anyway, I thought I'd start counting what's come in so far. Get ahead of the game, you know?"

She nodded. "Very smart!"

Jonathan stood up a little straighter. "I'd ask you to help, Rox," he assured her in an important voice as he pulled the chair out, "but then you wouldn't be surprised when the winners are announced at the dance. I'd hate to spoil the fun for you."

"That's sweet," she purred, perching on the edge of another desk, while Jonathan prepared to count the ballots. She leaned in close to him.

He gulped and looked up at her face hurriedly. "And I think you're right to consider confidentiality a very important issue," she continued. On the other side of the room, Frankie coughed. "I admire your integrity for maintaining it."

"Well, I, uh . . . it's nothing really," Jonathan gazed helplessly into Roxanne's eyes. "I'm glad you feel the same way."

For a moment Jonathan and Rox stared at each other while Frankie typed quietly on the Apple's keyboard. Then the door to the student government room flew open again. This time it was Matt, looking rough but incredibly sexy, Rox thought, in his usual torn blue jeans and a flannel shirt. "Hey, what's happening?" he greeted them. His friendly smile widened as he approached Roxanne after barely pausing to nod at Frankie. "Putting them to work already, eh, Preston?" he asked Jonathan.

"Sure am. They're my new right-hand men! I mean, women," Jonathan amended gallantly. Rox broke into a big smile. "I'm counting Sweetest Sweethearts ballots and fabulous Frankie over there is working on the Valentine's Day Dance match-up. We've got our work cut out for us."

"Sure looks like it." Matt shook his head. "Better you than me."

"I hope you at least filled out one of the questionnaires, though," said Jonathan.

"You bet." Matt glanced quickly at Roxanne, who smiled innocently, and then back at Jonathan. "I wouldn't pass up the chance to meet the girl of my dreams!"

"What about Pamela?" Jonathan reminded him. "Isn't *she* the girl of your dreams?"

"Yeah, right," Matt replied flatly. He turned toward the door. "I was actually just on my way to meet her at the sub shop."

"Catch you later," Jonathan said. He went back to the ballots, noting the votes on a pad of paper. Rox saw her chance.

"Wait, Matt!" she called after him. He paused with his hand on the doorknob. "I'm on my way out, too. I'll walk with you."

Jonathan's face fell, while Matt beamed. "Great!" he exclaimed. He held the door for her. As Rox glided past him, she caught Frankie's surprised expression. She could tell what her friend was thinking — Roxanne had the car today and Frankie was depending on her for a ride home later. "Don't worry, I'll be back," she mouthed. Then the door slammed shut and she and Matt were alone in the deserted hallway.

"Heading out to the parking lot?" She figured a car buff like Matt wouldn't ride the bus.

"Yep." He pushed his hands deep into the pockets of his jeans as he ambled along. "Do you need a ride?"

Roxanne hesitated. It certainly was tempting. But what would she do when he dropped her off and her car was still stuck in the Kennedy lot? "No, thanks," she said regretfully. "I have my own wheels today."

"That's too bad." Matt flashed her a shy smile as he ushered her out of the front entrance of the school. "I was kind of hoping for a chance to show off my car. . . ."

Rox gloated silently. Matt would be easy to butter up with a new car she could gush over. "Oh, you have a new car?" she said out loud in a thrilled, tell-me-more tone. "How exciting! What kind is it?"

"Actually, it's an old Mustang," Matt informed her proudly. "But it's a real beauty if I say so myself."

"I'd absolutely love to see it," she breathed, her eyes aglow.

"You would?" Matt was clearly pleasantly surprised by her interest. "Come on! It's over here."

In a few moments they were standing in front of what looked to Roxanne like a nondescript, beat-up old clunker. Matt waited expectantly for her to comment. Somehow Rox managed to *ooh* and *ahh* over the car as if it was a vintage Rolls Royce. "Matt, it's gorgeous!" she declared. "It's wild! Mustangs are my favorite, but this one's really hot."

"You like Mustangs, too?" he looked back at her enthusiastically.

"Of course. Who doesn't? They're so. . . ." Roxanne paused, looking off into the distance as if searching for the right word.

"All-American?" Matt supplied.

"That's it. You know, I would never drive anything but an American car."

"Really! What kind of car do you have?" he asked.

"Uh, um, a BMW," Rox admitted with a slight stutter. She quickly added, "But it's my mom's. When I buy my own, it'll definitely be a Mustang. The older the better."

"Yeah? What year would you look for?"

Rox wracked her brain. How old was old? Ten years? Twenty? "Nineteen seventy-three," she said decisively.

"Oh," Matt looked puzzled and Rox held her breath. Then he shrugged. "Well, this one's a sixty-five." He leaned on the hood and folded his arms across his broad chest. "You really like it?"

"Do I ever! Mind if I look at it a little closer?"

"*Mind?*" Matt shook her head in disbelief. "I'd love it! Here let me show you a few things. . . ."

For the next fifteen minutes, Matt gave Roxanne a thorough tour of the car's many special features. She carefully kept her mouth shut and let him do all the talking, storing away all the technical terms for use in future conversations with him. She didn't want him to notice that she didn't know a drive shaft from a dip stick. But she *did* want him to notice that beneath her open coat her cashmere sweater and slim black skirt flatteringly skimmed her slender curves. Her long red hair also looked great against the Mustang's bright blue finish, and even better against the interior — specifically when she was posing in the passenger seat, as she was right now.

Matt looked at her, his hands lightly caressing the steering wheel. He paused in his lecture on transmissions. "You know, Rox," he began, his voice soft and a little bit husky. "It's really nice to meet a girl who likes cars. I mean, most girls are bored by them, you know?"

Rox shook her head. "Yeah, I just can't understand it." She locked her eyes onto Matt's, mirroring the warmth and openness of his expression as best she could. She was looking at Matt's face, but in her head she was seeing as clear as life the information he'd written on his computer Valentine questionnaire. It might as well have been printed on his forehead. She smiled encouragingly. "I'm just glad I'm not *like* most girls! It's hard sometimes, though. I mean, some people think girls should only care about fashion and *art*" — she emphasized the word carefully — "and stuff like that! It burns me up when they cut down my interest in cars. There's nothing worse than a snob." Her eyes flashed. "But I say, let them think what they want. I'll like what I like!"

Matt ran a hand through his hair and smiled oddly. "It's wild, Rox." He looked straight ahead, as if he suddenly felt a little shy. "You feel exactly the way I do. I've never met a girl who's felt that way before."

He had been tapping his fingers against the steering wheel and now he clenched them. Roxanne could tell a confession was coming. She leaned ever so slightly toward him. "I know what you mean," she agreed softly. "It's not often I can talk like this to someone. Even though I have a lot of friends who are guys . . . I don't know. They're not . . . special."

Matt turned to look at her. Her gentle smile convinced him she was sincere. Suddenly he was spilling out his frustration about Pamela, about how they'd been together for a while now and she was a wonderful person but all she cared about was her art. When he first got his Mustang she could hardly even bear to ride in it! Rox was more than sympathetic. She made sure to look like she understood him from the depths of her heart. When he finished talking, she could tell he was feeling relieved — almost light-hearted. They sat for a minute in silence.

"Yep, she doesn't like cars. That's never going to stop *me* from liking them, though," Matt concluded. "Someday I'll have this baby fixed up in mint condition and then I'm just going to take off — drive across the country on back roads. If she's not with me that's her loss!"

It really will be, Roxanne thought, drinking in Matt's ruggedly handsome profile. Out loud she said dreamily, "Drive across the country! I've always wanted to do that myself. I love traveling. Anywhere, near or far, just for the freedom of it."

A slow smile crossed Matt's face. "I'll tell you what," he said, pushing a shock of dark hair out of his eyes. "Let's go for a drive right now! A short one, I mean." He laughed wryly. "That's all this particular car is up to at the moment."

Rox was eager. As Matt leaned forward to put the key in the ignition, she settled back in her seat. She might as well get comfortable, make herself at home. She planned to spend a lot of time with Matt Jacobs and his blue Mustang.

Katie and Molly, both dressed in sweat pants and sweat shirts, blew into the sub shop on a gust of chilly air. Katie hardly felt the cold, though. She was still hot through and through from her workout at the Fitness Center. She'd had a session with her private gymnastics coach, Mr. Romanski, while Molly taught her Wednesday afternoon aikido class, and afterward they'd gone jogging on the cushiony indoor track. Molly, a lifeguard and expert swimmer, had just decided she'd like to train for a triathlon.

"You run a marathon and then you swim the English Channel and then you bike across the Sahara or something like that!" she explained enthusiastically as they scanned the room for a free table.

Katie grimaced. "Sounds real fun, Moll. Look, there's Pamela. Let's go and sit with her."

They made their way toward the back of the restaurant, bopping along to the fifties music playing on the old-fashioned jukebox. Molly stuck her tongue out at the moth-eaten moose head on the wall, making Katie giggle. They

111

noticed Dee Patterson and Marc Harrison at a dark, corner booth, and waved. Pamela had picked one of the more secluded booths, instead of the one that the gang usually occupied, and was sketching intently on a pad on the table in front of her. She was alone and didn't notice Molly and Katie until they were practically on top of her. "Boo," Katie said, dropping her gear on the floor next to Pamela.

"Oh!" Pamela jumped. Her stubby charcoal pencil flew from her hand. "You scared me!"

The two girls slid in the booth across from her. "Come here often?" Molly joked.

"Not usually by myself," Pamela answered gloomily.

Only then did Katie notice her woeful expression. "Pamela, what's the matter?"

Pamela sighed, digging into her brocade satchel for a new charcoal pencil. "I was supposed to meet Matt here an hour ago," she explained morosely. "Looks like I've been stood up, huh?"

Katie frowned. "That's not like Matt," she observed, shaking her ponytail.

"It's really not," Pamela admitted. "But the fact is, I'm here and he's not."

"Maybe his car broke down," Molly suggested, trying to be comforting. "It looked kind of unsteady last time I saw it."

"Maybe." Pamela laughed; bitterly, Katie thought. "Yeah, that's probably it. His dumb old car." She stroked the charcoal across the drawing paper in a hard, straight line, pushing down until the point broke. Then she shook her head and forced herself to smile with false brightness at Molly and Katie. "Forget about Matt. What are you guys up to?"

"Making up for a tough afternoon at the gym with as many calories as possible! Anybody else for a large order of fries?" Molly asked, hopping back onto her sneakered feet.

"Me!" Katie raised a hand eagerly.

"How 'bout you, Pamela?"

"No, thanks. A cup of tea would be great, though."

While Molly waited at the counter for her order, Katie studied Pamela as she sketched. Her friend really looked blue, too down to be just because of Matt being late, or even missing an informal date. She was curious but didn't want to pry. Pamela could be pretty private. There was no point in quizzing her. If she wanted to talk, she would, eventually.

Katie decided to change the subject from Matt and cars, which was obviously problematic, to something more upbeat. "So, Pamela," she said, "you're going on the school ski trip this weekend, aren't you? Molly and I both are. I got new equipment for Christmas and I can't wait to try it out!"

"I didn't sign up," Pamela confessed, closing her sketch pad and shoving it into her bag. "Matt's going, though. He loves the snow, but it's really not my thing." She smiled briefly, but then her sad look returned. "I don't know, Katie.

It just seems like one more thing he and I don't have in common. Sometimes I really worry."

Katie leaned her elbows on the table and rested her chin in her hands. "What about?"

"About the fact that our interests are so different." Pamela sighed. "We seem to be growing further and further apart lately."

Just then Molly set the fries and the tea down on the table. She looked from Katie to Pamela and back again. "Boy trouble?" she guessed, taking a seat on Pamela's side of the booth this time.

"Mmm-hmmm. Pamela needs a little cheering up," Katie advised her.

"Really, it's no big deal," Pamela protested with a laugh. "Things'll turn out okay. They always do."

"If you're worried that you two don't like the same things, maybe you should try liking some of the things *he* likes." Katie thought this was a pretty good theory.

Pamela waved her hand impatiently. "Believe me, we've tried that. He's looked at the paintings in my house and I've looked at the engines in his cars."

"What about the ski trip?" Katie suggested again.

"No," Pamela answered. "I'm not about to risk breaking my leg bombing down some ski slope just to please him! I really don't think that's the answer."

Katie reached for the ketchup. "Just a thought," she said, pouring a little pool of it onto her fries.

"Thanks, Katie." Pamela softened. "I appreciate it. It's just — Hi, Greg!" she interrupted herself.

Katie twisted around eagerly. Greg was coming up behind her. She could see the top of his head brushing along the banners printed with the names of schools and sports teams hanging from the rafters.

"Hey, just the person I'm looking for" — Katie smiled with satisfaction — "Pamela Green!" Katie's face fell. "Sorry, K.C.!" Greg apologized as he tugged on her ponytail. "But I've got a message to deliver. Matt's still in the parking lot at school," he told Pamela. "I guess he went to start his car and nothing happened. Roxanne Easton was there keeping him company while he worked on it." Greg slid in next to Katie, whose playful pout had deepened into a frown at the mention of Roxanne. "I talked to Rox for a few minutes myself while Matt was checking under the car," he continued, helping himself to Katie's fries. "You know, she's really great. It turns out she's a big crew fan. Not only that, but she's into politics and political cartoons!" Greg seemed astonished that anyone could have the taste to like all the same things he did.

Katie caught Molly's eye and made a disgusted face as Greg raved on about Roxanne's virtues.

115

"And she's really burning to be a success in everything she does. She's not going to let being new at Kennedy slow her down. I like that sort of ambition. I have a feeling she'll be a great addition to the junior class." He grinned. "Not that we were ever short of talent!"

Katie glanced at Pamela, who was looking even more defeated than before. She could imagine what was running through her friend's head — the same image that was running through hers, probably. Their boyfriends and Rox Easton cruising off into the sunset . . . *blecch.* Katie practically choked on her fries. She wasn't sure how someone she didn't even know could put such a bad taste in her mouth. It really wasn't fair of her, she knew. After all, Roxanne could easily be a very nice person. But somehow, Katie doubted it.

As if to make sure that Pamela would feel as terrible as possible, Greg finished his story by adding innocently, "Anyway, Pamela, Matt asked me to tell you that he probably wouldn't make it. Actually, I think it had slipped his mind. When I mentioned *I* was going to the sub shop he sort of hit himself on the forehead and looked surprised!"

He laughed, and Pamela joined in a little weakly. Katie remained silent. She wanted to say something to Greg about the funny feeling she had about Roxanne Easton. Before she had a chance to, though, he turned and wrapped both his arms around her in a big bear hug. She gave

116

in to his playful mood, realizing that he'd only accuse her of being jealous and competitive again if she bad-mouthed the new girl. But inside, Katie made a decision. Maybe the rest of the crowd, especially the guys, she thought grimly, wanted to welcome the Stevenson kids with open arms, but she was going to be on her guard. She looked at Pamela, who was sipping her steaming tea, a pained expression on her pretty face. Yep, definitely on her guard.

Chapter
9

"Come on, Zack, baby. You can do better than that."

Zachary smiled weakly and took a deep, icy breath. His dad was standing in front of him, a foot or two away from the garage. Overhead, like an orange halo, a basketball hoop beckoned. Zachary dribbled, lunged away from his dad, and tossed the ball.

"YES!" his father yelled. "That's my boy."

Zachary laughed. It had been a pretty easy shot. His father was slow and about five inches shorter than he was. His body was low and wiry where Zack's was wide and tall, and when his father wasn't playing basketball, he complained about fallen arches and sore knees. But Zack's dad, unlike a lot of middle-aged fathers, was always ready for a game, be it basketball, touch football, or just slugging a whiffle ball around the backyard with one of those big, funny, plastic bats. That was the way it always had been and, as far as Zachary could tell, the way it always would be. His dad had wanted to be a jock, and he was thrilled to have a son as gifted as Zachary. He expected Zack to take full advantage of his athletic talent and not care about anything else. So far, Zachary had done exactly that.

"Okay, your old man's bringing this one down the court," Mr. McGraw shouted. His breath made frosty clouds.

"Dad," Zachary said in a quieter voice, "maybe we should call it a game. It's freezing out here. And I've got studying to do and that ski trip tomorrow. . . ."

"You're just trying to press the advantage because your dad's behind. There's no quitting now." His father dribbled a couple of times and then moved toward the basket. The steps he took were awkward and too many but Zachary let him go by. He wasn't that interested now in playing, and he'd just as soon get it over with.

His father shot the ball, and it rolled around the hoop a couple of times. Finally it fell in.

"Whoa! Maybe your old man's not so old after all," Mr. McGraw shouted.

"Good, Dad. But I've got to. . . ."

"C'mon, c'mon," his father insisted. "Just because you're not as good at this game as you are at football. Don't quit now just when your old man is sneaking up on you."

Zachary looked at his dad and then caught the ball as it was tossed to him. He immediately pushed it under one arm and leaned against the garage. "Dad, I got some homework. We've been playing out here for almost an hour."

"It's good for you."

"But what about my home — "

Mr. McGraw frowned and held up one hand while fanning himself with the other. "Ah. That school stuff isn't where it's at for you, Zack. Leave the studying to the eggheads."

Zachary sighed. He was tired of playing. In fact, sometimes he wondered if he weren't tired of being such a good athlete. His father thought sports was the only thing that mattered. He was always telling Zack that if he'd only been big and talented — like Zack — he would have been a pro ball player instead of managing a Safeway store all his life. He'd push and goad Zack, telling him not to follow in his footsteps, to work hard at sports and make something of himself. Zack had done that. He'd made first string quarterback last year when he was only a sophomore, lettered junior year in B-ball and track. But the more involved he got in sports and the more successful he became, the more worried he got that he was forgetting something else. Something important.

"You gotta pay attention, Zack, baby," his father teased, suddenly whipping alongside him and grabbing the ball.

Zack ran after him but his mind wasn't with

the game. He was thinking about his new classes. He felt even more behind than usual with this whole transfer thing. He hadn't missed anything, but some of his Kennedy teachers seemed to assume that he'd covered things last semester that Zack had no recollection of. Maybe his teachers at Stevenson had left out that part about right angles or the French-Indian Wars, or maybe he hadn't been listening because he figured it wasn't as important as his football games.

"Dad," Zack asserted, finally stealing the ball back and holding it. "I have to stop now. I have an English paper due on Monday and I haven't even started it."

His father shrugged, and almost pouting, started walking toward the lawn.

Zack rolled his eyes. "Dad, it'll just take me a half hour or so. How about if we play some more after dinner? We'll turn on the outside lights."

His dad was all smiles again. He looked back at Zack before running toward the house. "It's a deal. Only don't worry too much about that English paper. It'll ruin your game."

"Okay."

His dad winked and ran in the back door.

Zack pitched the ball at the backboard and let it ricochet into the yard. Why *was* he suddenly worrying about that paper? He'd never worried about school before, and it had never seemed to matter. Like his dad, all he'd cared about was sports and that had suited him just fine. So what had happened to make him suddenly feel so different? Zachary got a tight, burning feeling inside his chest as he realized the answer.

Holly. The girl in the library. The minute he'd looked into her face, into those clear, intelligent eyes, everything inside him had gone haywire. He'd fallen for her — instantly. But what was her impression of him? Instead of seeing him throwing and running down the football field, her first impression of Zachary McGraw was of some dopey junior who didn't even know how to use the library.

Zack wasn't sure what tack to take with Holly. She was so different from the girls he'd dated at Stevenson: frilly cheerleaders or girl jocks. He didn't know where to begin. Maybe he should get help from Frankie. Good old Frankie. She was always there when he needed her. And even though she was about the smartest person in the whole school, she never made him feel slow or stupid when she explained a problem he was having with geometry or general science. Frankie would know how to help him win Holly.

Zack picked up the ball one last time and tossed it. Swish. Perfect. Maybe there was a chance for him and Holly, he decided. Maybe he could prove to her that he was worthwhile and important, even if he wasn't a sophisticated brain. Come to think of it, he'd seen something in her eyes in the library — a warmth, a sparkle, a sign that he might have a chance. Maybe she even liked him for being slow, nice, jockish Zack McGraw. Maybe he just had to gather his courage, go in for the tackle, and pray that he didn't get hurt.

Back at Kennedy High, Katie was still at gymnastics practice. It was like that every Friday afternoon. Katie stayed until the last minute — leaving just enough time to change and meet Greg or the crowd. Then first thing Saturday morning she went to the Fitness Center in Georgetown. Of course, she *could* work out on her equipment at home, but Katie always trained harder when other people were watching.

Tomorrow would be a break in Katie's routine. Instead of the Fitness Center she would be skiing up on Mount Jackson. She loved the snow, and skiing was good for her balance and her strength. Still, she'd miss a workout. So this would be her last good session until Monday.

"K.C.," yelled Terry McMahan, a gangly, short-haired junior who specialized in the parallel bars, "watch me."

Katie kept her eyes glued as Terry jumped up and started to swing. Terry was one of the few other gymnasts who was as devoted to the sport as Katie was. Coach Muldoon, Terry, and about six others were the only ones still working out.

"I'm watching, Ter," Katie encouraged.

Terry swung. Back and forth, back and forth.

Faster and faster until she was going over the top like the spoke in a bicycle wheel. She let go.

THUNK.

"Stick it!" Katie ordered as Terry wobbled and wavered, flapping her arms to keep her balance. Finally Terry tumbled back onto the mat and sprawled.

"Darn," Terry groaned, punching the mat with her fist, "I'll never be as good as you are. Never."

Katie walked over and helped Terry up. "Don't get discouraged. You're getting there."

"No, I'm not. That was pathetic."

"Ter, you just have to bend your knees more when you land. Sink into your landing and keep your feet farther apart." Terry watched carefully as Katie demonstrated. As the team star and a senior, Katie had become sort of a role model and mentor to the younger gymnasts. "You'll get it," Katie cheered. She patted Terry on the back. "Try it again right away."

"Okay." Grateful for Katie's attention, Terry smiled, jumped back up, and grabbed the bar. "Ready?"

Katie nodded. She liked Terry's guts and determination. Terry didn't have Katie's athletic talent, but sometimes Katie thought that spirit and desire were even more important than ability. Terry swung, let go again, and landed. This time she still wobbled, but she stayed on her feet.

"Yes!" Katie yelled, applauding her teammate. "That's much better."

Terry blushed. "Thanks, K.C. You were right. I wasn't bending my knees enough. Thank you."

A little embarrassed by Terry's gratitude, Katie waved a hand and walked back to the mat. "You did it, not me. I'd better get back to work myself or Muldoon will ask me to do another perfect double flip."

Terry laughed. "That's no problem for you. I really do appreciate your help."

"Any time." Katie eased down and started doing her cool down stretches while Terry went back to the bars.

Katie tried to relax her muscles. She folded her body in half and rested her face on top of her thighs. Suddenly she heard herself whisper, "See, Greg Montgomery, I don't always have to show people up. I'm not so competitive!" She laughed softly, realizing that the whole spat with Greg was kind of silly. Roxanne Easton was just trying to get to know people, to fit in at a new school. Katie had made much too big a deal out of it. Stretching further, Katie grabbed her toes, took a deep breath, and tried to wipe her brain clean as a new blackboard.

Soon Katie's muscles were feeling long and loose. She reached farther and farther and didn't raise her head again until she felt an icy draft that sent a sharp cramp into her left foot. "Close the door!" she hollered, sitting up. She heard Ms. Muldoon echo the order as they both looked over at the gym entrance.

"Sorry," giggled a young-looking girl who was standing just inside the doorway. She was small and preppy-looking with lush blonde hair. Her jeans and sweater were speckled with fresh snow.

Katie guessed immediately that the girl was a transfer student. She had that lost look and stayed in the entrance as if she were waiting to be invited in. Proving to herself — and Greg — that she could be hospitable to the kids from Stevenson, Katie walked over.

"Can I help you?" Katie asked in a warm voice. "Are you looking for someone?"

"Sort of," the girl said, looking around the gym. She hugged her books, which still had Stevenson High covers on them. "Is this where the girls' gymnastic team meets?"

"Yes."

"I was going to come before, but I've been busy," the girl explained cheerfully. "There are so many new people to meet and all. And then today a bunch of us from Stevenson got together for sort of a TGIF party." She giggled again. "Anyway, I guess I'm finally here."

Katie had no idea what this girl wanted. She looked like a real social type. Maybe she was on the Valentine's Day Dance committee, or looking for one of the boys' teams. "Here for what?"

The girl smiled and stepped further into the gym. "To join the gymnastics team."

Katie almost burst out laughing. She couldn't believe this girl was serious! "Our team?" The girl nodded. "Isn't it a little late for that? We had tryouts last semester."

The girl from Stevenson merely shrugged, as if joining the team wasn't all that important anyway. "Well, if it's too late, I guess I'll wait until next year." She started to leave.

Katie stopped her, aware again that Greg would think she was being unfriendly or unfair. "Listen," Katie explained, "the girls who transferred from Stevenson were allowed to try out first thing this semester, but that was weeks ago. If you want, you can talk to our coach."

Ms. Muldoon was already walking over, looking curious. Katie explained the situation, and the coach took over.

"I'm Stacy Morrison," the girl told Ms. Muldoon.

Ms. Muldoon looked even more skeptical than Katie. "What year are you, Stacy?"

"Sophomore."

"Were you on the freshman team at Stevenson?"

Stacy shook her head. Her long hair bobbed. "I didn't really want to tie myself up with practice and all. But I've taken classes at the Y since I was little."

"Why did you suddenly decide you wanted to try out?"

"I don't know. I thought it might be fun."

Ms. Muldoon and Katie exchanged looks, both agreeing silently that this girl was a real flake.

"Stacy, did you bring a leotard with you?" Ms. Muldoon asked with a frown. "I need to see what you can do."

"Okay. I can show you." Suddenly Stacy set down her books, gathered her hair and stuck it in the neck of her sweater. Then, without warning, she ran toward the mat, almost plowing into Terry and two other girls who were just finishing their workouts. Everyone stopped what they were doing and stared.

Stacy gave a hoot like a cowboy and threw herself across the mat. Over and up. *Whoosh, thump, whoosh.* From a front to a back flip without any hesitation. She flew, unhindered by her street clothes and tennis shoes. Her moves were rough and without polish, but she was fearless and amazingly fast. Raw talent. When she finished, Stacy stood on the edge of the mat panting slightly and giggling.

There was a long pause while everyone gawked, amazed. Finally Terry started applauding and the other girls joined in. Except for Katie. Katie merely stared, her stomach getting tight as a handball and her adrenaline starting to pump the way it did before she competed in a meet.

Stacy walked off the mat and over to Ms. Muldoon. Katie knew right then that Stacy would be on the team. She also knew that if Stacy wanted to, she could eventually become as good a gymnast as Katie was. Maybe even better. Stacy looked back at Katie and smiled, but Katie couldn't quite get the corners of her mouth to turn up.

"Show up for practice on Monday," Coach Muldoon told Stacy. The coach went on to give detailed instructions about what to wear and who to talk to about changing her gym class and the schedule for practice and meets, the first of which was in about a month.

Katie didn't stick around to listen. Something inside her was bubbling over and she suddenly couldn't stand still. Before she even thought about it her legs were pumping and she was running out to the center of the mat, to the exact place where Stacy had just shown so much promise.

Katie ran and leaped, throwing herself into her floor routine, going through her moves as flashily as she could, leaving out any rest space in between. She added an extra flip at the end, making Stacy's demonstration look like child's play. By the time Katie finished, everyone — including Stacy — was watching *her*. Then Katie let out a forced laugh, as if her stunt was one big joke.

Ms. Muldoon's voice told Katie that she was not amused. The coach marched over. She was looking at Katie as though her star gymnast had just lost her mind. "K.C., you know better than to do your routine at that speed without a spotter! Especially at the end of a workout when you're tired. What are you trying to do?"

Katie shrugged and attempted an innocent smile.

The coach shook her head and headed for the locker room. Katie turned and started to follow her. But before leaving, she stopped to look back at Stacy Morrison. The sophomore from Stevenson was gazing at her with awe. Katie smiled and walked a little taller. Keep that one in mind, all you new girls from Stevenson, she felt like saying. Just keep that in mind!

Chapter

10

The day of the school ski trip was clear and unseasonably warm. Eric rolled over in bed, still half asleep. When a ray of sunlight slanted in the window and hit his face, his eyes popped open and he fumbled for his clock radio. *Eight-fifteen!* His alarm never went off. "Geez!" he shouted, leaping out of bed and stepping with a shock on the cold wood floor. It was a quarter after eight and the buses left Kennedy at eight-thirty!

Somehow he managed to dive into his long johns, jeans, turtleneck, and sweater on the way to the car while simultaneously juggling his ski gear. He peeled into the Kennedy parking lot at 8:28, completely out of breath. When he opened the car door his extra pair of socks, which he'd rolled in a ball, bounced out onto the pavement. They were soon followed by his goggles and a

131

ski boot. "Darn!" he muttered, dropping on his hands and knees to gather everything up.

He heard someone laughing over the sound of the idling bus engines. He squinted upward. Molly had pushed down a window on the side of the bus marked "1" and stuck her head out, grinning at him. "Nice going, Shriver!" she called. "Get up on the wrong side of the bed this morning?"

"I almost didn't wake up at all!" he quipped back. He finally had his stuff together and now he hoisted his long skis onto his right shoulder and strode over to the bus. He could see some of his other friends making goony faces at him through the smudgy glass. Matt, Jonathan, Katie, Greg, Diana, Holly. . . .

Eric was about to jump onto the bus when the driver held up a large, forbidding hand. "Sorry, this one's full," he pronounced. "You'll have to ride on number two."

"But I was one of the first people to sign up!" Eric protested. "I was assigned to bus number one!"

"Sorry." The driver yanked the door handle and the door shut in Eric's face. He turned to trudge over to the other bus. Great, Eric thought, lowering his skis as he stepped on board. I'm stuck on the bus with the people who signed up at the last minute — Stevenson kids I've never even met. Eric stifled a sigh of aggravation as he clunked down the aisle. Oh, well, he thought, it really wasn't that big a deal. He'd catch up with

132

the gang at the slopes. And this would give him a chance to get to know the Stevenson kids better. In fact, all the ones he'd met so far were really nice. For example there was that football player, Zack McGraw, who was in his government class. Eric waved but Zack, who waved back, was already sitting with someone. Then Eric's gaze lit on someone with thick auburn hair, very green eyes, and a very big smile. There was also a very empty seat next to her at the back of the bus. Roxanne Easton! Eric walked faster in case somebody popped out of nowhere and beat him to the seat.

"Hi, Eric!" Roxanne called out with obvious pleasure. "I hope you're planning to sit with me. I was starting to feel like a social outcast, sitting back here all by myself!"

"You bet I'm sitting with you," Eric declared, carefully maneuvering his skis into the rack over the seat. "I thought I was going to miss out by being late but it looks like I lucked out instead!"

Rox laughed and shook her head. "You Kennedy guys are such teases."

"No, I mean it," Eric said sincerely as he shut the storage compartment and dropped down into the seat next to Roxanne. He'd been hoping for a chance to get to know her better, and an hour and a half bus ride was the perfect opportunity. He didn't want to come right out and say it, though — it might sound too pushy. Instead, he just smiled engagingly. "It's nice to run into you again," he said. "I do feel lucky. What about

133

you, though? You realize you're stuck with me for the whole day now, unless you think you can get rid of me once we're on the slopes." Eric raised one eyebrow, his expression mischievous. "Think you can stand it?"

"Oh, I think so," Rox assured him. She was smiling but her eyes were serious. "I think so."

Eric smiled back at her. He wasn't sure if it was his imagination or not, but Roxanne appeared to be as pleased with the situation as he was. This is great! he thought dizzily. He knew the other guys would be green with envy if they could see him now. After all, Rox was definitely the most intriguing girl to come on the scene in a long time.

Ordinarily Eric would feel a little shy around someone so glamorous, but Roxanne's friendliness put him at ease. He was sitting in the aisle seat and now he turned to look out the window, using this as an excuse to lean closer to Roxanne. The sweet smell of her perfume tickled his nose in a pleasant way. He could see the bus had quickly left Rose Hill behind for the highway. Eric pointed to a big green road sign. "Sixty miles to Brimfield and Mount Jackson," he observed. "Might as well sit back and enjoy the ride."

Rox wiggled out of her short black ski jacket and Eric helped her wedge it behind her back for a pillow. Underneath she was wearing a white turtleneck and close-fitting hot pink ski overalls. She was so pretty and color-coordinated that

Eric thought she looked like an ad in a ski magazine. "That's a nice outfit," he complimented her in an offhand way.

"Oh, thanks," Rox said casually. It was obvious to Eric that she didn't know — or didn't care — that she looked great. He didn't know many girls who were like that. He realized he liked Roxanne's attitude. She was so unpretentious, so natural. Eric felt relaxed with her. Sometimes when he was with a girl she'd try so hard to impress him that he'd find himself unconsciously doing the same thing. But Roxanne was different, more easygoing. It really had been a stroke of luck getting stuck on the second bus.

"So, Rox, how's it been going?" he asked, curious to hear about her first impressions of his school. "Do you like Kennedy so far?"

"I love it!" she replied, putting a hand lightly on his arm in her enthusiasm. "It's a great school. There are so many good facilities and clubs and stuff. The pool especially is beautiful. I plan to start swimming laps during free swim hours as soon as I get adjusted to my new schedule."

Eric stared at her with interest. "You mean you swim?"

"Sure, do you?" Rox asked.

"Uh, yeah." He cleared his throat and smiled self-consciously. "Actually, I'm captain of the boys' swim team."

"Wow, that's right. I remember I heard that somewhere." Roxanne looked impressed. "You must be a great swimmer. Me, I just swim for

135

fun. I never actually considered joining a team. I'm just not the competitive type."

"Hey, I can really relate," Eric said with a sympathetic nod. "To tell you the truth, the competition's no longer my favorite part of being on the team. I just love the sport. I used to be a win-or-die type, but now I think the meets are fun whether you win or not. Katie Crawford taught me that — the hard way."

"Winning's really not what matters most anyway, is it?" agreed Roxanne. "As long as you enjoy yourself. People place too much emphasis on success sometimes, you know?"

"I know," Eric said with feeling. He really did know. Katie was a wonderful girl and he'd been incredibly in love with her at one time, but boy, he'd really felt that they were in constant competition. That drive to win was part of her, right down to her bones. She couldn't escape it and he couldn't escape it, either, when they were going out. Thinking back on it, it really was a lot easier just being her friend instead of her boyfriend. Rox, on the other hand, seemed laid-back. He didn't have to pretend he was something he wasn't with her.

"Take student government and all that," Roxanne continued, breaking into Eric's thoughts. "I'm trying to get involved at Kennedy, and Jonathan and the rest of you guys have been so nice to let me help with the activities for the dance." Eric liked the way Rox didn't draw attention to herself. She could have taken full credit for the computer Valentine idea but she was too modest. "But as much as I admire Jonathan for his school spirit, I could never run for office. Even school politics are too competitive in my book. You'd think they wouldn't have to be so intense, but they are." Rox smiled and shrugged. "Oh, well!"

With every passing minute, Eric was more impressed by Roxanne's sensitive, sensible outlook. He wouldn't have guessed he would enjoy talking to her this much. Right off the bat he'd been struck by her fabulous looks, but now he was finding she had a great personality, too. The bus ride passed in a flash. One minute he and Roxanne were chuckling together over a boating joke — they'd discovered they both preferred being *in* the water than on it — and what seemed like seconds later, the bus was pulling to a stop in the ski area parking lot.

It was a bit of a strain, but Eric managed to load himself up with Roxanne's skis, boots, and poles as well as his own for the short walk to the lodge. "Just making sure you'll be skiing with me all day," he informed her lightly.

"There's no one else I'd rather ski with," Rox confessed, zipping up her ski jacket. "I've met a lot of guys at Kennedy, and they're all so friendly that it's hard not to be friendly back! But I haven't had as much fun talking to anyone as I have with you." She smiled shyly. Eric's heart did a somersault and he almost dropped both pairs of skis. "I hope you don't mind my saying that," Roxanne added quickly.

"Mind?" Eric felt like he was walking on air. "Actually, I feel the same way."

Roxanne smiled with pleasure. "Good."

"So, what do you say?" he exclaimed. "Let's go ski up a storm!"

"You're on!" Rox was with him all the way.

"Shoot!" Holly Daniels tumbled headfirst into a drift of soft snow, her sunglasses and ski poles flying. She'd finally made it up the rope tow after falling off half a dozen times, and now she hadn't even gone ten yards down the beginner's slope before wiping out again. If only she'd remembered to sign up for a lesson! Diana, who had grown up skiing in the Rockies, had offered to stick with her, but Holly didn't want to cramp her style. In the end, Diana had gone up the chair lift with Molly to a steeper slope. Now Holly wished she hadn't been so unselfish. She was crazy to think she could teach herself how to ski. The bunny run might be nothing more than a molehill to expert Diana, but to her it looked more like Mt. Everest!

She took a deep, determined breath and got shakily to her feet again. At least I haven't lost my skis yet, she thought gratefully. The bindings were supposed to release if she took a bad enough spill. She had had enough trouble getting her heavy awkward boots to click onto the rented skis when she was on flat ground at the bottom of the slope; she'd never manage it here! Holly slipped her hands through the straps of her ski poles. Her mittens were cold and sopping wet, and so were her blue jeans. Her teeth chattered. She clenched them as she faced diagonally down the hill again. "Here goes nothing!" she said bravely to herself.

For a few yards, Holly managed to keep her skis facing forward and roughly parallel to one another. As she picked up speed she felt almost exhilarated. Hey, skiing is kind of fun! she thought. Then suddenly she was going *too* fast. The trees that had been on the far side of the slope a moment before were rushing closer and closer. Holly didn't know how to stop. She threw her arms up in the air, losing her balance. This time when she fell, her bindings did release — on both feet. She sat, covered from top to bottom with powdery snow, and watched helplessly while her skis raced off by themselves, finally crashing into a tree a short way down the hill.

Holly didn't know whether to laugh or cry. She was ready to give up and head for the lodge, but it was starting to look like she'd never even make it to the bottom of the trail! She sniffled, feeling more than a little lonely and sorry for herself. She looked over at her skis, wondering how she was going to get down to them. They certainly weren't going to ski back up to her. It looked like she had no choice but to slide down on her fanny. How humiliating! But it was either that or sit here and freeze.

Before she'd gotten very far, Holly was surprised by a spray of snow. A young man had skied to a swift, graceful racing stop right next to her. He lifted his goggles and Holly's heart lifted, too. It was Zachary. "Sorry about that!" he said in greeting. "Did I just get snow all over you?"

Holly burst out laughing. "There's so much on me already I can't even tell!"

"Here, let me give you a hand." Zachary reached down, and Holly put her small mittened hands into his large gloved one. He pulled her easily to her feet. "I saw you from the other slope and it looked like you could use some help," he explained, smiling in such a nice way that Holly couldn't feel awkward and stupid. "If you want, I'd love to teach you how to ski."

Holly's cheeks turned pink and she felt warm all over despite her wet clothes. She was glad to see Zachary again, maybe too glad. She'd thought a lot about him since that day in the library. Bending over, she made a show of brushing the snow off her jeans so she wouldn't have to meet Zachary's eyes. "Thanks, but you go ahead," she said nonchalantly. "I'll be okay, really! I'm actually starting to get the hang of it, I think."

Holly looked up. She knew she didn't sound convincing. Zachary raised one eyebrow. He didn't contradict her, saying instead, "Maybe you are, but with a few tips it'll come even easier." Before Holly could protest again he held up a hand. "I insist. Hey, you bailed me out in the library! You've got to let me pay you back."

Zachary's gentle, good-humored smile was irresistible. Holly grinned, relenting. "I'd love a few tips. If you don't think I'm too much of a lost cause, that is!"

Zachary shook his head firmly. "You've got lots of natural talent! Great balance. I could see that right away. You just need someone to point you in the right direction, that's all." He snapped his fingers. "Then you'll pick it up in no time."

Holly looked at him hopefully. "Where do I start?"

He laughed. "By getting your skis back on your feet! Wait here and I'll go get 'em." Before he turned to head down the hill, he took both Holly's hands and pulled off her damp mittens. "Here, try these," he offered, removing his own gloves and handing them to her. "They should be more comfortable."

Holly slipped her hands into the softly lined ski gloves and watched Zachary as he retrieved her skis and began sidestepping back up the slope to where she was waiting. The gloves were a little big but they were warm and, more importantly, *dry*. Holly felt a rush of gratitude for Zachary's thoughtfulness. He was ready to ski bare-handed just so she could be a little bit warmer. How incredibly sweet.

As soon as her skis were once more securely

141

on her feet and her poles were in her hands, Zachary began Holly's lesson. She was scared at the prospect of falling again, but Zachary quickly calmed her fears. They'd start slow. No more barreling down the slopes completely out of control! He showed her how to bend her knees and lean forward slightly instead of sitting back on her skis, and he explained how to plant her poles to steer some simple turns rather than trailing them uselessly behind her. Holly fell down a few more times, but she didn't get discouraged. She could feel herself improving with every cautious minute. Zachary, who was clearly an excellent skier, seemed like he was just as happy to be on the beginner's slope instead of the advanced one. He was a kind and patient instructor, and Holly couldn't get frustrated or upset over falling down, especially when she looked up to see his encouraging smile.

Another thing Holly quickly noticed about Zachary — every girl who skied by turned to look at him. A lot of them were good skiers and beautiful, too. Zachary, however, was oblivious to everyone but Holly. He gave her his undivided attention, applauding her increasing skill while being careful not to make her try anything too ambitious.

There was something very innocent about the way he didn't seem to notice the girls admiring him. Holly could tell he wasn't pretending. He really *didn't* notice them. She couldn't help mentally comparing him to Bart. Bart would have had a field day in a place like this. He'd flash every cute girl on the slope his famous smile, and call hello. He would probably even offer a few ski tips, too, if needed. As for Holly, she'd most likely still be stuck headfirst in a snowdrift! No, she reprimanded herself, you're not being fair to Bart. He's not that bad! Yes he is, another inner voice corrected her. If anything, he was worse!

She and Zachary rode the rope tow up and took one more run. This time Holly made it to the bottom without falling once. She was so excited she threw her ski poles in the air. Luckily no one else was within striking distance. "I did it!" she shouted joyfully. "Zack, I stayed up the whole way!"

"You were fantastic!" Zachary was as thrilled with Holly's accomplishment as she was herself. He put an arm around her shoulders and gave her a congratulatory squeeze. "I think you're ready for the chair lift and the intermediate run. Come on, it's over here!"

A few minutes later the chair lift was lifting them high above the heads of the other skiers. Holly wanted to swing her feet but Zachary put the safety bar down and made her rest her skis on it. "I don't want to lose you," he explained lightly. They chatted on the way up, and Zachary told Holly he'd been in the Ski Club at Stevenson. He added that he wished there was one at Kennedy.

"Why don't you start one?" Holly suggested, reaching up to pull her fuzzy pink beret more securely over her ears.

"Me?" Zachary seemed surprised by the idea. "I don't know. I don't know that many people at Kennedy yet. And anyway, I wouldn't know how." He smiled uncertainly.

"Well, you could try." Holly winked. "If you can teach me how to ski, you can start a club!" Just then the chair lift jolted to an abrupt stop. Holly's eyes widened. "Wh — what happened?" she yelped.

"Don't worry." Zachary's voice was reassuring. "Someone probably just fell as they were getting on the chair. It happens all the time. The lift'll start up again in a sec."

Then he gave her a mischievous look and began gently rocking their chair. Holly squealed and hid her face in his sleeve. "Zack, stop! We're going to fall!" He laughed, but stopped rocking. Slowly the chair swung until it was still again. For a moment, Zachary and Holly were surrounded by a deep, velvety hush. The only sounds came from snow slipping off tree branches and the occasional swish of a skier passing below. Suddenly Holly realized Zachary's face was very close to hers. The look in his eyes made her blush.

She glanced quickly down at her gloves, or rather, at Zachary's gloves. He had looked away, too, and now pretended to be very interested in the tip of his left ski. "Um, Holly," he began in a low, hesitant voice.

"Yes?" she said, too eagerly.

The warm note in her voice seemed to encourage him. He turned to her with a hopeful half-smile. "Uh, I was wondering. If you don't have — I mean, if you're not already. . . . Would you . . . would you like to go to the Valentine's Day Dance with me?"

All the color left Holly's cheeks and then rushed back into them, making them even rosier than before. For a long moment she was completely speechless. Zachary's invitation was absolutely the last thing she'd expected. . . . Or was it? Holly knew she was starting to fall for him as hard as he was obviously starting to fall for her. Still, a ski lesson was one thing and the dance was another. Things had gone too far and it was up to her to tell him so. She curled her fingers up into balls inside the gloves and took a deep breath. "Gee, Zachary," she said in a rush, "that's nice of you, but I'm — I have. . . . Jonathan signed me up to help with the refreshments and so I really wasn't planning to go with a date. Thanks anyway, though," she ended, somewhat lamely.

Zachary looked disappointed but he didn't seem to pick up on the awkwardness of Holly's story. "Maybe next time," he said with an easy, unoffended smile.

"Sure," Holly said. To her relief, the chair lift lurched into motion again a moment later. Very soon they reached the top and were skiing down the ramp. Holly caught sight of Diana and Molly.

She waved a ski pole at them and called out, "Look, you guys! I'm skiing!" When they beckoned to her to join them, Holly turned to Zachary. "Do you want to take a run with Di and Molly?" she invited, pushing a windblown curl away from her eyes.

"No, you go ahead. I think I see someone I know over there." He gestured vaguely in the opposite direction from where Diana and Molly had pulled to a stop.

"Well, okay." Holly gripped her ski poles and straightened her sunglasses. "Oh! Your gloves! I almost forgot."

Before she could take the gloves off, Zachary shook his head vehemently. "No, you keep them. You can give them back to me at the end of the day."

"Oh, um, thanks." Holly suddenly felt shy. "And thanks for the lesson. It was such a help."

"My pleasure!" The warmth and sincerity of Zachary's smile made her tingle. She pushed off with her ski poles and coasted toward her two waiting friends. As she skied, Holly replayed in her mind the conversation she'd just had with Zachary about the dance. Why hadn't she been able to nip things in the bud by just telling Zachary about Bart? What did her reluctance to admit she had a steady boyfriend say about her feelings for either boy?

Chapter
11

Katie gritted her teeth and dug the edges of her skis down hard in an extra sharp, extra fast turn. She wasn't sure she could take this much longer. As soon as they'd bought their lift tickets that morning, she and Greg had headed for the semiadvanced hill, with Jonathan and Matt not far behind them. When they arrived at the top of the mountain, though, who should they meet up with but Eric — and Roxanne Easton. Katie had made a special effort to be nice — she didn't want to give Greg any ammunition for ribbing her — and Rox was actually civil in return. What's more, despite her snow-bunny appearance, Rox was a decent skier and easily kept up with Katie and the four boys.

No, Roxanne wasn't necessarily the problem, although she was definitely the cause. The problem was that Katie had become the invisible woman again. All morning she'd been looking forward to playing games on the slope with Greg, maybe racing a run or two. Now it looked as though she might as well race her shadow. Greg was as bad as Matt or Eric or Jonathan. It was as if all of a sudden the guys had been transformed into Abbott and Costello times two. They threw themselves down the mountain eagerly, skiing backward, taking jumps, anything to outdo one another — and to impress Roxanne. Then at the bottom of every run, there was a jostle in the lift line to see who would get to ride up on the chair with Rox. Katie felt like she was the consolation prize, if that.

Now she took in an angry, shaking breath of cold, snow-dusted air. Whoa, calm down, she told herself. There was no point in ruining the whole day. Just because they were acting like fools didn't mean she couldn't still have fun.

Katie slowed down a bit, trying her best to relax. She had been skiing apart from the others at the edge of the trail, taking the whole scene in. Now she skied closer to Greg. He gave her a wide but somewhat absent smile as she locked her arm in his so they could ski in unison. "Having a good time?" she asked cheerfully.

"Oh, sure." He squeezed her arm, but his eyes wandered to where Roxanne was making some flashy turns, weaving skillfully among her other three admirers. If the guys were going overboard, Katie noticed that Rox certainly wasn't doing anything to discourage them. She swallowed. I'll count to ten, she thought, and if this nonsense doesn't stop. . . .

Just then Katie saw Rox catch sight of her and Greg. Rox grabbed Matt's arm and skied toward them. "Let's form a chain!" she suggested in a peppy voice. Greg thought it was a great idea and in a moment his free arm was linked with Roxanne's. Katie had just been annoyed before but now she was steaming. She dropped Greg's arm as pointedly as she could and sped off to the bottom of the slope by herself.

Ugh! she wanted to shout. She'd had it with Rox stealing the show. She'd had it with Stacy Morrison and everyone else from Stevenson, too. She didn't mind not being the center of attention, but this was ridiculous. And she was a far better skier than Rox anyway. . . .

Suddenly Katie had an idea. It wasn't a very nice idea, but she wasn't exactly feeling nice. Rox looked pretty good on the intermediate hill, Katie thought, but she was by no means an expert. Maybe it was time to put her to a test, to see how far her toothpaste smile and hot-pink ski pants got her on the advanced trail.

Leaning on her poles, Katie waited for the others, who were still on their way down the hill, linked in a laughing chain. As soon as they reached her, they pushed off toward the lift they'd been riding all morning. "Wait!" called Katie, "let's try something different." She pointed to the double chair in the other direction. "Who's up for the advanced run?"

Needless to say, all the guys were. After all, it would be an excellent opportunity to dazzle Roxanne. They piled onto the lift: Katie and Greg and two strangers sat in one four-person chair, Rox, Jonathan, Matt, and Eric were right behind them. The ride was longer than any other they'd taken, since this time they were going all the way to the top of the mountain. Beneath them the steep, narrow trail was clearly visible. Katie twisted in her seat to look over her shoulder. Even from here she could see that Eric and Jonathan were turning a little pale. They were only intermediate skiers, so they had to be feeling a little more nervous and a lot less cocky than before. Well, Katie didn't have any sympathy for them. They deserved whatever they got!

When she turned to face forward again, Katie discovered Greg watching her intently. She did the best to wipe the gleeful smile off her face. "What?" she asked innocently.

Greg pushed his goggles up off his face and narrowed his eyes suspiciously. "You're up to something, aren't you?" he guessed.

"What do you mean?" Katie tried to look as guiltless as she sounded.

"This." Greg gestured toward the top of the mountain. "This 'let's try a steeper run' business. There's something behind it, isn't there?"

Katie dropped her genial pose to glare at Greg

through her wind-ruffled red bangs. "Maybe there is. What of it?" she challenged. "Is it such a crime to want to get off the baby slope for a change? Or did you have a few more circus tricks you wanted to impress Roxanne with?"

Greg slapped the heel of his hand to his forehead and groaned. "Not that again, K.C. You really are too much!"

"*I'm* too much!" Greg was chuckling but Katie was not amused. "I'm too much!" she repeated. "That's really a laugh. Obviously you don't know how ridiculous you look, all of you. You'd think she was the only girl in the world!"

Greg's grin faded. "At least she's fun to be around," he observed coolly.

Katie blushed, outraged. "And I'm not, is that it?" she snapped. "Well, excuse me! This is just the first time anyone's bothered to speak to me all day! I guess my social skills are a little rusty."

"Come off it, Katie," Greg advised, pulling his goggles back down over his eyes. "Jealousy isn't your style."

Katie couldn't believe her ears. Greg had some nerve, preaching to her about *her* behavior! "It isn't, huh?" She inched forward on the chair, ready to hop off. "Are you telling me not to be jealous just because you've been entirely wrapped up in Roxanne Easton ever since we got to this stupid mountain?"

Greg shook his head as they pushed away from the lift and down the snow-packed ramp. "I'm telling you to grow up and stop playing

151

these competitive games. The only person you're going to hurt is yourself."

Katie was more than a little miffed. Greg's unbearably patronizing attitude only proved that she was right about Roxanne. Rox had them all brainwashed. Well, this steep slope would teach all of them a lesson, and Katie, for one, couldn't wait.

A minute later they had all gathered at the top. Katie was secretly delighted to see that even Roxanne's enthusiasm had dimmed. Eric and Jonathan looked downright ill. There were two trails down, both marked by the black diamonds that indicated the most difficult slopes. In silence, they skied to the nearest of the two, then paused for a moment. The cold wind, much colder than it was farther down the mountain, whipped everyone's hair.

Katie was about to warn everybody to take it easy; she wanted to teach the guys a lesson, but she didn't want them to kill themselves in the process. But Rox spoke up before Katie had a chance to. "Let's race!" she declared flirtatiously, leaning forward over her skis in readiness.

Race? Katie wanted to shout. Roxanne had to be kidding. It was bad enough to encourage a little playful showing off, but goading the boys into racing this slope was like asking them to jump off a cliff.

"It looks pretty rough," Jonathan observed. "Maybe we should go slow until we get used to it."

"Yeah," Matt agreed. "We can race later."

Her eyebrows raised, Roxanne challenged them. "You're not afraid I'll win, are you?" She turned, ready to take off. "Coming?"

Before Katie could protest they had started enthusiastically down the slope at a breakneck pace.

The trail was twisty and liberally studded with moguls. No one was clowning now, and the same look of intensity was mirrored on all six faces. Even Katie had to concentrate. Greg was skiing with as much flair as before, his experience making the black diamond trail look no more than mildly challenging. But Katie could tell Eric, Matt, and Jonathan were in over their heads. It was clear that Rox, too, was struggling. The faster they went, the harder the less skillful skiers had to work just to stay on their feet. It occurred to Katie that maybe coming up here had been a mistake. It was a difficult trail and Roxanne's challenge to race was turning it into a perilous one.

Eric seemed to be having the hardest time staying in control of his speeding skis. Concerned, Katie watched him out of the corner of her right eye as they approached a particularly sharp bend. On her left, she saw Rox take the first tumble. She couldn't help feeling a twinge of satisfaction. Suddenly Eric was flailing across the snow directly in front of Katie, on his way apparently to Roxanne's rescue. Instead, with a loud shout he fell unexpectedly himself, right in

Katie's path. She tried to avoid a collision but there wasn't time. They hit and Katie screamed. The whole world turned upside down. Katie was aware only of hard snow, jammed limbs, and a sound like a tree branch breaking. Then she felt an awful sickness in her stomach and a terrible, raging pain. Then everything stopped cold for Katie. Except the pain.

Greg reached his girlfriend's side first, his eyes wide with fear. "Katie!" he shouted hoarsely. His panic grew as he saw that she was clutching her right leg. "Katie, are you okay?"

Katie shook her head fiercely. She doubled over, the tears streaming down her face to splash, burning, on her cold shaking fingers. "My leg," she sobbed.

Matt and Jonathan had just skied to a stop nearby but Greg waved them on. "Go get the ski patrol!" he ordered. "Hurry!" Then he knelt carefully at Katie's side, smoothing her hair away from her pale face. "You're going to be all right," he whispered, tears starting up in his own eyes. Katie, still crying, hardly seemed to recognize him. Her wide, brown eyes were glazed over with pain and fear. Greg gently stroked her forehead, trying to soothe her. "It's all right," he repeated.

Katie squeezed her eyes shut and bit her lip so hard it bled. "No, it's not," she moaned. "It hurts. It's not all right at all." Suddenly her fear blazed into anger. "It's your fault!" she cried. "All you stupid people! If you hadn't been skiing like lunatics — "

"Shh, Katie, quiet." Greg eased her head onto his lap and cradled her shoulders in his arms. "It's no one's fault. It was an accident."

Roxanne had been standing quietly with Eric a few yards away. The two were brushing the snow off their clothes, unhurt. Now she spoke up. "It was your idea to go down the black diamond run," Roxanne reminded Katie.

Roxanne's I-told-you-so tone set Katie off again. "So it was all my fault!" She turned to Greg and asked sarcastically, "Was I being too competitive?"

Greg shot a furious look at Rox, who blinked innocently. "It wasn't your fault," he insisted to Katie gently, keeping his voice as calm as he could. "It wasn't anybody's — "

"You're lying." Katie was shivering uncontrollably now. Her voice shook, too. "It's all *your* fault!" she accused. Tears sprang again to her eyes. She'd never felt such pain and despair. "It's all your fault," she repeated, feebly pushing him away. "I never want to speak to you again!"

Before Greg could say anything, the ski patrol arrived. In seconds they had Katie securely bundled onto a rescue sled and were streaking down the slope with her. The only thing Greg, Eric, and Rox could do was follow, slowly this time.

The ride on the rescue sled was bumpy and fast. The speed scared Katie — all she could think of was the possibility of crashing, and more pain. She unclenched her jaw when they reached the bottom and slowed down. Through

the tears that stung her eyes, she could see someone in a navy blue parka peering at her anxiously.
It was Molly, who must have been told about the
accident by Matt and Jonathan. She had taken
off her skis and was waiting by the ambulance,
nervously shifting her weight from one clunky
boot to the other. It looked to Katie as if Molly
were holding her breath. She's probably really
concerned, Katie thought. She managed a weak
smile in Molly's direction.

Her friend's knees buckled with relief. "Katie,
are you okay?"

She grimaced as the rescue team lifted her
gently from the sled on to a stretcher. "Moll,"
she said, a tremble in her voice. "don't leave
me."

With the rescue team's permission, Molly
scrambled into the ambulance along with Katie.
She took her friend's hand and gave it a comforting squeeze. Katie didn't let go for the whole
ride to the nearby medical center. She kept her
eyes closed, concentrating on the pressure of
Molly's fingers in an effort to ignore the pain.

The trip only took a few minutes, but it felt
like hours to Katie. Once they got to the hospital, the paramedics shifted her onto a hospital
gurney, and rolled her in through the emergency
entrance. When they reached the examining
room, Molly was told she had to wait outside.

Katie tried not to cry while the doctor probed
her leg, but it was hard. Even the most gentle
touch was agony. The doctor finished her ex-

156

amination in just a few minutes. Katie knew what she was going to say before she said it. "I'm afraid it's probably broken. I'm going to have your friend call your parents so they can drive over and get you. Meanwhile, we'll do some X rays and get you set up in a cast."

Katie nodded. She stared up at the white ceiling, not really seeing it and not caring. She didn't care if her parents ever came, or if she spent the rest of eternity lying on this examining table. *Broken . . . broken . . . broken . . .* echoed through her brain. Her leg was broken. She couldn't walk, she couldn't ski, but that wasn't the devastating part. Gymnastics. It had been in the back of her mind the whole time, but Katie hadn't let herself think about it. Now it was a reality. Katie's chances of recapturing her state title were as shattered as the bone in her right leg. She closed her eyes as the tears started up again. Her life might as well be over.

Chapter
12

"One, two, three, run!" Diana pushed open the door of the Little Theater to let Holly charge outside and then dashed after her. It couldn't have been a more miserable day — cold, but not cold enough to snow. Instead, it had been alternating between sleet and an icy rain since dawn. Right now it was sleeting and Holly, landing awkwardly with one foot on a particularly slippery patch, just managed to catch herself before the other foot could fly out from under her as well.

The two girls had been scrounging around in the storerooms at the theater all afternoon. They were looking for creative decorations for the Valentine's Day Dance, which was less than two weeks away. They hadn't come up with much besides some rather moth-eaten old pink satin bunting, which might do if the lights were dim enough. And now it was wet, moth-eaten pink satin bunting, thanks to the glorious weather, Holly thought wryly.

They reached the main school building and grabbed the door handle simultaneously, then scrambled inside. "Brrr!" Holly dropped the bunting and held her arms out. "How is it possible that I got soaked to the skin in less than three seconds?"

"Don't ask me!" Diana flipped her long blonde ponytail over one shoulder and rang the water from it with her hands. "Whose smart idea was it to leave the umbrella in her locker, anyway?"

"Well, it wasn't coming down that hard when we went over there!" Holly defended herself. She grinned, looking down at her wet clothes. "We might as well just head to the cafeteria and dry out."

The two girls sloshed down the hall, leaving a trail of soggy footprints behind them on the industrial carpet. Diana shook her head glumly. "Not only did we get drenched, but we didn't even find anything good at that dumb theater!"

"It didn't help much that we didn't even know what we were looking for," Holly pointed out. "The decorations committee hasn't even come up with a theme yet."

"Well, we'd better think of something fast, and then we're going to need to go on a major shopping trip. Any ideas?"

Holly raked a hand through her hair, attempting to fluff up her damp curls. "This bunting actually gave me one," she admitted. Diana looked doubtfully at the sodden bundle in Holly's arms. "No, really," Holly insisted. "It did! How about a Victorian look? You know, soft lighting and lace and those funny antique Valentines on the wall. . . ."

Holly was partial to anything old-fashioned and romantic. Her own bedroom at home was decorated in a Victorian style and furnished with quaint, curious knickknacks she'd picked up at secondhand stores.

Diana pursed her lips thoughtfully. "That wouldn't be bad," she said, not sounding entirely convinced. "I don't know, though. With a computer Valentine service being the big draw, don't you think something a little more, I don't know, *up-to-date* would be appropriate?"

"Maybe we should ask the rest of the decorations committee," Holly suggested in the interest of democracy. This time she opened the door for Diana.

"Good idea," her friend agreed, preceding her into the noisy Kennedy cafeteria. After loading up their lunch trays, the two headed without thinking for the crowd's regular table in the usually sunny north corner of the cafeteria. Maneuvering through the enormous room was like running an obstacle course. Holly had hurdled over three backpacks, four empty trays, and a basketball before Diana stopped her with an ominous "uh-oh."

"Uh-oh, what?" Holly followed Diana's gaze. "Oh, no." Simply put, their usual table *wasn't*. Instead of a gang of their friends, boys and girls alike, there were two strangers at their table — Stevenson kids, maybe — looking lonely among the unoccupied chairs. At a smaller table to the left sat Molly, Pamela, Karen Davis, Katie, and a pair of crutches. At an even smaller table to the right were Greg, Eric, Jonathan, and a few other guys. The two tables were like opposing camps facing off across a deserted battlefield. Except that no one was facing anybody. People's backs were turned wherever possible.

"This couldn't all be because of what happened at Mount Jackson on Saturday," Holly said in disbelief.

"It looks like the mess didn't end on the ski slope," Diana confirmed Holly's fears. "And to tell you the truth," she added with some sharpness, "I can't say I'm surprised."

They detoured toward the girls' table and plunked their trays at the two empty spaces. "Hi, everybody!" Holly greeted in an overly bright voice.

"Hi!" Pamela answered eagerly. She sounded glad to see them. It was obvious that the conversation around the table wasn't exactly running along cheerful lines.

Holly fussed for a few moments with the food on her tray and then turned to Katie, who hadn't said a word to the newcomers. As she opened her carton of chocolate milk, she said, "I worried about you all weekend, K.C." Her eyes were warm with caring and concern. "How are you feeling?"

"Okay," Katie answered dully. She looked tired and Holly imagined that the pain from the broken leg had kept her from sleeping very well.

"Well, I'm glad you at least didn't have to miss any school!" Holly said, trying to look on the bright side.

"Yeah."

Holly looked at Diana, who shrugged helplessly. The five girls sat eating in silence for a minute. Holly, feeling very uncomfortable, was on the verge of demanding the whole story behind the crowd's eating at separate tables when Molly dropped her soup spoon with a clatter. "I can't believe it!" she exclaimed in a low, disgusted voice. "I absolutely can't believe it." All five heads turned to follow Molly's daggerlike gaze. Roxanne Easton, wearing a clingy, black sweater and extra-slim, extra-faded pegged jeans, was weaving her way — sort of like a snake, Holly thought — toward a table. And not just any table. Jonathan half-rose in his chair as she approached, while Greg and Eric quickly, and it appeared delightedly, moved their trays aside to make room for her. "I'm sorry," Molly continued, her eyes angry. "I'd just agreed that if I couldn't say anything nice about her or any of those . . . those *other* people I wouldn't say anything at all. We decided that right before you guys showed up,"

162

she explained to Diana and Holly. She shook her head and her shaggy brown hair swung against her face. "But this is just too much. I really can't believe they're still playing up to her after what she did to Katie!"

"What *she* did to Katie?" Karen objected, pushing the red plastic frames of her glasses up on her nose. "From everything you told me, the guys are just as responsible. If they hadn't been falling all over each other trying to show off for her, the accident never would have happened."

"Yeah, well, they're all to blame, then," Molly conceded. "But if the guys were hoping to redeem themselves, they just lost their last chance. Being so nice to Roxanne is a slap in Katie's face!" Molly was furious.

"Maybe they don't mean it that way," Pamela suggested in a gentle attempt to be diplomatic.

"They mean it," Molly said decidedly. Her delicate dark eyebrows knit together as she frowned. "You weren't at Mount Jackson, Pamela. You should've been with Katie in the ambulance — then you wouldn't bother trying to make excuses for them. They don't deserve defending!"

"Lucky for you Matt's not over there," Diana added. "What did he tell you, anyway, about the ski trip?"

Pamela looked surprised. "I. . . . To tell you the truth, I — I haven't even spoken to him since then." She seemed worried as she admitted this, and a little upset. Pamela, always the dreamy artist, had been comparatively oblivious to the Roxanne Easton phenomenon all along. Now it looked like it was occurring to her for the first time that her own romance might be threatened by the new girl. How could she have been so blind? Just the other day Matt had broken a date with her to give Roxanne a spin in his Mustang.

Holly had been following the exchange between Molly, Pamela, and Diana as if she were watching a complex Ping-Pong match, looking from one girl to another, and then back again. Now she sneaked a glance at Katie out of the corner of her eye. Katie had been strangely silent so far, idly stirring her chicken noodle soup but not eating any. Molly's latest outburst seemed to have drawn the first real response from her. "You know, you guys don't have to feel sorry for me," she said, staring intently at a spoonful of steaming noodles. "I'm okay, and the accident can't be undone by fighting about it."

Molly put an arm around Katie's shoulders and gave her a supportive hug. "It can't be undone, but it never should've happened in the first place. That's the real point here! Don't tell me *you've* stopped being mad at them."

"No, I haven't." Katie shot a tired, unhappy glance in the direction of Greg's broad, implacable back two tables away. Suddenly she pushed her chair back. "I'm thirsty. Anyone want a soda?"

"Sit still, I'll get it for you," Karen offered.

"No, I want to do it myself." Katie's delicate jaw was set in a stubborn line. "I have to get the hang of using these things!" She got herself awkwardly up and onto her crutches, and hobbled off at a snail's pace. Her friends watched sympathetically.

"Do you think it upsets her, our talking about the accident and everything?" Pamela wondered.

"I don't think so," said Molly. She crossed her arms over the front of her faded red jumpsuit. "In spite of what she says, I think it makes her feel better to know we're on her side."

"And I'm sure on her side." Karen reached up to refasten the red comb holding back her thick, wavy black hair. "I had a funny feeling about Roxanne Easton from the start. The very first day she transferred here from Stevenson, she stopped by the newspaper office. She pretended she wanted to write for *The Red and the Gold* but all she really did was ask a lot of nosy questions and snoop around. She hasn't submitted an article yet!"

"Basically, she has all the guys acting like fools," Diana said flatly. "No offense, Pamela," she amended quickly. "I don't mean Matt so much." Pamela looked more disturbed than ever. "But Eric and Jonathan and Greg . . . and even Jeremy!" She added her boyfriend's name and then snorted. "He wasn't even on the dumb ski trip and he told me this morning during study hall that he didn't think it was necessarily Roxanne's fault. Or the guys'. I swear somebody brainwashed him!"

Molly pushed her soup bowl away and reached for her banana. "All I can say is, I considered Eric my friend and I know Katie did, too. And what about Greg? He's supposed to be her *boyfriend*! I don't blame her for saying she never wants to speak to him again."

"Did she really say that?" Pamela's eyes widened in shock.

Molly nodded. "Mm-hmm."

Holly got a sick, sad feeling in her stomach. Poor Katie. On top of having a broken leg, she didn't even have Greg to lean on and turn to for love and sympathy. Holly had been fairly neutral when she first sat down at the table, but now she was beginning to feel as angry and indignant as Molly. How could Greg be so cold? There he was, sitting only a few tables away with his back turned while Katie struggled on her crutches, too proud to let one of her friends get her a stupid soda. Greg must have some reason to feel guilty or he could never behave this way, she thought. As for Eric . . . Holly was suddenly distracted by a conversation taking place at the table behind her. A few Kennedy sophomores she knew vaguely were whispering, but loudly enough that she could hear. They were talking about the ski trip and Katie's accident. Obviously the story had already gotten around school. It never took long, and this time the gossip was probably spread even faster because practically half the upperclassmen had been on the trip in the first place.

"What I heard," one of the boys was saying in a low voice, "was that Eric fell intentionally. He never forgave Katie for leaving him for Greg."

Holly sat bolt upright in her chair. She knew that what the boy was saying couldn't possibly be true, but just the thought was so terrible it made her look at Eric differently. She'd always thought he was such a nice guy. And he was a nice guy, she reminded himself. Or was he? She gave up trying to figure out who was right and who was wrong. It was too confusing.

Holly looked up to see Katie make her way back to the table and ease herself into her chair. She had a can of Coke stuck in the front pocket of her mint-green overalls. Katie smiled thinly. "See, I can still take care of myself," she joked.

Holly caught Diana's eye. The two friends silently agreed on the same thing — this would be a good time to change the subject and talk about anything but the Mount Jackson disaster. Holly cleared her throat.

"Does everybody want to hear Diana's and my idea for decorating the cafeteria for the Valentine's Day Dance?" She described the two options they'd come up with so far, putting a special pitch in for her own favorite, the Victorian theme. "So, we thought the whole decorations committee should vote on one or the other before we went ahead with anything."

167

"That seems fair," Karen observed. "Who's on the committee, anyway?"

"Me and Di for starters. Plus Jonathan, Eric, Molly. . . ." Holly's voice trailed off. She gulped. So much for changing the subject! she thought dismally.

"Great committee, huh?" Molly commented sarcastically. She tossed her banana peel into a nearby trash barrel. "I'm sure we'll work together really effectively!"

Holly sighed and looked down at her ham and Swiss cheese sandwich. She hadn't even taken a bite, but after all this discouraging talk her appetite had pretty much deserted her. It was starting to seem pretty clear that the crowd's disagreement over whose fault Katie's accident was or wasn't ran pretty deep. With Greg and Katie not speaking, Molly furious at Eric, Matt and Pamela completely out of touch, and even Diana and Jeremy in a spat, there wasn't a single couple who hadn't been affected. Sitting at separate lunch tables looked like just the beginning.

Listlessly, Holly picked up half of her sandwich and was raising it to her mouth when she caught a glimpse of a blond boy in a red chamois shirt on the other side of the cafeteria. In all the fuss over Katie, she had practically forgotten her ski lesson with Zachary and their conversation on the chair lift. Once again, seeing Zachary had a funny, confusing effect on Holly. On the one hand, her worries about Bart and their relationship were instantly revived. On the other, her heart beat a little faster at the possibility that Zachary might see her — maybe even come over to talk to her. She watched him discreetly, hoping he might walk by her table but dreading it, too. But he only grabbed a sandwich in the lunch line and raced right back out of the cafeteria again. Holly sank back in her seat, relieved and disappointed at the same time.

Diana noticed her friend's sudden discomposure. "Is something wrong, Holly?" she asked, her blonde eyebrows raised.

"No, uh, not at all," Holly assured her hastily. She took a bite of her sandwich and chewed it vigorously, trying to look ordinary and unconcerned. "Everything's fine."

"Well, you shouldn't worry," Diana told Holly, in a low voice. "You're one of the lucky ones! At least Bart's away at college and not part of this mess."

Holly nodded, all of a sudden feeling limper than the sandwich she'd dropped back on her tray, unfinished. If Diana only knew! Holly shivered at the thought. She certainly couldn't explain her dilemma to Diana. Dilemma! she thought to herself. Holly stifled an anxious sigh. Inside she knew she wasn't the lucky one at all.

Chapter 13

Zachary took a big bite out of his roast beef sandwich as he hurried down the near-empty hallway to the student government room. Too big a bite, he soon realized — it was going to take him about five minutes to chew and swallow it. That turned out to be just as well, though, because somewhere along the way he took a wrong turn and ended up at the wrong end of the south wing. Shoot, he thought, shaking his head with frustration at his own slowness. Am I ever going to be able to find my way around this place?

He backtracked at an even quicker pace, and in a minute he was standing outside his destination. The door was closed. Zachary took a deep breath, his hand raised, then gave a tentative rap with his knuckles. A small voice called, "Come in." He pushed the door open. Just as he'd hoped, Frankie Baker was alone. Zachary exhaled, relieved.

Frankie looked up from the computer. Now, at the sight of Zachary, her light eyes almost sparked. "Oh, Zack, it's you!" she exclaimed.

"Hi, Franko!" The two exchanged sincere smiles. Zack crossed to her desk and gave her an affectionate, football player-type slap on the back. "How's it going? Working hard?" He peered with distrust at the brightly lit computer screen. "Never could get the hang of these things," he admitted, shaking his head sowly.

"They're not that bad, once you get used to them," Frankie said. Her cheeks flamed bright pink. "Seriously. I used to be afraid of them myself!" She smiled wryly. "You just have to convince yourself that you're smarter than they are. Then you're all set!"

"Maybe." Zachary looked and sounded doubtful. "But, hey, Frankie, I have a question about the computer Valentine form. That's actually why I'm here."

If Frankie was disappointed, she didn't show it. "Sure, Zack." She tipped her head to one side and adopted a helpful attitude that made her look sort of like a librarian, or so Zachary thought. "What do you want to know?"

"Well." He paused, almost losing his nerve but not quite. "Um, there's a place on the form where it asks if there's one special person you want to be paired with. You know the part I mean?"

171

"Yeah, I know." Frankie's cheeks went pink again.

"Well. . . ." Zachary cleared his throat and shuffled his sneakered feet awkwardly. His own face was a little red. "What I want to know is, will the computer really put you with that person?"

He looked at Frankie hopefully. She looked down at her hands, which were still resting lightly on top of the keyboard. "The computer's programmed to respond to that question only if both people put each other's names on the form," she explained shyly. "So if . . . she . . . puts you, too, then you'll get paired. Otherwise, well, it could happen if your interests and all were totally compatible, but it would sort of be a long shot."

Zachary nodded thoughtfully, fighting back a sigh of disappointment. So it wasn't going to be enough just to write Holly Daniels' name on the form, then. He wasn't guaranteed that she would be his Valentine, and he wanted her to be, so badly. First, in the library, then on the ski trip this past weekend, he'd thought she was the prettiest, the nicest, and the smartest girl he'd ever met. He'd dreamed about her every minute since then. But she was keeping her distance. She was as friendly as anything, but she was definitely keeping her distance. There wasn't really any other way to interpret the other day on the chair lift when he'd asked her to the dance and she'd said no.

He leaned forward with his elbows on his

knees and rubbed his forehead. Was it because he was younger? Maybe, Zachary thought. He pictured her sitting with her friends in the cafeteria where he'd just seen her. Most of them were seniors, he knew. From everything he'd heard so far, they were a bright, popular group. Holly was probably backing off because she'd found out that he wasn't a good student. He had to have another chance to prove that brains weren't everything!

Zachary glanced up at Frankie, who was quietly watching him, her attitude patient. He'd made up his mind. He really didn't want to pull anything sneaky, but on the other hand he really *did* want another chance to show Holly that he was a good guy, even if he wasn't a senior or Mr. Brilliant. "Uh, Frankie," he began slowly, a shy expression on his handsome, freckled face. "I understand how this is supposed to work, but I wondered . . . I mean, I don't want you to get in trouble or anything, but . . . that is, is there any way I can arrange to get paired with a specific person? Or rather, can *you* arrange to pair me with her?" he finished in a rush.

Frankie put her hand to her ponytail to twist it, looking a little nervous. Zachary held his breath, sure she was going to say no. Then she shrugged and smiled a faint smile. She tipped her head on one side. "Well, why don't you tell me who the girl is and I'll check on the computer to see what she wrote on her form."

Zachary gulped. "Um, her name is Holly

Daniels," he managed to get out. Despite his embarrassment, he couldn't help a smile from creeping onto his face. Holly's name sounded even more beautiful when he said it out loud like that, he thought.

Frankie hit a few keys on the computer and then Zachary saw her type in Holly's name. An instant later the computer chirped twice, its screen still blank. He raised his eyebrows. "It looks like Holly didn't even turn in a questionnaire," Frankie informed him.

She looked at Zachary and shrugged as if to say that was that, but his expression was still pleading. She sighed deeply. "She didn't turn in a form, but I'll tell you what," she said, coming to a decision. "As long as Holly shows up at the dance and gives her name at the door, you'll have a date."

Zachary's appreciation showed in his shining blue eyes. He grinned boyishly. "Franko, you're the greatest!" he exclaimed, giving her another friendly swat on the shoulder. "This is going to be great! Thanks a lot, thanks a real lot."

"Sure." Frankie dismissed the favor. "Just don't tell anyone I did this for you, okay?"

"Not a soul," he promised her, jumping to his feet. He couldn't sit still a second longer. He was too psyched. After mussing Frankie's hair affectionately, he then sprinted to the door. "You're the greatest," he repeated over his shoulder. "See ya!"

" 'Bye, Zack."

Zachary barreled out of the student government room so blind with happiness that he almost ran over Roxanne on her way in. "Oops! Sorry there, Rox," he said, distracted.

"Why, Zack McGraw." Roxanne lowered her eyelashes and treated him to a dazzling smile. "I'm sorry to see you're on your way out. We haven't talked in the *longest* time!"

"Uh, yeah, right, Rox." Zachary raised an eyebrow in her general direction. "It's really too bad." He continued down the hallway without pausing. "Oh, well!" He didn't have to turn around to picture the piqued look that accompanied Roxanne's indignant "hmmph!"

Zachary had seen all Roxanne's looks and he didn't take them too seriously anymore. Like every other guy from Stevenson, he used to be wild about Roxanne. But one by one they'd all learned their lessons. He'd learned *his* lesson when he arrived at her house to pick her up for a movie date a year ago to find Doug Zuckerman's car in the driveway on the exact same mission. Rox had merely lifted her hands and smiled helplessly. What could she do? She'd just gotten the dates on her calendar all mixed up! Zachary shook his head, amused. Yep, Rox was really a number. He was sure that by now she had at least two dozen Kennedy guys swooning for her. Poor fellas, he thought, feeling sorry for them.

But now Zachary dismissed Roxanne from his thoughts. There was no point wasting any energy on her. He had Holly to think about. And at the

Valentine's Day Dance, maybe, just maybe, he'd discover that she'd been thinking about him, too.

After Zachary said good-bye and raced for the door, Frankie turned back to the computer. She bent her head and squeezed her eyes tightly shut. For a moment she'd thought that Zack had come in just to see her. But no. It would never occur to him that it might be painful for her to be treated like a second-string linebacker who was a good guy, but spent a lot of time sitting on the bench. Frankie sighed, her breath coming out loud and shaky. Zack liked someone else . . . a Kennedy girl, she guessed, named Holly Daniels.

The door had barely clicked shut behind Zachary when it flew open again. Frankie jumped. This time, Roxanne breezed in. "How's the little computer whiz?" she asked affectionately. She flung her books onto the couch and bounced across the room to Frankie's side. "Slaving away, even during your lunch hour?"

Frankie nodded. "It's really not so bad," she assured her friend. "I'm almost done entering forms and then I'll be able to run the program that pairs everybody up." She forced a smile. She didn't want Rox to notice how upset she was and tease her about her hopeless crush on Zack. Rox could really be merciless. "Let's just hope it works!"

"Well, I can save you a little trouble." Rox pulled up a chair and sat down, fiddling with the small gold heart she wore on a chain around her neck. Her tone was still playful but her eyes, now locked with Frankie's, were very purposeful. "Frankie, I want you to arrange a Valentine rendezvous for me during the dance with Greg, Matt, Eric, and Jonathan. At different times, of course. If you do that, you'll have that many less people to worry about!"

Roxanne tossed the suggestion out as lightly as if she'd recommended that Frankie bend down and tie her shoe. Frankie gaped at her friend in utter disbelief. Rox might as well have asked her to schedule a rendezvous with King Kong on top of the Empire State Building. It was impossible! Fixing a date for well-intentioned Zachary was bad enough, but arranging for Roxanne to lead on four perfectly nice boys was just too much.

"Rox," Frankie began. She was surprised to notice her voice almost sounded stern. "I can't do that. It's against the rules and besides, it's . . . it's *wrong*."

"What's wrong about it?" Rox looked genuinely puzzled.

"Well, it's just . . . it just is," Frankie floundered. "It's cheating. Those guys filled out the questionnaires thinking they'd be matched with one special date. And besides, maybe the computer wouldn't even have matched you with any of them!"

"If you're trying to say that I wouldn't be a good match for them, that's absolutely untrue." Rox tossed her long red hair imperiously to punctuate her statement. "I assure you, Frankie, if they get dates with me they'll be eternally grateful to both you *and* to the computer! You'll do it, won't you?"

Frankie shook her head, but she didn't look quite as sure of herself as she had before. "No, Rox. I just can't. That still doesn't make it right. And anyway, why those four? I mean, don't Greg and Matt have girlfriends? Why don't I just match you with Eric or Jonathan?"

Rox snorted. "They may have had girlfriends, but girlfriends are no longer an issue." She narrowed her eyes, which made her appear superior. "Not since the ski trip! I'd say all four of them are up for grabs now."

Frankie did her best to hold her ground. "That still doesn't make it right," she repeated mechanically.

Roxanne took a deep, determined breath and went on less subtly. "Look, nobody'll even find out. And you're so smart to have designed this whole *complicated* program." Rox lingered for a moment over this thought, her expression admiring. "You can set up those dates in a flash and it'll be between you and me."

"But, Rox. . . ."

"Please?" Roxanne batted her eyelashes. Frankie wouldn't have been surprised if she'd dropped to her knees.

For a long minute she thought about it, evading Roxanne's probing, pressing gaze. It was hard to say no to her best friend, especially when she obviously had her heart set on these dates. Frankie understood that it was probably difficult for Rox, being new and not knowing as many people as she had at Stevenson. She knew how important it was to Rox to have a wide circle of admirers. She hesitated a moment longer, but for perhaps the first time, Frankie's conscience won out over her loyalty to her strong-minded friend. She gripped the arms of her chair, prepared for the fireworks. "I can't Rox. Sorry."

To her surprise, Roxanne didn't explode. Instead her eyes narrowed and her lips curled into a threatening sneer. Frankie shrank back in the chair. "Look, Frankie," Rox said in a cold, even tone. "All I'm doing is asking you to do me one simple favor. That's not too much to ask from your best friend is it? And don't forget I *am* your best friend." She laughed harshly. "Face it, Frankie, I'm your *only* friend! Who do you have besides me? Without me, you'd be. . . ."

Roxanne didn't finish her sentence. She didn't have to. Her words trailed off, and Frankie filled in the blanks on her own. I'd be alone, she thought. I'd be a loser, the original girl nerd. With Roxanne, at least she had something that resembled a social life. Frankie hung her head, defeated. "I'll fix the dates for you," she said, simply and sadly.

Rox lunged forward to give Frankie a big hug. Her cruel coldness was instantly replaced by forgiveness and warmth. "I knew you'd see the light!" she exclaimed with an exultant smile.

"I've really got to run now. Matt was going to teach me how to change a flat during lunch today." On her way out the door, Roxanne paused. She looked back at her friend. Frankie felt small sitting in front of the computer. "Thanks, Frankie," Rox said sincerely. "You're the greatest!"

The greatest, Frankie repeated silently after the door had slammed behind Roxanne. She wanted to laugh. Both Zachary and Rox had said that to her in the space of about five minutes. They thought she was the greatest because she was so spineless that she'd let them take advantage of her, walk all over her. In reality she wasn't the greatest at all. She was the smallest, the weakest, the least *everything*. Frankie's sigh was nearly a sob. She'd never really thought about how a doormat felt, but now she knew.

She typed for a moment, calling up Zachary's computer entry. A second later she scheduled his date with Holly Daniels. She sighed again, this time wistfully. Imagine going to your Valentine's Day Dance rendezvous and finding Zachary! For Frankie it would be a dream come true. She wondered how Holly would feel. But all she was left with was the dream part. There was no chance that Zachary could ever like her. Helping him along with another girl was about the closest she was ever going to get.

Frankie looked up Greg's file, then Eric's and Matt's and Jonathan's. It really wasn't that hard to do what Roxanne had asked. But while her

180

fingers typed effortlessly, inside, Frankie felt a little sick. It really wasn't right, but as usual, she'd given in to Roxanne. And to Zachary, although his motive was a lot easier to accept than Roxanne's.

So here I am, Frankie thought gloomily. Her hands dropped from the keyboard into her lap, and for a moment, she was motionless. She stared down at the front of her gray Shetland sweater and matching corduroy skirt. Twice today I let myself be bulldozed into doing things I really didn't want to do. Why? Just so they'll like me? Frankie couldn't answer her own question. That was the worst thing. She really didn't know why she let people push her around, or how to change.

Chapter
14

Molly picked a piece of green pepper off her slice of pizza and studied the string of mozzarella that stretched from it, her face gloomy. "So I opened the letter," she concluded with a sigh. "It was one of those thin envelopes they warn you about. I guess it doesn't take much paper to write 'No thanks, we don't want you.'"

Katie reached across the table to pat Molly's hand. "That's pretty rotten," she agreed. "But hey, Moll, there are a lot of other schools out there. Right this minute, good news is probably on its way from someplace else!"

Molly pushed her pizza away, shaking her head. "Yeah, but other schools aren't James Madison University," she pointed out. "And they don't have Ted. Now there's no chance he and I will be together next year."

Katie and Molly met at Mario's after school, or rather, after Molly went home and found the rejection letter from James Madison. In another half hour some of the other kids were supposed to show up for a meeting of the relatively informal Valentine's Day Dance committee. As Molly explained to Katie, Jonathan had chosen Mario's as a neutral gathering spot — supposedly the guys involved refused to meet at one of the girls' houses and vice versa. Even the sub shop had been ruled out for various reasons.

Molly and Katie decided the meeting was bound to be a disaster. Nobody wanted to talk to anyone else because everyone was still taking sides over the ski trip, and Jonathan was crazy to think that the group might be able to make any decisions about decorations, music, or refreshments. Katie had already planned to leave before the meeting even started. She really didn't want to get caught in the middle of all the fighting, even if that was where she belonged, considering she was the one with the controversial broken leg.

Now Katie was doing her best to cheer up a very discouraged Molly. "Okay, so you've found out the worst — you didn't get into James Madison," she began matter-of-factly. She reached up to adjust the royal blue bow tying back her hair. "You know I'm sorry, too. But maybe James Madison isn't even the right place for you." She waved a hand vaguely. "Which means the right school is out there somewhere! You could even

183

end up at some other college in Virginia; you can still see an awful lot of Ted, if that's what you really want."

Molly rested her elbows on the table and watched as Katie lifted another slice of pizza off the pan with a knife and fork and deposited it on her plate. "You're right, Katie. I mean, I know it's not the end of the world. I just assumed I was going to have to make the choice myself." She laughed halfheartedly. "To follow Ted, or not to follow Ted!" she pronounced in a theatrical voice.

Katie raised one eyebrow as she wiped a dab of tomato sauce from her chin. "That's really not how you've been viewing it, though, is it?" she asked, surprised.

"No, I guess not," Molly admitted. "I never was very good at follow the leader! I like having my own way too much." She had to laugh and Katie joined in. "But this is different somehow. You know?"

"I know." Katie finished off her third piece of pizza without blinking. "But it'll all work out. You'll see."

"I suppose it will," Molly said brightly. "But you've got to admit it's a complicated situation. I mean, what do you think'll happen when you and Greg are at different schools in different places next year?"

"Greg," Katie began, her tone chilly, "could move to Alaska next year for all I care!" The angry spark in her eyes fizzled out. "And for all the difference it would make," she added sadly.

Molly frowned. "You mean you still haven't gotten a formal apology from him yet?"

Katie shook her head. "We might as well be total strangers for the amount of communication that's taking place between us these days."

"It just goes to show," Molly said in her best gloom-and-doom voice, "that we're absolutely right not to forgive any of those good-for-nothing guys. If they're not sorry — "

Molly sounded ready to deliver a few more dire prophecies, but Katie didn't give her a chance. She glanced at the clock over the counter and then put both hands on the tabletop to ease herself up on to her feet, or rather, foot. "I'd better be going," she said. "My mom's probably done with her shopping by now."

"Sure you don't want to stay for the meeting?" Molly tried again to persuade her. "I can't guarantee it'll be a laugh a minute, but after all, this is your Valentine's Day Dance, too. You deserve a say in things."

Katie laughed dryly. "I think I'll pass."

Just then Katie's attention was drawn to the door of the restaurant by a flash of color. She remembered that particular shade of very electric blue. Sure enough it was Roxanne Easton, in the minidress she'd worn on her first day at Kennedy at the beginning of the semester. With her was her sidekick, Frankie Baker. Katie froze in position, half in and half out of the booth. "Don't look now, Molly," she warned, "but everybody's favorite new transfer just strolled in."

Needless to say, Molly spun around in her seat to look. Katie ducked back into the booth so she wouldn't be conspicuous, standing there and staring herself.

"What are we going to do?" Katie whispered.

"What do you mean what are we going to do? It's a free country." Molly paused and then wondered aloud, "But what do you think they're doing here?"

"What do you mean 'what do I think they're doing here?'" Katie questioned this time. "They felt like having pizza, just like us."

"Don't be so sure," Molly cautioned. "With the meeting supposed to start in about three minutes, their timing seems awfully fishy to me. Besides, they're not ordering pizza or anything. They just picked up sodas, see?"

She looked pointedly at Katie. Katie shrugged. "Well, I don't know about fishy, but I *do* know I don't want to sit in the same room with that girl any longer than I have to. I'll talk to you later, okay?"

"Okay. I'll call you tonight," Molly told Katie. She shot a dark look at the table for two by the window where Rox and Frankie were now sitting. "See ya."

"See ya." Katie adjusted her backpack more securely across her shoulders and then, with the help of her crutches, started on her slow way to the door.

After Katie left the sub shop, she decided to have her mom drop her off back at school so she could watch her teammates work out. But by the time she'd hobbled all the way to the gym from the parking lot, she was exhausted. The crutches made her arms hurt and her palms sting. Her good leg was weary from supporting the rest of her body. In fact, as she sat watching her fellow gymnasts run and tumble down on the floor, all positive energy seemed to seep out of her. It was as if she'd given all her cheer to Molly, and all that was left inside was one big ache.

"Hey, K.C., maybe you could watch me!" called Janice Adams, a clumsy senior who'd barely made the team. "Tell me what you think of my form."

"Okay."

Janice climbed onto the balance beam and managed a half turn. She looked at Katie, then lost her balance and jumped down. "Well?"

Katie tried to smile. "Janice, you have to remember to keep your hips under you."

"Oh, yeah." Janice thought for a moment, then heaved herself back onto the beam.

Katie stared down at the floor, but soon Stacy Morrison climbed onto the beam, replacing Janice. Stacy giggled and made faces at some boys who were peeking in the front door. The sophomore waved her arms and pretended to lose her balance. Then she did the splits. Smooth. Limber. Rock steady. Stacy tossed her hair and giggled some more. Katie looked down at her broken leg. Stacy Morrison had just gone to the top of the list of people that Katie did not want to think about right now. Right up there with Roxanne Easton.

But Katie was thinking about Greg again, about the crowd and the ski trip and her stupid, useless leg. Using both hands, she eased her cast sideways along the bench, then tried to rub her calf beneath the plaster — but of course she couldn't feel anything. Her cast was already starting to get gray and dirty. Molly had written "Get better, leg, that's an order," near Katie's ankle. Karen had signed her name, as had Holly and Diana and the other girls. Pamela had even painted some pink and yellow flowers down the outside. But there was no cartoon by Greg, or funny quote from Eric or Jonathan. Not one word.

Katie heard her voice being called again and looked down at Janice. But Janice was across the floor now, flailing and flinging in an attempt to stretch her legs. Instead, Ms. Muldoon was jogging up the bleachers, waving at Katie. The coach sat down next to her.

"Hi. I'm so glad to see you here, K.C.," Coach said. "Another girl might quit the team. But not you."

Katie shrugged.

"How's the leg feel?"

"About the same. Maybe a little better."

Ms. Muldoon patted Katie's shoulder. "I had an idea, K.C.," the coach began in an excited voice. "I'll explain it to you, and you tell me what you think."

"Okay."

The coach leaned forward to keep her eye on the floor while she explained. "I'd like you to come to practice as much as you can, even though you can't work out for a while. You have the best attitude and competitive edge of almost any girl I've ever coached. The team needs you around." Ms. Muldoon glanced down at Stacy on the balance beam, shook her head, then turned back to Katie. "K.C., I was thinking. How would you like to help me coach? Just until your leg heals. You could start with Stacy Morrison. See, Stacy is really talented. She could be the girl to take your place. But she has no discipline and very little technique. She needs lots of help if she's going to be the kind of competitor that you are." There was a long pause, filled with Stacy's laughter and the *clunk* of someone landing after a vault. "Well, what do you think?"

Katie's voice stuck in her throat. The idea of sitting on the bench helping Stacy Morrison take over her position on the team almost made her dizzy. Great. First she could give Greg to Roxanne, and then she could make Stacy the next gymnastics star. Perfect. Swell.

"I'm starting physical therapy pretty soon,"

Katie said quickly. "So, I don't know what my schedule will be. I may not be able to even come to practice for a while." She managed a quick, tight smile.

Ms. Muldoon looked concerned. "You're going to stay on the team, though, aren't you?"

Katie didn't answer.

"I don't want you giving up, K.C.," the coach warned. "You might still compete this season. You wait and see."

"Sure," Katie couldn't help mumbling sarcastically.

Ms. Muldoon faced Katie with a tough look. "Giving up is not your style, K.C."

"I know."

There was a small hubbub down on the floor as Caroline Bartlett took an easy spill off the uneven bars. Ms. Muldoon immediately shot up and started down the bleachers. "Think about it. You don't have to decide now," the coach called back.

Katie nodded and her eyes filled with tears. She turned away so that Ms. Muldoon wouldn't see her. Suddenly it was all getting to Katie — everything she used to love so much. The air in the gym felt heavy and stale. The echo made her head ache. The *thump-thump* of Stacy Morrison's graceful, talented feet made her want to scream.

Stacy Morrison was on her own, Katie decided. As far as she was concerned, everybody from Stevenson could be that way. Just like Katie was on her own now. Totally on her own.

190

* * *

Molly thought about the way Katie had left
the sub shop. How she'd greeted the two girls
from Stevenson. Katie handled it superbly. She'd
managed to give Frankie a genuinely friendly
smile, and at the same time she lifted her chin in
the air and bestowed a haughty glance upon
Roxanne. Molly giggled into her pizza. *Way to
go, K.C.!* she'd been tempted to holler. Then she
scowled. Only a few seconds after the door of
Mario's swung shut behind Katie, it swung open
and Jonathan and Eric appeared. The first people to catch their eyes were Roxanne and Frankie.
The first *person* was more like it. There was no
mistaking who had prompted their eager hellos.

Another thing Molly couldn't help observing,
even from her vantage point across the room, was
that while Eric and Jonathan were clearly delighted to see the girls, neither of them seemed
surprised in the least. It was looking more and
more like they'd invited Roxanne and Frankie to
the meeting. They'd planned it right from the
start. Molly was burning. It was bad enough to
have to force herself to be civil to the guys, but to
be expected to act the same way toward Rox
Easton was ridiculous.

But Molly was cornered. Jonathan was already
waving to her to join the others at a long, rec-
tangular table midway between her booth and
Roxanne's window. Leaving a few dollars for the
pizza, Molly rose to her feet reluctantly. She
reached the table and pulled out a chair on the

opposite side from where Jonathan, Eric, Frankie, and Roxanne were seated. "Hi," she said coolly to no one in particular.

"Hi," Frankie said with a small smile. Eric and Jonathan echoed the greeting. Rox simply nodded, her eyes expressionless. It was all Molly could do to keep herself from jumping to her feet and storming away in indignation. Before she had a chance to do anything, however, the rest of the Valentine's Day Dance "committee" straggled in. Pamela, Matt, Diana, Jeremy, and Holly all looked relatively uncomfortable already. They were together, but at the same time they weren't. Diana and Pamela were physically a little bit nearer to Holly than they were to their boy-friends; it was still girls versus boys. And when they sat down, Molly noticed that Matt and Jeremy chose the same side of the table as Jona-than, Eric, Rox, and Frankie, although they were supposedly sitting across from Pamela and Diana, who ended up on Molly's side, as did Holly.

Molly raised a dark eyebrow in Jonathan's direction. He pushed his fedora back from his forehead and cleared his throat with authority. "Ahem," he began, looking from one side of the segregated table to the other. "Well, everybody knows why we're here, right?" There were grim nods all around. Only Roxanne looked sunnily unconcerned. "There's still a lot of planning that needs to be done before the dance, which, believe it or not, is exactly a week from today. One piece of good news, though. I just heard from Brian

192

Pierson that he and Karen have confirmed the band we've been hoping to get, so we're all set there!"

Jonathan paused as if he expected his audience to break into applause. A few chairs were shifted and a few arms crossed, but that was it. Frankie broke the awkward silence by asking timidly, "What can we do to help?"

Jonathan tipped his chair back, anchoring himself by hooking one foot around a leg of the table. "Glad you asked," he said, relieved. "We've still got decorations to iron out, right?" He looked at Diana and Holly for confirmation and they nodded. "And food and drink and stuff. Plus chaperones — somebody's got to invite some teachers. Who's going to take pictures? So, who wants to do what?"

"Well, Dee already told me she wants to shoot a few rolls, and Holly and I have already gotten a start on decorations," Diana volunteered without much enthusiasm. "We can get all the supplies together if everybody agrees on a theme."

Holly jumped in to describe her Victorian scheme and then Diana added the suggestion of a computer-age motif. Jonathan sought opinions. "What does everybody think?"

Roxanne looked as if it was somewhat distasteful to her to choose either of the two, probably because they'd come from the wrong side of the table, Molly decided silently. Nonetheless she placed her vote. "I think the more state-of-the-art, the better," Rox purred.

I bet that's what you think, Molly thought cattily. Anything to showcase your cute little computer Valentine service. Molly might have spoken up for the other decorating option, but she didn't have a chance to. Matt, Eric, and Jeremy were so busy second-, third-, and fourthing Roxanne's opinion that nobody else could get a word in edgewise.

"Well, that was easy," Jonathan observed, casting an approving glance at Roxanne himself. "A space-age theme it is. How about refreshments? Any ideas?"

"Pizza," Matt said spontaneously. Everyone had to laugh at that.

Jonathan exercised the power to veto that came with the privilege of office. "Negative," he said. "Our budget doesn't cover pizza for a few hundred."

"How about chips and vegetables and dip?" Pamela suggested sensibly. "You know, the old standbys. And maybe even some frosted Valentine's Day cookies like Kim Barrie made last year."

"Excellent!" Jonathan affirmed. "You've just gotten yourself named refreshment chair, Pamela." Pamela lifted her slim shoulders in a disinterested gesture. Molly noted that Rox looked just a little miffed that someone else had managed to steal even a tiny sliver of her thunder. "This is a lot more painless than I thought it was going to be," Jonathan now announced. "The last thing is the chaperones. Who'd like to take a shot at lining up a few?"

Rox quickly made herself heard. "I'd love to do it," she offered, her smile bright and eager. "Frankie could help. It would be a great way for us to meet some more of the Kennedy faculty."

Roxanne was just too good to be true, Molly thought, rolling her eyes. She caught Diana's eye, then Holly's, then Pamela's. There was no doubt that the girls saw right through Roxanne's nauseating sweetness. The guys, meanwhile, were eating it up.

Molly had had as much of their false camaraderie as she could stomach. She started to get to her feet. Pamela, Diana, and Holly followed suit.

"This was really worthwhile, Jonathan," Molly said dryly. She slipped her worn black leather bomber jacket on over her cherry-red knit dress. "Thanks for asking for our advice."

"Hey, anytime." Jonathan didn't seem to pick up on Molly's sarcasm. At the same time, his own tone wasn't exactly warm. He clearly didn't intend to beg the girls to stay and hang out awhile.

Neither did Roxanne, but she had one last remark to make before Molly, Diana, Holly, and Pamela marched out of earshot. "Oh, Molly," she said, her voice silky. "If you see Katie, please tell her I hope her leg is feeling better."

For a moment Molly froze. Then she pivoted on her heel to face Rox again. "You hope her leg is feeling better?" she repeated. She laughed harshly. "That's the funniest thing you've ever said, I think. I didn't know you were a comedian!"

Roxanne widened her eyes guilelessly, but Molly detected a sharp edge to her innocent tone. "I'm not sure what you mean by that," she challenged Molly carefully.

Molly pushed a dark curl away from her very blue eyes. "You don't, huh?" she said. She would really have liked to try one of her more painful aikido moves on Roxanne just about now. "You don't see the humor in your asking about Katie when if it wasn't for you she'd never have hurt herself?"

The others, guys and girls alike, had been observing this exchange, stunned expressions on their faces. Now Jonathan tugged on the brim of his fedora and raised his voice to Molly. "Rox was just trying to be nice," he interjected. "You could at least do the same."

"Be nice? You've got to be kidding!" Molly shook her head in disbelief. The four boys — Jonathan, Eric, Matt, and even Jeremy — were obviously ready, one and all, to spring to Roxanne's defense. All four of them had fallen for her corny line; they all thought she was genuinely concerned about Katie

Now Molly couldn't believe herself — or that she'd just sat, by her own choice, with such heels for twenty minutes. Without another word she whirled around and headed briskly for the door. She could hear Di, Holly, and Pamela following her. As she grasped the door handle and gave it a tug, she tossed a last scornful glance over her shoulder. To her surprise, Matt was on his feet. Was he coming to his senses? Molly wondered hopefully. She touched Pamela's arm. Her friend's expression had lightened, too. Then Roxanne got to *her* feet as well and stood a little too close to Matt's side. He directed an apologetic look in Pamela's direction. "It's time for the Fix-it Club's Friday afternoon workshop," he announced, apparently to the customers of Mario's in general. He didn't actually meet Pamela's eyes. "Anyone want to head back to school and learn how to repair a leaky radiator?"

It looked like Roxanne was the only taker, but Molly and the other Kennedy girls didn't stay to make sure. They were out on the sidewalk and halfway to the parking lot before Matt and Rox had even reached the door. Molly was livid, and her friends weren't too pleased, either. The four piled into Diana's car. Diana started the engine and then blasted the heat, although they hardly needed it considering they were all pretty much steaming.

"I can't wait to tell Katie what a concerned friend she has in Roxanne Easton!" Molly joked grimly. The other girls laughed with equal bitterness, but no one else had much to say. The scene in Mario's had made everybody think. In silence they drove back to Diana's house, where they decided they were going to make dinner, rent movies, and spend the night. Molly was thinking hard herself, and things didn't look good. An hour earlier she'd been worried about getting rejected by James Madison University and how that might affect one relationship that was very precious to her — her relationship with Ted. Now it looked like a number of other friendships she really cherished and which were currently much closer at hand — her friendships with Eric and the other guys — were seriously on the line. If they weren't already lost. . . .

Chapter
15

Katie grimaced as she lowered herself onto the sofa in her basement. It had been almost two weeks since she broke her leg and every day she became more comfortable with the cast and more at ease on her crutches. For some reason, though, her leg just throbbed this afternoon. Maybe it was the weather, which was cold, damp, and cloudy. It made her bones ache, and her heart, too. She pushed such self-pitying, self-defeating thoughts from her mind, reminding herself that she'd brought her sociology textbook and her journal down with her intending to get some work done.

The basement had always been Katie's special retreat. In addition to serving as a family room, it also housed her gymnastics and exercise equipment. These days it was the only place she could go to get away from her mother, who had been coddling her too much since the accident, and her little brothers, who at first had been extra nice to her but by now were back to their usual annoying selves.

She opened her sociology textbook and tried unsuccessfully to focus on the page. The big block letters of the chapter heading blurred and merged into new shapes. For a second they almost looked like a skier after a nasty tumble, with skis and poles and legs all awry. . . . Katie slammed the book shut. She looked up abruptly to an even more depressing sight: her gymnastics equipment. The low balance beam, the mats. . . . She squeezed her eyes shut, suddenly fighting back angry, frustrated, forlorn tears. It just wasn't fair. She hadn't even gone to practice for the last two weeks, as Coach Muldoon had wanted her to. All her life she'd worked toward this year, this moment: her last competitive season when, finally, she would be unbeatable. And instead, here she was, sitting on her fanny, weighted down by a plaster cast. She could hardly *move* her leg much less stand on it, walk on it, leap with it, spring from it. And it was all because of, because of. . . . Katie wiped her eyes with the back of one hand. Because of Roxanne Easton? No, she had to admit to herself that it really wasn't Roxanne's fault, even if she was a witch and a flirt. It was the guys' fault, and most of all it was Greg's fault for being as ridiculously infatuated with Rox as the rest of them were when he was her, Katie's, boyfriend.

When he was her boyfriend. Katie detected the past tense in her thoughts and shook her head sadly. Her long red ponytail swung over her shoulder and she reached up to twist it the way she always did when she was nervous or serious. Greg was supposedly still her boyfriend, but when she was lying hurt on the ski slope she'd told him she never wanted to see him again. And so far he'd just about taken her at her word. Greg might not still love her, but he always had manners. He sent her flowers and a card, but all he had signed was "Greg." No personal message, like "get better," or "love always." Nothing. He was graciously blowing her off. Oh, why am I so furious with him, again? Katie wondered momentarily. Oh, that's right. Because he was stupid enough to fall for Roxanne's utterly fake sugary sweetness. Even worse, he was still hanging around with her. It was all the proof Katie needed that Greg didn't care that her leg was broken and her hopes for her gymnastics title dashed, and that he was practically responsible. Some boyfriend he'd turned out to be!

Even while Katie was thinking these bitter thoughts, lonely tears were creeping down her pale cheeks. No matter what she said to anyone, even to herself, the fact was that she missed Greg. He might at that moment be the biggest jerk on the face of the earth, but she still loved him and felt lost and lonely without him.

She sniffled and pulled her journal out from under her abandoned sociology text. She might as well record such depressing thoughts for posterity. Just then her ten-year-old brother Danny stuck his head around the door to the basement and shouted down the stairs. "Greg's here!" he informed her, making the announcement in the same sing-song, little-brother way he always did.

Katie sat up, her heart pounding. She put a hand to her rumpled bangs and then to the collar of her torn and faded navy polo shirt. "He is?" she squeaked, caught entirely off guard. Danny had disappeared and now Katie could see Greg's familiar loafers and then his long khaki-covered legs descending the staircase. It was too late to run and hide. Besides, I can't run anyway, she thought irrelevantly.

The last step creaked under Greg's weight and then he was approaching her. His sandy hair, damp from the rain, stood back from his forehead in comical spikes where he'd run his fingers through it. The expression in his eyes was guarded, and Katie, who had been smiling warmly and expectantly, now felt her smile fade and her own eyes grow cool.

"Hi," she said, with as little emotion as possible. "What are you doing here?" She started to shift her leg awkwardly from the couch to the low coffee table to make room for him to sit down.

Greg jumped, a cushion in hand, to help her. When she was comfortable again, he took a seat next to her. Next to her, but not *near* her. Katie suddenly felt anxious and unprepared, as if she and Greg were about to talk for the first

202

time. His stiff posture and the absence of his easy, confident smile made him look like a stranger. "So?" she questioned in an accusing, defensive tone.

"Katie," Greg began, looking at her cast instead of at her face. "I just came over to say I'm . . . I think we should talk.

"You do?" She was determined not to be helpful.

"Um, well, yeah." Greg appeared to be put off by Katie's sullen attitude. When he spoke again his own tone had become aggressive. "Don't you think we need to?"

Katie's shrug was noncommittal, and she leaned forward to flick a thread off her autograph-covered cast. Greg was about the only person she knew who hadn't signed it. Scratch that — Greg, Eric, Jonathan, and Matt were the only people she knew who hadn't signed it. "Maybe," was all she said in response.

Greg drew his breath in sharply. Now he looked and sounded irritated. "Oh, I get it." He sat back and crossed his arms over his broad chest. "You told me you never wanted to speak to me again and you're too stubborn to go back on your word!"

Katie gaped. The nerve! "I can't believe you're calling *me* stubborn!" she exclaimed. "*You're* critizing *me*? If you hadn't been acting like such an idiot over Roxanne, I never would have been put in a position to say such a thing in the first place!"

Greg shook his head, his jaw clenched. "So you're still blaming her for all this." He waved a hand in the direction of Katie's cast.

"Blaming her? I don't think so." Katie tried to laugh scornfully but she was so close to tears the sound came out an octave too high and sounded completely ridiculous. "No, sir. I'm blaming you!"

"But Katie," Greg said, his anger giving way to reasonableness. "Be fair. What did I really have to do with your fall?"

"You mean besides causing it?" she snapped.

"I didn't — !" he started to exclaim. Then he caught himself. When he started talking again his voice was lower and his eyes more serious. "I didn't come over here to argue with you," he said with a big sigh ."That's the last thing I had in mind."

Katie didn't give him a chance to explain any further. "Then why *did* you come over?" she demanded. She knew she shouldn't goad him any further, but she was so irritated she couldn't resist adding, "I'm sure your time could be better spent drooling over Roxanne!"

"What is all this anti-Roxanne garbage, anyway?" Greg burst out. He threw his hands up in the air. "What did she ever do to offend you except steal a little bit of the limelight?"

Katie could barely speak. Tears of fury and pain stung her eyes and caught in her throat. When Greg first walked in, deep inside she'd been incredibly happy to see him. But all he was doing was torturing her, reminding her of how bad everything in her life had become. "Go away," she managed to choke out. "Just go away and leave me alone!" She put her hands to her face.

Greg started to reach toward her but then got to his feet instead. "I'm sorry, K.C.," he said abruptly, his tone rough, yet tender at the same time. "That's really what I came over here to say. I came over to say I was sorry and to ask you if you'd go with me to the Valentine's Day Dance tomorrow night."

"I'd rather go with King Kong!" Katie cried, her face still hidden.

"Fine," Greg declared sarcastically. Katie could hear him stomping across the room. "You just do that!" She finally took her hands away from her face, but all she saw was his back retreating up the stairs. A second later, the image was blurred by her tears, and Greg was gone. He closed the basement door quietly behind him even though Katie knew he must have wanted to slam it. Good old Greg — always polite, even in a crisis. Where as she. . . . Katie suddenly felt ashamed of herself. Maybe Greg was wrong about the ski trip and a lot of other things, but he had been willing to apologize and she'd acted like a baby. She started to jump up to run after him and then collapsed with a cry. Her broken leg brought itself painfully back to her attention. She realized then that by the time she managed to hobble up the stairs and outside, Greg would be gone. It was no use.

Katie threw herself down full-length on the couch, her head buried in her arms. She pictured Greg driving away in his mother's Mercedes — too fast, probably, because he was mad. Where would he go? Would he leave her house and head right for Roxanne's? Would he ask Roxanne to the Valentine's Day Dance? It was a horrible thought, but only too likely, Katie realized. And she'd driven him to it. The trouble may have all started when one hundred Stevenson kids, including Rox Easton, transferred to Kennedy and threw the whole gang for a loop. But she wasn't helping matters any. It was the day before the dance and instead of making an effort to patch things up with Greg, she'd only forced him further into the hands of the enemy.

Mrs. Einerson beckoned to Diana from the hall phone as she shut the front door and stopped to wipe her shoes on the welcome mat. "It's Bart," Mrs. Einerson mouthed. "He wants to talk to you, so don't go away." Diana slung her coat and scarf over a hook in the hall closet and joined her mom. "Good luck on your geology test, dear," Mrs. Einerson was saying. "Miss you. Your dad does, too. Here's Diana, honey."

Diana took the prone and, uncoiling the extra length of cord, took it with her into the living room. "Hi, there!" she greeted her brother as she curled herself up in her father's favorite chair, ready for a long chat. "You have a test coming up?" For about five minutes all she did was nod and say "uh-huh, uh-huh" while Bart filled her in on every detail of his favorite class: geology. Rocks for jocks, she thought to herself with a smile.

Finally Bart paused. "So, what's up with you, Di?" he asked. "Is your semester getting off to a good start?"

"It's going okay," Diana answered. "And actually a lot is up!" She twirled the telephone cord around her finger, wondering where to start. She decided the beginning was probably the best place, so she hold him about Stevenson closing . . . the ski trip . . . everything. "And ever since Katie broke her leg," she finally concluded, "the crowd has been totally divided. It's like a seventh-grade dance, with the boys on one side and the girls on the other! You wouldn't believe it," Diana exclaimed to her brother. "Jeremy claims to be on Greg and the other guys' side even though he doesn't know the first thing about it."

Bart's laugh sounded reassuring, even over the long-distance line. "It'll all blow over," he predicted. "Just give it a few more days."

"I'm not so sure," Diana disagreed. "There are a few things that just aren't going to fade away. Katie's got a broken leg, for one thing, and she and Greg aren't speaking to each other, for another." Diana made a face. "And, of course, Rox Easton is here to stay."

"I'd kind of like to meet this girl," Bart joked.

"Don't even say that," Diana warned. "I bet you would!"

Bart laughed heartily. Then his voice turned serious. "How's Holly doing through all this?"

Diana moved the phone to her other ear, scrunching her shoulder up to hold it in place. "Okay, I suppose. She's sort of on the fringe of this whole scene, you know? But, she was on the ski trip, and I know she feels as badly for Katie as I do. She's just kind of out of things in general these days." Diana reached down to rub the silky ears of her golden retriever puppy, Sierra, who had come up to rest her head on her knee. "She seems a little down, a little lonely. Especially since it's Valentine's Day tomorrow, and then the dance and all that."

Diana could hear her brother heave a big sigh. "Yeah," he said in an uncharacteristically glum tone. "I know the feeling."

She pretended to be shocked. "Don't tell me *you* don't have a date for the Valentine's Day Dance!" she teased.

Bart chuckled good-naturedly. "I'm not saying I couldn't have a date for the dance if I wanted one, but there isn't even a dance in the first place! Luckily. Because I swear I wouldn't go. Honestly, Di, I don't want to be with any other girl besides Holly, even as a friend."

Diana knew her brother meant what he said. She couldn't remember ever hearing him sound so genuinely devoted. "I know she feels the same way about you," she assured him. "She didn't even want to go to the dance, but then a week or so ago she signed up sort of out of the blue to help with refreshments. I guess that's a good way to be there and see all her friends but also keep busy behind the scenes so she doesn't feel funny about going alone."

"Hey, I've got an idea!" Bart declared suddenly. "I already sent her a Valentine and of course I'm going to call her, too, but how about if — " He switched gears. "You said there was some sort of computer dating gimmick for the dance this year?"

"Yeah." Diana scratched under Sierra's chin and the puppy's tail thumped against the carpeted floor. Sierra had been a Christmas present from Bart. "Everyone filled out questionnaires and the computer paired people up and assigned them a Valentine rendezvous for some time and place during the dance. I filled one out just for fun," she admitted, "but I know for a fact that Holly didn't."

"Well. . . ." Bart paused dramatically. "What if you gave Holly a note at the dance listing a time and a place for a mystery date, and when she got there there'd be a bunch of roses and a card from me waiting for her? Do you think that would make her feel better?"

"Bart, she'd love it!" Diana exclaimed. "That's an absolutely inspired idea."

"The only catch is you've got to buy the flowers!" Bart pointed out to her. Diana could practically see his mischievous, irresistible smile. "But I'll pay you back — double!" he promised. "As long as Holly's happy."

"Well, I'll do anything to help," his sister volunteered enthusiastically. "And I think the flowers will be a fantastic surprise. I can't wait to see Holly's face!"

Diana and Bart gabbed for a few more minutes about some friends from their old high school in Montana that Bart had run into at the university. Then Diana hung up. That had to be the longest phone conversation she and Bart had had since he left for school last autumn. Bart really had a lot on his mind these days, she guessed.

Diana leaned back in the chair, and stared thoughtfully at Sierra. It made her sort of sad to know that Bart and Holly were lonely for each other, but in a funny way it also made her glad. Her brother and her best friend were still in love with each other, even though they were more than a thousand miles apart. A relationship *could* endure even against those odds. That was nice to know in light of the fact that a year from now she and Jeremy would probably be at different schools — Jeremy might even go back to England to study at Oxford. Although, at the moment, they were hardly speaking to each other because of the feud. Well, as Bart said, that had to pass. At least, she hoped it would!

Yes, long-distance relationships were a real challenge, and Diana knew they didn't always make it. So she was more than happy to play good fairy for Bart and Holly — maybe someday someone would do the same for her.

Chapter
16

The night of the dance was clear and mild for February. Molly called Katie at five o'clock to remind her that a bunch of people were meeting at six in the transformed cafeteria to set up the refreshments and put a few last-minute touches on the decorations. "Be there or be square!" she ordered Katie, who managed to get away without committing herself. Now it was seven and Katie still wasn't at the cafeteria setting up. She didn't plan to be there at eight, or nine, or ten either. The gang wouldn't be surprised when she didn't show up at the dance. They probably wouldn't even miss her. After all, no one besides Molly had seen much of her since her accident.

Katie flipped on the TV. Boy, there are a lot of dumb shows on Friday night! she thought, turning the TV off again in disgust. She hadn't actually stayed home and watched TV on a Friday since her baby-sitting days. There was always something fun going on — a party, a sports event, a date, a dance.

Suddenly Katie couldn't bear to sit alone in the family room any longer. She was tired of being a recluse, especially tonight when everyone she knew was at the Valentine's Day Dance. She had to do something, go somewhere. It didn't matter where, as long as she got out of the house and distracted herself from the thought of how her broken leg had ruined her gymnastics career and the whole second semester of her senior year.

Fifteen minutes later, Katie was on the bus to Georgetown, her crutches stashed behind the bus driver's seat. Her parents hadn't let her take the car even though she assured them she was able to drive perfectly well with one foot. When she tugged on the cord that ran above the window, a bell rang and the driver pulled over at the next stop, right in front of the two-story, stucco building that housed the Fitness Center. Katie made her slow way down the aisle of the bus, tentatively resting her weight on her plaster-encased right foot. She knew she probably shouldn't be walking on the cast this soon but it didn't hurt and she could get around so much easier this way.

Once inside the center, Katie took the elevator to the second floor where the gymnastics studios were. She opened the door to studio A, one of the larger rooms. Bleachers had been set up on one side. Mr. Romanski must have held a meet there earlier in the day, Katie thought. Neva, his assistant, was coaching a class now. It looked like the eight-to-ten year olds. A nostalgic pang tugged at Katie's heart. She remembered when she was a little girl and gymnastics lessons were the highlight of her life. Three times a week she'd be barely able to sit still in school because she was so impatient for the end of the day. When it finally came, she would rush home and change into her tiny leotard and tights, and her mother would take her to the gym. She had worked so hard at it — she'd try anything — and it didn't matter how many times she fell off the balance beam or the uneven bars. Bumps and bruises couldn't deter her. She was fearless.

Katie sighed as she rested her crutches against the lowest level of the bleachers. Those really were the days, she thought morosely. But bruises are one thing; a broken leg is another. She was about to take a seat when she noticed a pale, familiar face up in the far corner of the bleachers. It was Frankie Baker, one of the new Stevenson students who seemed to Katie to be a really nice girl despite her unfortunate choice of friends. "Hi, Frankie!" she called up to her, pleasantly surprised. "I'd join you, but I don't think I can make it up that far!"

Frankie smiled shyly and rose to her feet, retrieving her coat before making her way down to where Katie was sitting. "I was sorry to hear about your accident, Katie," she said with sincere concern as she took a seat.

"It's getting better every day," Katie said lightly. She didn't want to pursue this topic. Roxanne was Frankie's best buddy, and Katie wasn't sure she could trust herself not to say something nasty. "But what brings you here, Frankie? Are you a gymnast?"

"Oh, no!" Frankie shook her head hurriedly. "I could never even do a cartwheel! No, I'm just waiting here for my sister, Carol." Frankie pointed to a tiny, blonde girl who was tumbling energetically across a mat. The little girl did resemble Frankie, but to Katie's eye, she had a sparkle her older sister lacked. Frankie was glancing at the clock over the door. "Her class should be over in ten minutes or so."

"And then you're going home to get ready for the dance." Katie's words were more of a statement than a question but to her surprise Frankie shook her head, seeming embarrassed.

"No, I'm not going to the dance," she confessed in a small, apologetic voice.

Katie bounced in her seat, jolting her broken leg painfully. "Not going to the dance!" she exclaimed, astonished. "After all your hard work putting the computer Valentine service together? How could you miss it?"

Frankie was blushing furiously. She looked as if she wished she could disappear into thin air. For a moment she was silent, then she turned to face Katie despondently. "The guys I like never like me back," she said simply. "No one will ask me to dance, so what's the point of going?"

Katie stared back at her, flabbergasted. From her perspective, Frankie was a very pretty girl. Maybe she wasn't the sharpest dresser, but her hair and her eyes and her figure were very striking. And not only was she pretty, but by all accounts she was incredibly smart, too. Even though Katie didn't know her very well, she also judged her to be a genuinely kind person. But now Katie forced herself to look at Frankie through Frankie's own eyes. She was Roxanne Easton's best friend and constant companion — even Marilyn Monroe might have felt pale in comparison. It was obvious that Frankie had given up on herself, on her ability to be interesting and attractive. She'd spent too much time hiding in Roxanne's shadow.

Frankie's hopelessness lit a fire under Katie. She hated to see someone like Frankie quit, no matter what the reason. "Frankie, you shouldn't think like that," she urged. "If you're sure no one will ask you to dance, then no one will. They certainly won't if you don't even give them a chance to by not going at all!"

Frankie frowned. "Katie, you just don't understand what it's like," she said sadly. "There is this one guy . . . but he likes another girl. It's always been that way with me." She shook her head, her expression miserable. "You just couldn't know how it feels."

Katie waved a hand. "Cut!" she declared. "I *do* know how that feels. Honest. I've been there myself."

Frankie raised an eyebrow. "You have?" she asked, sounding doubtful.

"I sure have!" Katie laughed ruefully. "I can't tell you how many hopeless crushes I've had on guys who didn't even know I existed! Too many to count. Seriously. And it's discouraging, I won't deny that. But then one day a guy I liked, liked me back!" Katie smiled, thinking back to junior year when she first started dating Eric. "If I'd hidden myself away from the world, that never could have happened."

Frankie nodded obediently but Katie could see she hadn't changed her mind. To her, Katie's story was a nice fairy tale and that was all. Frankie was staring down at the tips of her shoes. Now she turned her head to look up at Katie as she bent down to retie one of her laces. "What about you?" she asked, shifting the focus of the conversation away from herself. "Aren't you going to the dance?"

Katie's smile faded. "No," she said quietly.

"Why not?" Frankie wondered.

Katie looked at her blankly. Suddenly she realized that she was giving up just as much as Frankie was. Who was she to preach when she was hiding from the world herself? And Katie had never given up before. Even last fall when she'd quit the crew team over a misunderstanding with Greg, she'd fought back. She'd gone back to the team and helped them win their biggest race of the season and she and Greg had overcome their problems at the same time.

216

Frankie's lack of spirit seemed to give Katie back some of her own. She would go to the dance. She had to; she couldn't live with herself otherwise. Maybe she couldn't actually dance, maybe she and Greg were really finished this time, but it was better than sitting here in the Fitness Center thinking about Stacy Morrison and all the things she couldn't do anymore. Katie saw now that she'd been wrong to think her life was over. She hadn't lost anything really valuable by breaking her leg. Just her mobility, and only for a while. No, her life wasn't over because she broke her leg, but it would be over if she gave up on herself and quit trying. She wasn't ready for the sidelines yet.

Katie scrambled to her feet, grabbing her crutches to steady herself. "Come on, Frankie!" she cried, her eyes glittering with excitement and determination. "We're going to the dance!"

Frankie attempted a smile but she didn't budge. "Thanks, but I really have to wait for my sister."

"Okay, I'll wait, too," Katie said agreeably. She winked. "Then you can give me a ride to the dance. It beats catching the bus home and having my dad take me!"

Frankie hunched her shoulders. She looked to Katie like she was protecting herself, retreating back into her shell. "I'd be happy to give you a ride home, Katie, but I'm not going to the dance."

Frankie's tone was very final, and Katie realized there was no use trying to persuade her. She was disappointed, more for Frankie than for herself. "Well, I'm sorry I won't be seeing you there," Katie said. "Thanks for offering me a ride, and I'll look for you in school next week. Have a nice night tonight, whatever you decide to do."

Frankie seemed to see through Katie's forced brightness. She was going to spend the evening alone at home and both girls knew it. "Have a good time, Katie," she said, a forlorn note creeping into her voice despite her attempt to sound casual.

"See ya, Frankie." Katie made her way slowly toward the door, being careful to avoid the floor mats. As she propped the door open with one crutch so she could hop through, she glanced back one more time at Frankie. The other girl was a small, sad splotch of faded color against the dark wood of the bleachers. She seemed nearly invisible, but only because she wanted to be, Katie was convinced. Oh, well. She didn't have time now to worry anymore about Frankie Baker. Katie Crawford had to catch the next bus home and change into a party dress fast before she missed the Valentine's Day Dance entirely.

"Hey, Holly — I think we need more punch," Pamela called, eyeing the near-empty punch bowl as she pushed some pink-frosted, heart-shaped cookies into a more artistic pattern on the paper plate. Holly, who had just returned from the kitchen with as many bags of chips and pretzels as she could carry, grabbed the punch bowl and headed back again. The pink lemonade punch sure was going fast! People were thirsty after dancing up a storm to the music of the band, which was appropriately named Lover's Leap. Everyone seemed to be in a romantic, Valentine's Day mood. The cafeteria looked fantastic, and Holly appreciated the transformation all the more because she'd helped to create it. True, the modern look had won out over her suggestion of a Victorian theme, but she had to admit it was effective. Strings of blinking pink and cherry-red lights along the walls and ceiling bathed everything in a warm, space-age Valentine's Day glow, and a huge banner hanging over the door read "HAPPY VALENTINE'S DAY! DISCOVER THE FUTURE OF ROMANCE." As kids came in, they stopped inside the door at a booth draped in the pink satin bunting she and Diana had revived from the Little Theater. There, they were handed a computer sheet with a time, a numbered location, and a code word with which they'd be able to recognize their computer Valentine. A chart posted next to the booth served as a key to the locations: number 1 was the lobby outside the principal's office, number 2 was a back stairwell, numbers 3 through 6 were the four dimly-lit corners of the cafeteria, and so on. From her post at the refreshments, Holly had already seen dozens of people sneak out of the dance to return as part of a couple. Sometimes they came back laughing hilariously, or with starry eyes and arms around each other, and sometimes they kept their distance and looked as if they felt sort of silly.

Dee Patterson, in a flattering black, frilly-skirted dress, was having fun snapping pictures of the returning couples. Her boyfriend, Marc Harrison, followed her, somewhat resignedly carrying a flash and extra film.

Yep, Holly thought to herself, amused, everybody's in a Valentine's Day mood. Then she corrected herself. Everybody except me and my friends that is! The crowd was still completely on edge. Greg had arrived looking extremely handsome in a neat navy blazer, gray trousers, and a red tie with little white hearts on it. But he also looked extremely pained. You'd think he was the one with the broken leg. He'd picked up his computer Valentine date and stuffed it into his pocket without even reading it. Holly hoped he looked so uninterested because there wasn't much chance he'd be paired with Katie — everyone knew she wasn't coming to the dance.

Meanwhile, Jonathan and Eric, who also looked terrific, were avoiding the refreshment corner. Holly, Diana, and the other girls hadn't had much to say to them lately, just out of principle. And then there were Pamela and Matt, who supposedly were at the dance together, although you wouldn't have known it to look at them. Pamela, very elegant in a simple pale pink silk dress that reached almost to her ankles, was spending more time than was really necessary overseeing the level of the punch bowl and the chips-and-dip supply. Matt drifted in and out on his own, checking his watch every minute or so. He was clearly looking forward to his computer Valentine date and, when he bolted out of the cafeteria at eight-thirty and Pamela remained posted at the refreshment table, Holly couldn't help wondering how the evening would turn out for them.

At least Diana and Jeremy were having a relatively good time, she thought. They'd both had early dates and had gasped with joy when they bumped into each other at rendezvous spot number 8, on the stage in the dark, deserted school auditorium. But considering they'd just discovered that they were really and truly meant for each other, even by the standards of a computer, they didn't appear that blissful to Holly. The tension over Katie's accident hadn't been lessened by the festivity of the dance. It seemed inescapable.

As for me, Holly thought as she scooped up some dip with a potato chip and then, careful not to spill any on her dress, popped it into her mouth, I might as well have stayed at home like Katie! Valentine's Day doesn't mean that much when you don't have anyone to share a romantic moment with. She looked out with envy at all the chattering, laughing, dancing, snuggling couples. I'd be the happiest girl in the world if only Bart were here, she said to herself loyally, if somewhat mechanically. Then she stopped, wondering. Would she really? She tossed her brown curls to shake away such traitorous doubts. Of course she would! Why, she'd even made a new dress for the dance, choosing a style and colors she knew Bart would have liked. The delicate floral print and feminine cut of the dress were very flattering. In an uncharacteristic splurge, she'd even bought a new pair of shoes to match.

Holly adjusted the tie at her waist with a sigh. There was really no use in pretending to herself that she'd made the dress for the sake of someone who wouldn't even see it. She was wearing it because she knew it looked nice on her and she was hoping another boy who might very well show up at the dance *would* see it and appreciate it. But so far there was no sign of Zachary Mc-Graw. Maybe after she'd turned him down he'd decided not to come. Holly didn't acknowledge how disappointed she'd be if this were the case.

At that moment, someone tapped Holly on the shoulder. She jumped, and her potato chip went flying. Fortunately no one was standing nearby. For a brief, wild instant Holly thought it might be Zachary coming up behind her, but it was only Pamela. She was holding a slip of paper, which now she held out to Holly. "Here, Holly. I was just over at the booth helping hand out the last few computer date assignments and I found this. You forgot to pick yours up. You're lucky you didn't miss your date!"

Holly took the sheet wordlessly. Pamela didn't seem to notice her perplexed expression and before Holly could tell her that there must be some mistake — that she hadn't even filled out a computer Valentine questionnaire — Pamela had bustled off to the kitchen with yet another empty punch bowl. Holly watched her leave, baffled. Then she raised the piece of paper up close to her face so she could read it in the dim, erratic light. There was her name, HOLLY DANIELS, as big as life, and in neat columns next to it "10:00" and LOCATION 10. She had a Valentine's date at ten o'clock at. . . . She walked rapidly over to the chart on the wall by the booth, her heels clicking evenly. Location 10 was by the flagpole in front of the school. A pretty chilly spot for a romantic rendezvous! Holly thought wryly.

Just then she glanced up to see Diana watching her with a very peculiar expression on her face. Her best friend looked pointedly at the slip of paper in her hand and then gave her a knowing, secret smile. Holly had a sudden flash of intuition. She waved the computer printout as she approached Diana. "Did you have something to do with this?" she asked suspiciously.

"Why, whatever do you mean?" Diana could not have appeared more innocent. Holly pressed her but Diana insisted she didn't know. Finally Holly gave up. She folded the sheet and tucked it in the pocket of her coat, which was hidden under the refreshment table. Diana soon left her holding down the fort alone while she hit the dance floor for a few songs with Jeremy.

Holly thought for a moment as she ladled out cups of punch. She squinted thoughtfully. Diana wouldn't admit it but she knew something, that much Holly was sure of. Diana had a secret and Holly had a mystery date. . . . Suddenly Holly's cheeks went white. The ladle slipped from her fingers and landed with a splash in the punch. It could only mean one thing! Somehow Bart must have flown home for the weekend and was waiting to surprise her! No, that was impossible. Or was it? As she retrieved the ladle and wiped her fingers on a paper napkin printed with multi-colored hearts, Holly decided it might be un-likely, but it wasn't impossible.

At first Holly was too flabbergasted to feel anything but numb. But with every passing min-ute she became more and more nervous and ex-cited. Before long she found herself praying that her hunch was true, that it would be Bart waiting for her by the flagpole. Obviously she'd love to see him — it had been weeks! She wanted to see him, but also she *needed* to see him, and not only because he was her boyfriend and she missed him. Holly knew she needed to see Bart right now because seeing him might be the only way to wipe Zachary McGraw from her mind.

She started watching the clock as eagerly as Matt had been just a while before. There was still more than an hour to go until her date, and Holly wasn't sure she could stand the wait.

Chapter 17

Matt tugged nervously at his tie. He hated wearing one — he felt like a dog with a too-tight collar — but this was a dance and he couldn't exactly have come in his gas station uniform. He grinned to himself, thinking of what Pamela's face would have looked like if he'd arrived tonight to pick her up in his oil-spattered coveralls. Although, he thought, his fading grin replaced by a preoccupied frown, he might as well have been wearing them for all Pamela had noticed.

And they'd hardly said a word to one another during the ride to the dance. The silence was partly due to the fact that they were theoretically on opposing sides in the ski trip controversy, but they had agreed in honor of Valentine's Day to put that aside for the evening at least. Mostly the silence had seemed to spring from the fact that neither of them had much to say. It hadn't been a hostile silence, but it hadn't been a companionable one, either. It had just been empty, and Matt was glad when they got to the dance. Pamela immediately busied herself with the refreshments, freeing him to wander off on his own and think.

He'd checked his watch about twenty times in the first five minutes after he arrived at the dance and discovered that he had an early date. It was lucky that he did, too, because he was so impatient he could hardly stand still. At 8:30 he would meet . . . *somebody* . . . outside the principal's office. He'd been dreaming about who might be waiting for him tonight, secretly hoping but not wanting to admit it to himself. It was a long shot. Longer than a long shot. Still. . . .

Matt sneaked out of the noisy cafeteria a shade before 8:30, casting one last guilty look back at Pamela. He needn't have worried, though. She was concentrating on repinning the pink bunting that decorated the computer Valentine booth and had her back to him. Now he gulped and yanked on his tie again, this time giving in and loosening it as well as unbuttoning the top button of his pale yellow oxford. His casual style shouldn't matter to the girl at the rendezvous, he reasoned. If the computer was right, she'd hate ties and formalities as much as he did. Once well into the darkened hallway, Matt quickened his pace. His heart also started to beat faster. In a few seconds, he was pushing open the glass door to the lobby, which was even dimmer than the hall had been. It was so quiet Matt imagined he could hear someone else breathing on the other side of the murky space. He crossed the floor with eager yet cautious steps. As he got closer he detected the outlines of a tall, slender girl in a low-cut dress. When she stepped forward out of the shadowy corner, her green eyes shining, he realized it was Roxanne.

Matt was thrilled, but for an instant he was petrified, too. Having his computer Valentine turn out to be Rox Easton was a dream come true for him, but what if she was disappointed? Maybe he wasn't as smooth and elegant as the guys she was used to. Matt didn't have to wonder about how Roxanne would react for long, though. Before he could even say his code word, she had wrapped her arms around his neck and they were kissing.

For a split second he didn't respond, because he was so surprised and also because he thought of Pamela. He knew *she* wouldn't rush right into the arms of her computer date. She'd shake his hand and maybe even dance with him but she'd never forget that she had a boyfriend. But although kissing Roxanne might not be fair to Pamela, Matt couldn't stop himself. At this moment Rox was everything he was looking for. She was daring and beautiful and carefree and spontaneous. Her kisses, her body . . . he couldn't have resisted them even if he'd wanted to. And even as he was kissing Roxanne, Matt decided that he didn't want to resist her or whatever temptation she represented. What this said about his love for Pamela, he wasn't sure. He'd just have to figure it out later.

By now Matt and Roxanne had been kissing for a couple of minutes straight, and Matt was starting to lose his breath. They both pulled back at the same moment with similar reluctance. Matt's dark eyes were glowing with joy and discovery. Rox flashed him her most bewitching smile. "I was hoping it would be you!" she exclaimed softly. "I've been imagining this moment ever since we met."

Matt's jaw dropped. "You were? You have?"

"Of course!" Roxanne reached up to loosen his tie further. "I knew from that first time we really talked — out by your car, remember?" Matt nodded dumbly. "I knew you and I could be something special to each other," she explained. "Share something once-in-a-lifetime."

Matt could hardly believe what he was hearing. He was really and truly on cloud nine. He started to draw Roxanne close again, but this time she resisted. She glanced nervously past his shoulder in the direction of the door that lead back to the hall and the cafeteria. "What's the matter?" Matt asked, following her gaze but seeing nothing.

She smiled apologetically. "I'm so glad we were paired," she breathed, squeezing his hand. "I'm just worried someone'll see us."

"Why?" Matt felt bold all of a sudden. He wouldn't have cared if Pamela herself had walked into the lobby just then. "We don't have anything to hide." He searched Roxanne's eyes intently. "Do we?"

"Of course not!" She stood up on tiptoes to peck him on the cheek. "It's just . . . Matt, I have to confess something." Matt waited patiently. Rox looked embarrassed. "I've only just realized that a few other Kennedy guys — Eric, Jonathan, and Greg actually — like me, too." When he frowned, she hastened to add, "You're the only one I really care for! I just think that for *now*, we should keep our romance a secret." She lifted her bare shoulders delicately. "I don't want to hurt their feelings."

Matt was touched by Roxanne's sensitivity. She was really a sweet, wonderful person. And she liked *him*. Matt Jacobs! It was his wildest fantasy come to life. He leaned toward her to kiss her again, but before he could put his arms around her she had slipped past him. He had to take a few giant steps to catch up with her.

"A secret, remember?" she urged, stepping through the door back into the hallway. "We don't want anyone to see us!"

"But the dance!" Matt nodded toward the cafeteria entrance. "Can't we be together there?"

Roxanne dropped her eyes from his. "Maybe . . . maybe later," she said evasively. Matt looked disappointed. "Definitely later," she amended.

"We'll sneak a slow dance. But right now, I . . . I have to go to the girls' room."

"Half an hour?" Matt persisted.

She glanced unobstrusively at her watch. "An hour."

After flashing Matt a provocative, promising, good-bye smile, Roxanne hung back while he continued on to the cafeteria. Matt, for his part, was too overwhelmed with his good fortune to notice that instead of entering the girls' room, Rox darted back to the shadowy hallway toward the lobby. He hardly even felt the floor beneath his feet — he was flying. Being with Roxanne just now had been like racing a brand-new Camaro down a straight, wide empty road. He'd never been so exhilarated.

Luckily, Pamela was still preoccupied with the refreshments when Matt returned from his rendezvous. She was also helping Jonathan put the finishing touches on the crowns for the soon-to-be-announced winners of the Sweetest Sweethearts contest. Pamela was too busy to dance, even too busy to ask about his date. It was just as well. Matt wanted to be alone with his secret. One close look, and Pamela would see that something had happened to change him right down to his bones.

Roxanne barely had time to scurry to her next appointment. She quickly touched up her lips with the fire-engine-red lip gloss she kept tucked in her sequined clutch. Three minutes after she parted from Matt she had doubled around to the back door of the cafeteria to take up her position in the dark northeast corner. Just in time, too. A tall boy in a rumpled white shirt and baggy pin-striped trousers was weaving his way toward her.

She pushed one flimsy red spaghetti strap back up on her shoulder and smiled uncertainly. Jonathan returned her smile, equally uncertain. There were a few other people milling about and he tried to appear nonchalant as he came up next to her. Jonathan offered his code word in a low, hopeful voice. Roxanne happily gave the appropriate response.

Three minutes later the two had shared a warm, thrilling kiss; Roxanne had assured Jonathan that he was the only one she cared for; confessed that she knew some of the other boys liked her, too, and begged him to keep their romance a secret a while longer. They'd parted with another clandestine embrace and a whispered promise to meet later for a slow dance. "A very slow dance," Jonathan added with a wink.

Rox giggled. "Very slow!" she echoed, tossing him a good-bye kiss.

Rox slipped into the girls' room and leaned against the closed door. She let out a long sigh. All this sneaking around was getting exhausting. And she still had two dates to go! Fortunately she had fifteen minutes before she was supposed to meet Greg, plenty of time to rest and refresh herself. She pulled a tiny brush from her clutch and ran it through her hair, then shook her head so the long strands fell over her bare shoulders. She couldn't help smiling into the mirror. Date-hopping like this might be exhausting, but it was also *fun*.

In fact, Roxanne couldn't remember ever enjoying herself more. Before the night was over she would have four of the best-looking, most popular guys at Kennedy High at her feet, which was no small feat for the new girl from Stevenson. Four boys. "What more could a girl want?" Roxanne whispered to her reflection. In the silence of the otherwise deserted bathroom, her smile crumbled just a little. She turned away from the mirror before she had a chance to doubt herself. With this kind of social success, I *do* have everything I want, she thought aggressively. Nothing could make me happier. *Nothing*. Slowly the triumphant smile returned to her face. Two down, two to go, she thought. Rox was ready for date number three.

Greg heaved a large, lonely sigh. He was slouching against the wall under a string of flashing pink lights not far from the band. He'd been there for an hour now. It was a good spot for keeping an eye on the door and for keeping out of the way of people who might want to talk or dance with him. Greg was trying his hardest to feel festive but it wasn't working. He just didn't have the heart for a Valentine's Day Dance. No pun intended, he thought grimly. Not when dozens of girls had walked through that door — a lot of them cute, some even with red hair and one actually on crutches — but none of them Katie. It just didn't look like he was going to get another chance to apologize to her. He'd been willing to get down on his knees yesterday, which wasn't exactly easy for him to do, but she hadn't let him. No, things definitely didn't look good.

And speaking of other girls, he was supposed to meet his computer Valentine in five minutes at location number nine, wherever that was. Greg couldn't help smiling wryly to himself. He was going to be a fun date tonight! A real barrel of laughs. Poor whoever-she-was was sure in for a disappointment. Just then he caught sight of Eric who was on his way back to the refreshment table with an empty punch cup. Greg suddenly had an idea. "Hey, Eric!" he called out, raising his voice to be heard above the band's somewhat feeble rendition of "Dancing in the Dark." "Come here!"

Eric joined Greg, slapping him on the back. "Hey, buddy, had your Valentine's Day date yet?"

Greg shook his head. "That's where you come in, pal." He stuck his hand in his jacket pocket and took out the computer printout for his appointment. He unfolded it and read it again, totally uninterested. "I'm just not in the mood, you know?"

"Katie?" Eric guessed, sympathetic.

"Yeah, Katie." Greg spoke her name lightly but his expression was dull.

"Okay, so you're not in the mood for Valentine's Day romance. What does that have to do with me?" Eric wondered.

"You could do me a big favor," Greg explained. "Would you go for me and tell whoever it is that I'm sorry but something came up?"

"Well. . . ." Eric took the sheet from Greg and glanced at the code words and also the time and place. Finally he nodded. "Sure." Then he checked the time again. "Geez, I'd better run!" he grinned. "Don't want to keep the lady waiting. She'll be disappointed enough as it is."

"Thanks," Greg said gratefully. "I owe you one."

"Hey, no problem." Eric shrugged. "And who knows, maybe I'll be the one who owes you. You could be passing up a hot date!"

Greg laughed and waved Eric off. "I'll take that chance. Thanks again."

He watched his friend weave his way across the dance floor to the door and was about to turn back to face the band when a flash of red caught his eye. It was Roxanne, looking unbelievably gorgeous in a very slinky dress. She was sneaking out of the cafeteria, too. Greg saw her glance surreptitiously over both shoulders before disappearing into the hall. No, he thought, shaking his head disbelievingly. It couldn't be! Rox has to be heading for another rendezvous. She couldn't have been my date. Or could she? After all, they did have a lot in common. The computer might very well have picked up on it.

Greg was ready to laugh out loud, at himself this time. Eric might have been right. He may have just thrown away the chance of a lifetime, an opportunity any other guy at Kennedy would kill for. Make that *any* guy at Kennedy, Greg thought. He might as well admit he was no exception. Roxanne was hot. But even so, Greg wasn't exactly about to run after Eric and reclaim his date. He sighed deeply as the band faded into a love song and the dancing couples he'd been watching idly from the sidelines pulled one another close. Roxanne was hot, but she wasn't Katie.

Eric studied the computer printout Greg had given him. He was supposed to substitute for Greg at location number nine and say the code word "sail." Easy enough, but it didn't leave him much time to butter up Greg's date before he met his own date in fifteen minutes. Oh well, he thought, puffing himself up a little, if I can swim the 100-meter freestyle in under a minute, I can handle this!

The lobby outside the principal's office was pretty dark and Eric's eyes hadn't adjusted yet from the colorful blinking lights at the dance. He squinted. There was someone there in a red dress, that much he could tell. He cleared his throat experimentally and then delivered Greg's code word in a loud whisper. "Sail?"

The response, "boat," came immediately in a

soft, husky feminine voice. A girl emerged from the shadows. Rox Easton! Eric's jaw dropped. She looked as surprised as he did, if not more so. She took a half step backward and then stuttered, "Stroke!"

Now Eric was really confused. He snapped his jaw shut again. "Stroke" was the response to his own code word, "back." How come Roxanne knew his code word if she was supposed to be Greg's date? Or was it the other way around? "Wait a minute," he protested, confused. Something was definitely fishy here. "I don't get — "

Before he could say another word, Roxanne had placed her hands on his shoulders to greet him with a long, warm kiss. If she'd been taken aback for a moment herself, that moment had passed. Eric, meanwhile, forgot about code words. Backstroke, sailboat, what did any of that matter when he was kissing Roxanne Easton?

"Eric, I'm so glad it's you!" Rox exclaimed, her voice vibrant with passion and sincerity. She had pulled back slightly to flash him a heart-stopping smile. Eric gazed into her eyes, an awed expression on his face. "Of all the guys I've gotten to know since I've been at Kennedy," she continued rapidly, "I like you the best. We have so much in common."

Eric could hardly get a word in edgewise as Rox rambled on. He nodded when she said that she wanted to spend the entire evening with him. After all, that was just what he wanted, too, more than anything. And he nodded again when she explained that some of the other boys also liked her and because she cared about them as friends and didn't want to hurt them, she thought she and Eric should keep their romance a secret. They shouldn't spend too much time together that night. That was fine with Eric, too. He was ecstatic that Roxanne should single him out like this, and he had to acknowledge that he felt vaguely triumphant. But he would never want to rub it in the faces of the other guys. They were his friends, after all.

Eric had been thinking as rapidly as Roxanne was talking, but now he abandoned himself to the excitement of the moment. He didn't need to analyze the situation. Roxanne was wild about *him*, and that was all he needed to know.

After a few more minutes, Rox and Eric went their separate ways, arranging to meet on the dance floor in half an hour. Eric walked back to the cafeteria, as bouyant as if he were floating. Ever since the ski trip bus ride, he'd thought about Roxanne constantly. In a lot of ways that had been a terrible day. He felt responsible for Katie's accident, even though it really had been just an accident. Even worse was that Katie still wouldn't speak to him. But in other respects it had been a fantastic day. Since then, he'd been hoping that Roxanne might pick him out of the crowd, and now it really looked like she had. He was the luckiest guy in the world!

Eric hopped up and kicked his heels together as he reentered the dance. It was time for his own computer Valentine appointment, but it had completely slipped his mind. He'd already found his dream girl.

Chapter
18

Katie waved good-bye to her father in the Kennedy High parking lot. How embarrassing! Being dropped off at a dance by your dad when you were a senior! She gripped her crutches and hopped up onto the curb and across the flagstones to the front door of the school. Well, it was just one of the many indignities that came with a broken leg. She was getting used to them. Another was having to wear a knee-high stocking on one leg with a semi-formal dress and a thick wooly sock, along with a cast, of course, on the other. Talk about a *Glamour* magazine fashion "Don't"! How *not* to dress for a Valentine's Day Dance. Katie giggled to herself.

But at least I'm here, she added silently. I'm not moping at home by myself. She pushed the door open. From the dark, empty entryway she could hear the far-off, muffled sound of the band. Suddenly Katie's heart started beating a little faster and she smiled despite herself. The band sounded pretty good. Hey, I almost feel like dancing! she thought.

By the time Katie had made her way into the cafeteria, however, the music had stopped. As she slipped inside, glad it was dark so she could make a relatively inconspicuous entrance, she heard Jonathan Preston's voice rise above the buzz of chatter and laughter. Good old Jonathan, she thought, forgetting for a second that she was supposed to be mad at him. He never needed a microphone to make himself heard!

"Excuse me! Shut up out there!" Jonathan was shouting unceremoniously. The crowd quieted down a bit. "Thank you, fans," he said with a wide grin. "Okay, this is the moment — or one of them anyway — that you've all been waiting for. By now most of you have probably already met your computer Valentines, and we hope they're all matches made in heaven. Here to announce the result of the Sweetest Sweethearts contest, the lucky guy every gal wishes was her Valentine, is . . . student council president, Colin Edwards!"

Jonathan waved his arms with a flourish and the band provided a complimentary drum roll. The students cheered, and Colin took a bow. Then he drew a large, heart-speckled envelope from the pocket of his navy blazer. "This is it," he announced, straightening his tie and clearing his throat. "Mr. and Mrs. Sweetheart, King and

Queen Valentine. The winners are. . . ." Colin cleared his throat as he tore the envelope open and withdrew a slip of paper. Then his face went red. He cleared his throat again, this time nervously. When he spoke his voice had dropped an octave and lost most of its *oomph*. "Um, the Sweetest Sweethearts of Kennedy High are, uh, Katie Crawford and, er, Greg Montgomery."

The announcement was met with scattered applause and mumbled expressions of surprise. Katie's own cheeks were as red as her hair. She was rooted to her spot and seriously considered fleeing the scene in the hope that her dad might still by some miracle be waiting in the parking lot. The kids standing near her had all turned to give her curious, sympathetic looks. Katie could see Greg now on the other side of the dance floor waving his arms at a stumped Colin. It wasn't hard to read his lips. "Keep going!" Greg was mouthing to the emcees. "Skip this part!" Jonathan held up a delicate crown made of pink rosebuds and baby's breath and shrugged helplessly.

Katie took a deep breath. Strangely, she and Greg had been chosen Sweetest Sweethearts. Maybe she wasn't sure if they were even a couple anymore, but what did she have to lose? There was no reason to put a damper on the whole dance. If she was going to get back in to the swing of things, this was as good a place as any to start.

Leaning on her crutches a little but not really

using them, Katie limped to the front of the crowd. Greg had moved forward, too, and when he saw her, his jaw literally dropped. Jonathan gestured frantically to the band to start playing while Colin carefully placed the crown on Katie's head.

She looked at Greg shyly and expectantly. As the music started up again, he stepped toward her. He took one of her crutches and leaned it against the wall and then he put his arms around her. They began dancing, slowly and wordlessly. At first Katie felt awkward dancing with one crutch, not to mention with the heavy, cumbersome cast weighting her down. Soon, though, she and Greg fell into step, their own familiar rhythm taking over. Her leg hurt a little but she was hardly aware of it; the feel of Greg's arms around her erased any other sensation. As the soft, husky vocals of the love song rose up around them, Greg pulled Katie closer. She rested her head gingerly against his chest, not ready to look up and meet his eyes. His heart was pounding under her ear; her own heart was beating pretty fast itself. It was clear that the special spark that lit every time she and Greg were near each other hadn't been entirely extinguished. As they continued to dance, Katie found herself hoping that in spite of everything, maybe she and Greg could work things out after all. Maybe they couldn't, but there was one thing she was sure of: She still loved him. Would that be enough?

* * *

When Colin announced Katie and Greg as the Sweetest Sweethearts, Matt was so surprised he dropped his punch, some of which splashed onto his tie. Now he was in the boys' bathroom trying to wash the spot off. First he tried rubbing at it with a piece of paper towel dipped under the faucet. No go, the wet paper only disintegrated and the spot remained. Next he leaned over the sink to hold the entire tie under the tap. The spot came off but Matt was left with a dripping wet tie. "Shoot," he muttered to himself. "I hate dressing up!"

Eric, washing his hands at the next sink, grimaced sympathetically. "I know what you mean," he agreed. "Coats and ties are more trouble than they're worth." He smiled slyly, pulling a comb from his inside jacket pocket. "Girls like 'em, though."

Matt was pressing the tie between two paper towels to soak some of the water out of it. He nodded, thinking of Roxanne loosening his tie provocatively a while ago. "That's true," he agreed, refraining from a grin himself.

Just then the door swung open. Jonathan and Jeremy breezed in, involved in an animated conversation. This bathroom is worse than Grand Central Station! Matt thought. He greeted his friends and then refocused his attention on his tie. One more paper towel treatment and it would be as good as new. When the name "Roxanne" popped up in Jonathan's banter, however, Matt's ears perked right up. And when he heard what Jonathan was saying about Roxanne, he forgot all about his tie.

"Jer, it's really amazing," Jonathan declared, leaning against the wall while Jeremy bent over the sink to check one of his contact lenses. He was talking in a low voice, but Matt couldn't help overhearing him. "I never would've dreamed I'd meet someone like her in a million years. And she feels the same way about me!" Jonathan puffed himself up slightly. "Yep, Roxanne could have anybody, but I'm the only guy she cares about," he boasted. "I guess it's not surprising, considering how much we have in common. Can you believe she loves mystery novels — I can't wait for her to meet my mom — and funky hats, and what's more, she hates traveling just like I do. And she's very community-minded — "

"Wait a minute!" Matt exploded. He'd been silent, first because he was curious and then because he was stunned. Now he gripped the edge of the sink to steady himself, staring at Jonathan in disbelief. "Roxanne *Easton*?"

Jonathan's smug look fell a little. "What other Roxanne is there?" he asked.

"Roxanne likes mystery novels and funky hats and hates traveling." Matt quoted Jonathan in a precise, persistent tone. "How do you know that?"

"Because she told me." Jonathan was now totally confused. "Look, Jacobs, what are you getting at?"

Matt shook his head, bewildered. "Just that Roxanne told *me* she *loves* traveling and *hates* books and fashion," he answered bluntly.

"What!" Jonathan exclaimed. The two boys started at each other and then, both thinking the exact same thing, turned in unison to look at Eric. It was a safe bet their friend wasn't combing his hair so carefully for their benefit.

Eric's ordinarily healthy complexion had gone pale. He stared back at them, comb in the air, openmouthed. "Roxanne told *me* she loves swimming and she's not all that interested in success and things like the student government," Eric stuttered.

It seemed to sink in first for Jonathan. "Oh, no," he groaned.

Matt was getting the picture, too. "Oh, *no*," he echoed.

"I can't believe this!" Eric tossed his comb down and it landed in the next sink with a clatter. "Are you trying to tell me that you guys had dates with her, too? That she's had a different story for each of us and has us all thinking we're the one she likes? What's going on?"

"It looks to me," Jeremy offered, his British-accented voice deferential, "as if Roxanne knows how to change her personality according to the personality of the guy she's with." He couldn't help laughing. "I guess I'm lucky I didn't appeal to her — she would've had to develop interests in film and photography on top of all the others!"

"Oh, *no!*" Eric hit his forehead with his hand.

"Then this explains her using the wrong code word when — Greg!" he shouted. Jonathan, Matt, and Jeremy looked more astonished than ever. Eric retrieved his comb and raced for the door. "Come on, you guys! We've got one more story to check."

The four sprinted down the hall, their ties flapping wildly, and ran into the cafeteria. They found Katie and Greg still slow dancing in the hazy pink spotlight. When Eric beckoned urgently to them, the pair followed the boys out into the hall. As soon as the cafeteria door swung shut, Eric gripped Greg's arm. "What did Roxanne tell you?" he asked, his face a serious as his voice.

Greg cocked his head to one side. Katie, her crown slipping over one eye, looked puzzled, too. "What do you mean 'what did she tell me'?" Greg responded.

"About herself," Jonathan filled in, waving his hands for punctuation. "You know, about her interests and stuff."

Greg shrugged, apparently still mystified. His face turned a little red, as if the prospect of discussing Rox — no matter what the reason — in front of Katie, might be just a little embarrassing. Nonetheless, he forged ahead. "Well, just stuff you guys probably know about her already — she and I aren't *that* close. She likes crew." He grinned. "Smart girl, eh? And she's really into politics. She's ambitious, too." He stopped, looking from Eric to Jonathan to Matt to Jeremy and back again. The first three had all put their faces in their hands and were slumped forward, totally humiliated. Even Jeremy looked none too proud of himself. "What am I missing here, guys?" Greg wondered, giving Jonathan a jovial slap on the shoulder. "Why the long faces?"

Jonathan swallowed. "We've all been made to look like complete fools, that's all," he informed Greg, too devastated even to crack a joke. "You, too, buddy. Roxanne made each of us think she liked all the same things we did. And we each had a secret rendezvous with her tonight!"

Eric added, "I'm sure if you'd shown up at yours she would've given you the same 'you're the only one for me' line!"

"Basically we all fell for her, hook, line, and sinker," Matt admitted. He rubbed his unshaven chin ruefully. "She took us all for a ride, but it couldn't have happened if we hadn't been such suckers for her flattery."

The boys filled Katie and Greg in on their recent discovery and compared their encounters with Roxanne that night. Greg whistled. Katie just watched the others as they talked, keeping quiet herself. Finally the group fell silent.

Eric turned to Katie, a guilty look on his face. "K.C., I'm really sorry, about everything," he began, sounding anxious and ashamed. "I'm sorry I skied like an idiot at Mount Jackson and made you break your leg and I'm sorry I took Roxanne's side over yours. What can I say, I was really and truly blind."

Before Katie could open her mouth, Jonathan and Matt and even Jeremy echoed Eric's apology. She waved a hand to cut them off. "Thanks, guys, but I should be apologizing, too. I'm sorry I blamed you for my fall. After all, it was my idea to go down the black diamond run!" She held Eric's eyes for a moment. "Besides, I have a feeling you're already paying pretty heavily for this Roxanne business. It sounds like she really put one over on you." Katie didn't gloat; her sympathy was sincere. Eric and the others smiled, awkwardly but with appreciation.

"Thanks, Katie," Eric said. He laughed, despite himself. "This whole farce is pretty funny if you think about it, I guess. I mean, I was just in the guys' room brushing up for a dance with Roxanne. Now I wouldn't touch her with a ten-foot pole!"

Matt and Jonathan were equally vocal about keeping their distance from Roxanne. Katie narrowed her eyes. She couldn't prevent them from sparkling even though she was trying to seem stern. "You really mean that?" she challenged.

"Scout's honor," Jonathan vowed. There were nods all around.

Katie laughed. "Then in that case maybe we should go find the girls. I bet they'll be happy to turn off the heat. If we can get them to believe this crazy story, that is!"

When the group reentered the dance, the band was between sets and Karen and Brian were deejaying. Couples flashed by, jumping to the beat of a Robert Palmer song. Katie scanned the crowd for Molly or Holly or Diana. Matt, standing next to her, did the same thing. He was looking for Pamela. He knew he owed her a big apology. Now that he thought about it, they hadn't really talked in weeks — not since he'd lost his head over Roxanne, to be more specific. They were long overdue for a talk.

In a few minutes, everyone had been rounded up — except for Pamela. "She left," Holly said in answer to Matt's question, "but just a minute ago. You might still catch her, if you run."

Matt headed for the door, and the others pulled out chairs at a corner table decorated with candles and a pink paper tablecloth. Greg and the other guys quickly filled Holly, Diana, and Molly in on the most recent developments in the Rox Easton/ski trip saga.

"We were so stupid," Greg admitted candidly. Eric and Jonathan nodded in confirmation. "It was a mistake to fall for Roxanne's tricks, especially since it caused such a rift in the crowd. I hope you'll forgive us."

"I've got to take credit for a lot of the problem, too," Katie was quick to add. "The accident wasn't anybody's fault. I was wrong to blame the guys — I was even wrong to blame Roxanne!" she admitted with a wry smile. "The important thing is, it's crazy to let a thing like that come between a bunch of people who are supposed to be friends."

"Phew!" Diana shook her blonde head and smiled brightly. She and Jeremy had pulled their chairs close and were sitting with their arms firmly around one another. "This is such a relief! I was starting to think Jeremy and I would have to stop seeing each other just on principle!"

Eric poked Molly gently in the ribs. "What about you, Ramirez?" he asked. "Can we be friends again?"

Molly mussed his hair. "Sure, Shriver." She laughed. "I'd pretty much decided you were a complete jerk, but on second thought, maybe you're not so bad!"

He gave her a brisk bear hug. "Thanks, Moll!"

"What do you say we celebrate all this by meeting at the sub shop after the dance?" Greg suggested. He looked around the table for a response and saw what he expected to see — more nods and grins.

Just then the band struck up a very lively dance tune. Eric jumped to his feet and grabbed Molly's hand. Diana and Jeremy rose at the same time. In a moment the table was empty except for Katie and Greg. He glanced at her out of the corner of his eye. She had her hands clasped in her lap and was studying her fingernails, her forehead wrinkled in concentration. Greg put a hand to his neck. Suddenly his tie felt really tight. His nervousness didn't help. He loosened the knot and then reached over the empty chair between him and Katie to rest a gentle hand on her shoulder. She raised her eyes to his. The expression in them was guarded, but underneath he thought he saw all the things he himself was feeling at that very moment — hope and expectation and love. "Katie," he began softly. "I'm very sorry. I have so much I want to say to you."

The tiny spark in Katie's eyes grew warmer and brighter. "Me, too," she began, turning in her chair to face him. "About Roxanne . . . the accident — "

Greg slid over into the chair next to Katie's. A second later he had his arms around her and she was looking into his eyes, which were only inches away from her own. "Shhh," he whispered. He leaned forward and kissed her hair lightly. Katie buried her face in his shoulder. "We have all night to talk." His tone changed. "For now, how about a dance?" he teased.

Katie giggled. She tapped her cast against Greg's leg as a reminder. "The slow dance I could handle, but this stuff . . . I think I'd be better off sitting out this particular song."

"Good." Greg hugged Katie so tightly she could barely breathe. "Because I was hoping we could get started on the kissing and the making-up stuff. What do you say?"

In answer Katie raised her glowing face to his.

Greg was right. They had all night, and plenty of time after that to talk. Right now it was Valentine's Day and, miracle of miracles, they weren't fighting but holding each other instead. In all their time together, no single moment had been more magical than this one. As the band broke into a romantic melody, their lips met. They didn't part for a long time, and then it was only so Greg could pull Katie onto his lap for another kiss that was even longer and sweeter than the first.

Chapter
19

Matt dashed down the dim hallway and took the stairs down to the main entrance three at a time, wishing he was wearing his old sneakers instead of the new leather loafers his mom had made him buy for the occasion. Pamela couldn't have gotten far. Holly said she'd only just left and besides, he'd driven her to the dance so she didn't have a car.

Once outside, Matt thought about running out to check the bus stop, but on a hunch, he headed for the parking lot instead. His Mustang was parked in the far corner underneath a big old maple tree, its bare, gnarled branches creating a stark silhouette against the pale yellow disk of the full moon. He more than half-expected to find someone waiting for him there, and as he approached the car he could see a girl with fair hair in a long, dark coat sitting stiffly on the hood. She watched him as he drew closer, her usual smile missing. It was Pamela.

Matt stopped and stood in front of her, shifting his weight uncomfortably from one foot to another. For a long moment neither of them said anything. Pamela had dropped her gaze and was nervously twisting the bracelet on her left wrist. Finally Matt cleared his throat. When he spoke his voice was gruff. "Uh, Pamela, do you want to. . . . Maybe we should, uh. . . . How about going for a drive?"

Pamela looked up quickly, half eager and half cautious. "Sure," she said in an even tone. "I think that would be a good idea."

Matt walked around to the passenger side to open the door for her and then closed it carefully once she was settled inside. Striding back around to the driver's side, he realized that his palms were damp and he was clenching his teeth. He was nervous. He couldn't pretend this was just an ordinary drive he and Pamela were about to take. The silence between them was loaded and it felt like a full, fat thundercloud that was very near bursting.

The first time Matt turned the key in the ignition, nothing happened. He patted the dashboard and tossed Pamela a sheepish grin. "We've been a little slow these days," he said lightly, hoping to break the ice. Pamela just nodded. On the second try the Mustang's engine sputtered to life and a few seconds later they were heading out of town.

Matt made an effort to relax; he had to consciously loosen his grip on the steering wheel. Sneaking glances at Pamela's profile out of the corner of his eye, he couldn't help thinking how ironic the situation was. It was such a beautiful night for a drive. The moonlight streaming through the car windows made Pamela's hair and eyes shine. He was in his car on the open road — his favorite thing in the world. And he was with his favorite person. But somehow they just didn't fit. All the elements were right but the mood was all wrong. And it wasn't only the general strain between them because of the post-ski-trip feud.

The silence in the car stretched on for a while longer, and Matt grew more and more tense. It was hard to start talking after so many empty minutes had passed, but he knew if he didn't do it now he probably never would. He rubbed his chin and then scratched his ear. "Pamela," he began, hesitant. "How come you left the dance in such a hurry?"

To his astonishment, Pamela laughed. He shot her a suspicious glance — she didn't *look* amused. "Matt, you don't have to bother acting innocent for my sake," she said dryly. "I'd have to be a whole lot slower than I am not to have caught on to you and Roxanne Easton by now." He started to protest but she cut him off with a violent wave of her hand. "I saw you with my own eyes," she informed him flatly. "On my way to meet my own computer date."

Pamela's voice had been sharp at first but she

finished sounding defeated and sad. She'd turned to look out the window and Matt couldn't see her face, but her words tore at his heart. He'd really hurt her, and it hurt him to know that. He realized it was time to stop driving and give Pamela all his attention.

He pulled the Mustang over to the side of the road, parking half on the sandy shoulder and half on the dry, brown dirt bordering a wide, moon-swept field. He turned the engine off and the car went dark; the only lights around belonged to a pair of farm houses just up the road. Matt unbuckled his seat belt and reached for Pamela with both arms. "I'm sorry, Pamela," he said quietly. "I'm sorry for hurting you, for acting like such a fool over Roxanne."

Pamela didn't push him away; she let him hold her but her own arms remained pressed to her sides, motionless. She sniffled. "Why did you run after me?" she asked, her voice muffled against Matt's denim jacket. "You seemed to be having such a good time with . . . with *her*."

Matt gave Pamela a squeeze and then pulled back so he could meet her eyes. The tiny, almost imperceptible quiver in her chin made him feel more ashamed than ever. "I discovered a couple things about her tonight, and about myself," he explained humbly. "She took me — and a few other guys, too — for a real ride. It was all an act. I guess she was just out for the conquest, but I'm not really sure. Whatever it was, I fell for it, but I know better now." He hung his head. "I guess I've been acting like a real jerk, huh?"

Pamela seemed touched by Matt's genuine remorse. Her eyes brightened just a little. "Pretty much," she admitted, trying her best to smile.

Matt was encouraged. "Well, I'm sorry, Pamela," he repeated eagerly. "I really am. It's over, all that stuff with Roxanne. Katie's not mad anymore, and me — I learned something. I don't have anything in common with Roxanne after all."

Matt had taken Pamela's hand and now she dropped her eyes to study their intertwined fingers. He waited anxiously for her to speak, to say she accepted his apology and that things were going to be okay. "Thanks," she said at last, her voice low. "I mean, for being sorry. I'm glad . . . I'm glad you don't really like her." She laughed, but it was a false, brittle laugh. "She doesn't deserve someone as nice as you! But, Matt, don't you think" — Pamela raised her eyes to his again and her expression was pained — "don't you sort of wonder if you and I have much in common anymore?"

Matt flushed and his throat went dry. Deep down he knew Pamela's question didn't really require an answer. She was only putting into words what he'd been feeling inside for a long while now. But saying it out loud like this was frightening. Matt suddenly found himself feeling scared. Something precious was slipping away from them and he was powerless to stop it from going. "Oh, Pamela," was all he could say. His deep voice cracked.

Tears sprang into Pamela's eyes. "It's true, isn't it?" she insisted. "You know you wouldn't have fallen so hard for Roxanne in the first place if you weren't looking for something — for someone — new." She shivered, pulling the collar of her nubby green wool coat closer to her throat, as if she'd felt a sudden chill. A single tear rolled down the curve of her cheek.

Matt was speechless. He could tell Pamela that that wasn't true but he'd be lying and she'd know it. "You and me, though," he attempted, struggling with the confused emotions. "What — what about us?"

"Maybe there isn't any *us* anymore," Pamela suggested with unhappy certainty. "Maybe that's something we both just have to face."

"Maybe," Matt allowed grudgingly. He wasn't ready to resign himself to that yet. "Maybe."

They sat quietly staring forward through the Mustang's broad windshield, each full of their own thoughts. As they watched, the moon slipped behind a slowly creeping bank of midnight-blue clouds. Suddenly Matt was aware of how cold the car had become. Pamela turned to face him. "Maybe you should take me home now," she said gently.

"Okay." Matt started to reach for the ignition, then instead turned to wrap his arms fiercely around Pamela. This time she hugged him back with all her might. The embrace warmed them, softened the sharp edge of the pain, but just for a moment. When Matt buried his face in Pamela's soft hair, he knew it was for the last time. "I'm sorry we're ending like this," he whispered, his voice catching. "I'm sorry we're ending at all. Pamela, I'll miss you so much."

"Me, too," she said, twisting her fingers in the dark hair that curled over his shirt in the back. "Me, too."

They held each other for a few long moments. When they pulled away, they both had tears in their eyes. Matt slid back into his seat, gazing through the windshield. He couldn't look at Pamela anymore or he would break down and beg her to stay with him no matter how little they shared or how unhappy they might make each other. After all, wasn't it better to be unhappy *with* someone than on your own? He started the car, thinking. Maybe it was, maybe it wasn't. It looked like one thing was far sure — he'd soon find out.

Pamela and Matt didn't bother making conversation on the way to her house. They'd said everything there was to say already. It would trivialize everything to talk about the moon, or the band at the dance, or how bad the potholes in the road were. After he pulled into Pamela's driveway, Matt started to open his door so he could walk her inside but she stopped him, placing a hand quickly on his arm. "That's okay," she said, a little too brightly. "I'll make it on my own."

"Yeah," agreed Matt. He leaned toward her and kissed her softly on the cheek. "You probably will."

Pamela tried to smile, but her lips trembled. " 'Bye, Matt," she said, so quietly he could hardly hear her. "I'll see you."

" 'Bye, Pamela." He sat in the car and watched her walk across the gravel and up the five steps to her door. As she opened it she turned and looked back at him, raising her hand in a farewell wave. Matt waved back at her and then backed the car around, heading for home. He had to bite back the tears as he drove. Everything was suddenly so empty — the night, the car, even himself. Pamela was gone. He'd probably still see her every day in school, but they'd never really be together the same way. The thought made his heart ache.

But the longer Matt drove, the better he felt. Maybe it wasn't so bad being unhappy by himself. Maybe being alone for a while was the only way to figure out how to be happy, on his own or with somebody else.

Matt flipped on the radio. Bruce Springsteen's "Born to Run" was playing. He turned it up loud, tapping his hands briskly to the beat on the steering wheel. He didn't really know what was ahead of him. Now that he'd lost Pamela, everything was that much more uncertain — but he was in his car, and he was going some place.

Holly had hardly heard what Katie and Greg and the others were saying about Roxanne's two-timing — or rather her four- or more-timing — and the end of the feud over Katie's fall. Her computer date was burning a hole in her pocket and she couldn't pay attention to anything but her own rambling, speculative thoughts. She hadn't filled out a form so there shouldn't be a date for her, but there was. And Diana was still smiling in that sly, knowing way! It was driving Holly crazy. It had to be because of Bart, she was convinced. Somehow he must have managed to come home from Montana for the weekend. And finally it was time to meet her Valentine!

Holly rummaged under the refreshment table for her coat. The weather hadn't been terribly cold lately, but her flimsy dress wouldn't offer much protection against even a mild February night. She pulled the coat on as she slipped away from the dance, hoping no one, not even Diana, would see her leaving. She'd been having strangely mixed feelings about the prospect of seeing Bart, but as she walked quickly to the front door of the school she got more and more excited. Outside the street lights were bright but the flagpole itself was not illuminated. There was a figure in the shadow, though, a boy of medium height with broad shoulders and narrow hips.

Holly's heart skipped erratically as she started toward the flagpole again, a welcoming smile already lighting up her face. She'd know Bart anywhere.

But when she got a little nearer, Holly could see that the boy waiting for her in the shadows had blond hair, not dark hair like Bart. She stopped, suddenly uncertain. Then the boy stepped toward her. It was Zachary.

Holly drew her breath in sharply. Zachary raised a hand and hurried to offer an explanation, as if he were afraid she might run away. "Holly, I'm so glad you're here!" he exclaimed, sounding shy but happy. "I hope you don't mind. I mean I know you didn't want a computer Valentine, but I thought — " He broke off and shrugged helplessly. His smile broadened into an appealing grin. "What can I say? I'm crazy about you. You've made this the best Valentine's Day ever just by showing up."

Holly listened to Zachary with wide eyes and a pounding heart. Half of her was astonished by the whole scene but the other half of her wasn't so surprised at all, by Zachary's presence or his words. She'd been aware of his feelings since that day on the ski slope. What was more, she'd felt the same way herself. Now all thoughts of Bart fled from her mind. She realized unconsciously she'd been hoping all evening that Zachary would be her mystery date. She was as nervous and hopeful as he was, but she forced herself to think calmly. She couldn't forget Bart altogether; it wouldn't be right. She knew she had to raise the subject of her boyfriend with Zachary. It was now or never.

Holly took another step in Zachary's direction. She knew what she *should* say: "I can't meet you like this. I can't share your feelings. I love somebody else. Good-bye." But instead she never got beyond "Zack, I——" As she stepped closer to him she was unable to resist his inviting smile and his warm, wishful eyes. The instant his hands touched hers, the last doubt was erased from her mind. She wanted to feel his arms around her and a second later they were. She wanted him to kiss her and when he did she kissed him back, her whole body melting against his. It was like magic and she could tell Zachary felt it, too. His expression was as deliriously happy as her own.

"I can't believe this is happening," he whispered in her ear. He hugged her, a goofy grin lighting up his face.

"Me, neither," Holly whispered back.

"Happy Valentine's Day, Holly."

Holly suddenly realized that what had started out as a lonely evening had turned into a surprisingly romantic one. She smiled. "Happy Valentine's Day, Zack."

Diana eyed the clock. It was finally time to tiptoe out to the steps of the library. A few minutes before, she'd leaned a dozen red roses wrapped in tissue paper against the bottom stair, a card reading "Love, Bart" tucked in the ferns at the top. She just hoped no one else would stroll along and snatch the flowers up before Holly got there and discovered them.

As she opened the door to leave the dance, something on the floor near the booth caught Diana's eye. It looked like somebody's computer Valentine date assignment. She picked it up. It was — in fact, it was the one Diana had made up for Holly. She'd typewritten the time and location, hoping Holly wouldn't notice that it wasn't a legitimate computer printout. Diana stared down at the paper in her hand, puzzled. It was smudged with footprints, obviously from lying on the floor for some time. It must have fallen off the booth sometime after she had placed it there and asked the student handing out assignments to file it with the others. Now Diana raised her eyes, her forehead furrowed. If this note ended up on the floor, then what was on the sheet Holly had received?

Wait, I know, she thought. This *is* the slip Holly got. She must have accidentally dropped it herself after she read it! That explains it. Diana continued through the door. Her step was springy and she was in high spirits. Cheering Holly up with roses from Bart was going to be the crowning glory on a wonderful evening. Her friends had stopped feuding, Jeremy was in a good mood again, everything was as it should be. She skipped down the main staircase and cautiously opened the front door to peer across the courtyard and the street to the steps of the library. She could see the conical shape of the flowers, but no Holly. Her friend was late for her "date." Maybe she wouldn't show up at all, Diana worried. Maybe she thought the rendezvous was a prank. Well if she didn't come, Diana would just have to deliver the roses in person. The effect would be about the same. She figured she might as well hide out and spy a while longer, though. Holly might be on her way.

Just then Diana glanced up toward the north end of the courtyard where the flagpole was. A couple was kissing passionately in the shadows. She smiled to herself. It looked like some of these computer pair-ups *were* matches made in heaven! Then her smile faded. No, she told herself firmly. It couldn't be. The girl had short dark hair an awful lot like Holly's and the same kind of coat, too. It couldn't be her! Diana had pulled back into the doorway so she wouldn't be seen, but now she inched slowly to get a better view. She didn't like being nosy but she really wanted to find out who those people were. The couple parted momentarily from their embrace, and Diana narrowed her eyes. The girl's coat was open in front, revealing a froth of flowery material. And her profile — that was Holly's upturned nose, all right.

Diana ducked back into the main foyer before Holly could spot her. She didn't even wait to find out who the boy with Holly was. Suddenly she felt sick — sick and betrayed. Leaning against a pillar at the bottom of the stairs, Diana took a

265

deep breath to calm herself but it was no use. Her best friend was cheating on her brother — and right out in front of the school where anybody could see! The idea was more than Diana could take. She could only hope no one else would see Holly and discover what a rotten friend and a rotten girlfriend she'd turned out to be. Bart got jealous easily, and his pride would really be hurt if other people knew Holly was fooling around behind his back like this.

Diana headed slowly back to the dance, a heated debate taking place inside her head. Half of her argued that it really wasn't any of her business who Holly kissed and whether she cheated on her boyfriend. The fact that Holly's boyfriend was Diana's brother shouldn't change that. But of course it did. Diana recalled Bart's voice on the phone when they'd talked the other day and had come up with the scheme for the roses. It had been so full of love and caring for Holly. He was so worried that she was going to be sad on Valentine's Day. Bart insisted that Holly be reminded of how much he was thinking about her even though they were far apart. He was probably sitting home in his dorm room right now waiting for Holly to get back from the dance and call him to wish him a Happy Valentine's Day.

Diana gritted her teeth. Half of her wanted to be fair, whatever that may have taken, but the other half just couldn't be. No matter how she looked at it, what Holly was doing not only hurt Bart, and Holly herself. It hurt Diana, too.

Diana strolled back into the dance trying to look unworried and nonchalant. Jeremy wasn't anywhere in sight — fortunately. She needed a few more minutes alone to compose herself and get back in the Valentine's Day spirit.

But it wasn't any use. Even when Jeremy rejoined her, all smiles, Diana couldn't make herself act happy. She was tense and gloomy, and the party mood had completely deserted her. By the time the dance came to a close and Holly and her mystery companion still hadn't reappeared, Diana was beyond cheering up.

Jeremy was eager to go on with the rest of the crowd to the sub shop, but Diana vetoed the suggestion. She asked him to drive her home instead, refusing to let on what was bothering her. As the strings of flashing lights were unplugged one by one and everyone, even Katie in her cast, cheerfully pitched in to clean up before heading out, Diana couldn't keep a disgruntled frown from stealing across her usually sunny face. Happy Valentine's Day, Bart, she thought sourly.

Chapter *20*

Roxanne lurked in the corner of the cafeteria, near where the band was dismantling its equipment, her eyes sharply focused on the exit. Katie, Greg, Eric, Molly, Karen, Brian, and some of the others were laughing and gathering up their coats, hats, and boxes of leftover food and decorations. Obviously they were about to leave the dance to finish up the evening at the sub shop. Rox fought back a swelling feeling of panic. Greg hadn't shown up for his computer date — for some reason Eric had come instead, and she'd almost blown her cover. But still, things had gone well with Eric and with Matt and Jonathan. So what could explain the fact that suddenly all four guys were keeping their distance? In the last hour, not one of them had taken her up on her promise of a secretive slow dance. Worse still, the whole gang was making unmistakable signs of taking off, and it didn't look like they were going to invite her to come along.

Rox shook out her long, glossy hair. She had to be imagining it. The whole scene really was too unlikely! Maybe — maybe they haven't noticed that I'm still here and would be willing to help, she thought doubtfully. The idea that anyone actually might not *notice* her was so foreign to Roxanne that it was nearly inconceivable. Still, there had to be some explanation. She steeled herself. There was nothing left to do but charge over there and find out for herself what was going on.

She avoided the girls — she certainly didn't expect them to bend over backward to make her feel welcome at post-dance activities. But Eric should be an easy mark. Roxanne sidled up just as he was hoisting a box full of empty punch bowls onto one of his broad shoulders. She opened her mouth to speak but before she had a chance to say a word, Eric cruised right past her without so much as a nod of recognition. Roxanne whipped her head around to follow him with her eyes, absolutely astonished. That couldn't just have happened! *Nobody* blew her off like that. Rox turned on her heel. Not far away, Jonathan was absorbed in wrapping strings of lights into neat bundles. There'd been no mistaking *his* response to her earlier in the evening, as Rox recalled. She'd had him wrapped around her finger. Sure, he'd never caught up with her for a dance, but that was probably because he was busy making sure everything ran smoothly. He was the head of the Dance committee, after all.

Roxanne approached him, her eyelids half lowered and her lips preparing for a tempting smile. This time she wasn't going to leave anything to chance. "Hi, Jonathan," she said sweetly. She waited. Without even looking up, Jonathan tossed the last bundle of lights into an overflowing carton, grabbed the carton, and headed for the door. Molly, Greg, Katie, and the others were already out in the hallway. Without a glance back, they headed off, leaving the stripped cafeteria nearly empty, except for Roxanne.

She stood there watching them go, her cheeks flaming in a very rare blush of discomposure. She wasn't at all used to being embarrassed — and she didn't like it. She didn't like it one bit. Well, it looked like the end of the evening to Roxanne whether she liked it or not. There was no reason to hang around here another minute. Besides, she needed to cool off in a big way. She snatched her coat from the rack by the door and stomped down the hall. It wasn't easy to stomp in such high heels, but she managed. She needed to stomp — she had to vent her fury somehow. How dare those jerks! she thought, practically kicking open the door of the main entrance. How dare those snotty Kennedy kids reject me, after all the work

I put in! If it wasn't for me, their stupid dance would have been a boring flop. But obviously they're not grateful in the least!

Rox paused just outside, taking a few deep breaths to calm herself. Now her anger took on a wistful quality. She'd been so close — so close to really making her mark on this school, and on this school's guys. It wasn't fun to find herself, for absolutely no reason that she could tell, back on the outside of things. She deserved better. Lifting her chin with determination, Rox headed across the courtyard for the parking lot. I'll figure out some way to get back in with them, she told herself. It can be done and I can do it. She smiled. Her self-confidence never deserted her for long. She *would* find a way to put herself where she belonged at Kennedy. She had to — she wouldn't stand for being left out, treated like a nobody. That was okay for someone like Frankie, but not for her.

Roxanne instantly felt better. Her step lightened. As she neared the flagpole, she suddenly noticed that there were two figures not far ahead of her. Or rather, one figure — they were standing so close together it was hard to tell they were actually two people. Rox frowned, feeling more than a little sour-grapish. That could have been her tonight. It *should* have been her — her and Eric — or Jonathan — or Greg — or Matt — Who was that anyway? She peered curiously in the couple's direction as she passed, careful not to jingle the car keys she clutched in her hand. The moonlight helped to expose them. The guy was Zachary McGraw. Hmmph! Roxanne could never understand why Frankie had such a thing for him. He might be cute, but he was definitely a hick. She hadn't realized he was dating anybody, though. Looking closer, she decided the girl sort of looked like Holly Daniels, who was in Roxanne's gym class. Rox narrowed her eyes. It *was* Holly Daniels. Very interesting, she thought. Obviously, some people hadn't had any trouble making social and romantic inroads at Kennedy! Rox wasn't sure what to make of this discovery, but she filed it away in her mind. It might come in handy someday.

She was still speculating about Holly and Zack as she unlocked her car, but as she drove out of the parking lot and turned toward home, those thoughts dissolved, leaving her feeling tired and lonely. She hadn't expected to leave the dance alone, and so early. She wasn't sure she wanted to face her mom and her brother and have them witness her failure, too, but it was too late to stop at Frankie's house. There was nothing to do but go home. With any luck, her mom had a date tonight and wouldn't be around anyway.

Roxanne glanced out her window as she drove through downtown Rose Hill past the sub shop. Even from the road she could see that the popular Kennedy High hangout was packed. Rox tightened her hands on the steering wheel and drove a little faster. She didn't care to be reminded that she wasn't welcome where everything was happening. Although, she vowed silently, that is going to change. She may have just experienced a setback to her fast start at Kennedy, but she didn't plan to be slowed down for long.

Katie nestled closely under Greg's strong, supportive arm. She smiled up at him, her lips still warm from his kisses. "Now, what were we talking about?" she teased.

The dance had been over for a couple of hours and the gang had left the sub shop thirty minutes earlier. Katie and Greg were alone in his car at the overlook in Rose Hill Park, the moonlit vista of Washington, D.C., spread out before them. Katie was as comfortable as she could be considering that her broken leg was wedged against the dashboard.

Greg bent down to nuzzle his nose against hers. "I did sort of lose the line of our conversation," he admitted with a mischievous grin. "What can I say? I can't think straight with you this near me! It's been a while."

Katie nodded. It did seem like forever since she and Greg last held one another. She hadn't realized how much she'd missed him — and this feeling. She sighed deeply with contentment.

Greg held a hand up to her mouth playfully. "No more heavy breathing!" he exclaimed. "The windows are steamed up enough already."

Katie laughed. "Well, don't blame me! It was all your fault. I was ready to talk, but you wouldn't let me get a single word in."

"Guilty as charged," Greg conceded, raising his eyebrows up and down Groucho Marx-style. "You're so irresistible, I can't just kiss you once. It's worse than eating a single potato chip."

Katie groaned. "And you're ridiculous!" she declared, slapping him lightly on the shoulder. "I've never heard anything so corny."

"I know, isn't it great?" Greg said with enthusiasm. "And I've got a captive audience." He reached down to pat her cast gently. "I love it."

"I can't run away," Katie agreed. She smiled despite herself. "And I've gotta admit I really don't mind."

Greg hugged her tightly. He had been gently rubbing her shoulders, but now he lifted his hands to run them through her silky hair. His eyes, locked onto Katie's, had become serious. "Let's not ever fight again," he said in a husky voice.

Katie shivered. It was hard to believe that only a few hours ago she'd been angry and lonely and sad. It had really been a long night. So much had happened since she'd wandered over to the Fitness Center in an attempt to escape from her problems. She didn't like to think what her evening would have been like if she hadn't forced herself to come to the dance. It would have ended the same way it began: miserably. "No," she seconded solemnly. "Let's not. Ever."

"I am sorry, Katie," Greg told her, his gaze locked on hers. "I know I've said it already, but it's important to me that you know how much I mean that. I'm sorry for the way I've acted these last few weeks. And for the way I acted before your accident, too."

"I know. And thanks." Katie squirmed a little in the seat to reposition her leg and then reached up to touch Greg's cheek affectionately. "But I was to blame as much as you were. I really over-reacted. There's no rule that says that just be-cause you're my boyfriend you can't act friendly to other girls! I guess I just couldn't help being jealous."

"You really didn't need to be," Greg assured her. "Roxanne's a pretty girl but that's about it. There's not much beneath the surface." He laughed wryly. "Or rather what I found out to-night is what *is* beneath Roxanne's surface isn't as pretty as the rest of her!"

"Hmmph!" Katie snorted good-naturedly. "Took you long enough! I could have told you that right from the start."

"Well, we had to give her a chance," Greg reminded Katie. "She was new and it couldn't have been easy, transferring from Stevenson half-way through the year."

"No," Katie conceded. "I suppose not. But she's here now. She and all the Stevenson kids. Don't you think the rockiest part is over?"

"Hope so." Greg idly traced his index finger

across Katie's forehead, along her cheekbones, and over her nose. His expression was thoughtful. "It's funny, though. At the beginning of the semester we really didn't think we had anything to worry about. Remember?" he laughed. "Boy, were we wrong!"

"Everybody'll bounce back from this." Katie was confident. "Just like you and I are bouncing back!"

Greg grinned. "You bet! We'll show them how it's done." He pulled her close, and for a long moment neither of them said anything. Their feelings for one another spoke for themselves. Then Greg kissed Katie on the neck under her ear and whispered, "No matter what you say, my apology still stands. When you were hurt, these last couple of weeks, all I wanted to do was take care of you and make you feel better." A note of shame and regret entered his voice. "You needed me and I wasn't there for you."

"Because I wouldn't let you be there," Katie pointed out. "I was too stubborn to admit I needed you. I kept thinking of you with Roxanne — and I just made myself more and more bitter and jealous."

"Silly girl," Greg said fondly. "You never had anything to worry about and you never will. Trust me."

Katie smiled. "That's what I'll do. I'll trust you. And if you trust me, too, I guess we'll be okay, huh?"

"No doubt about it." Greg's voice was firm. "We'll be stronger than ever." He looked down at her cast. "Well, in a manner of speaking," he added.

Katie grimaced. "Don't remind me," she said, trying to laugh herself but not quite managing it.

Greg cupped a hand tenderly on either side of Katie's face. "What are you going to do about your leg, K.C.?"

"Ms. Muldoon asked me to help coach this new sophomore. I never even went back to practice to tell her if I'd do it or not. Maybe I should try and coach."

Greg gazed at her. "If you want to."

"There's not much else I can do," Katie said with a resigned sigh. "The doctor says my chances of competing in gymnastics this spring are just about zero. He said I — "

"Wait a minute," Greg interrupted. " 'Just about zero' doesn't mean it's impossible! There's still some chance, right? Maybe it's only a tiny one but it's still there."

"I guess so," admitted Katie without much conviction.

"Well, then, that's what you have to work for," Greg encouraged her. "That tiny, improbable chance. I'll help you out. I'll make up for the last few weeks." He bent forward to kiss her, and suddenly Katie found herself feeling a crazy, ridiculous spark of hope. Maybe her leg *would* heal faster than Dr. Merwin predicted. Maybe she could be back on her feet in time for gymnastics finals. She looked deep into Greg's eyes, and the love and belief there made her feel stronger and more whole than she'd ever felt before, even before she broke her leg. As long as she and Greg had each other, Katie knew almost anything was possible.

Coming soon . . .
Couples #29
TAKE ME BACK

The applause was loud in Holly's ears as she walked back to the table and sat down. "Great job!" Greg, her debate partner, whispered.

"You, too," she replied. "Shhh!" The judge was coming up to the platform to announce the winner. Holly closed her eyes for an insant. Whatever the decision, she couldn't do anything to affect it now. Opening her eyes again, she looked out in the audience and caught her boyfriend Bart's eye. He and Diana were sitting in the middle of a row of seats. Holly could sense that he was watching her. Whether the judge agreed or not, she felt she had spoken and argued very well in the debate. Did Bart think so, too? Was he feeling as proud of her as she had hoped he would? She would know in a few minutes.

As the audience burst into applause, Holly

jumped up and gave Greg an excited hug. They had won! The debate was theirs and so was third place in the whole tournament!

Holly looked out into the auditorium. Diana and Bart were starting down the aisle to the platform. She smiled and raised her hand to wave to them.

Suddenly someone grabbed her and lifted her into the air. "What . . . ?" she gasped.

"Holly, you were great!" Zachary McGraw exclaimed.

"What are you — "

He put his arms around her again and swung her through the air.

"Let me down!" she cried. "Let me go!"

"I thought I'd surprise you by coming," Zack said.

Holly whirled around and glared at him. "You fool! You total idiot! Didn't I tell you to leave me alone? I never want to see you again in my life!"

Bart and Diana were staring at Holly from twenty feet away. Bart's eyes glared coldly at her. Before Holly could go to them or even call out, they turned and hurried from the auditorium.

Holly sank down onto the floor and the tears started to spill from her eyes.